Missing in Toscana

To Shelly and Roy,
all good wishes,
Alice Heard Williams
July 2008

Also by Alice Heard Williams

Novels

Seeking the High Yellow Note
Remembering Piero
Pensione Anastasia

Poetry

Anna Comes Today
When Wild Parrots Fly
Hey, Madame Matisse

Missing in Toscana

Alice Heard Williams

Copyright © 2008 by Alice Heard Williams.

Library of Congress Control Number:		2007909793
ISBN:	Hardcover	978-1-4363-0874-8
	Softcover	978-1-4363-0873-1

All rights reserved. No part of this book may be reproduced or transmitted in any form or by any means, electronic or mechanical, including photocopying, recording, or by any information storage and retrieval system, without permission in writing from the copyright owner.

This is a work of fiction. Names, characters, places and incidents either are the product of the author's imagination or are used fictitiously, and any resemblance to any actual persons, living or dead, events, or locales is entirely coincidental.

This book was printed in the United States of America.

To order additional copies of this book, contact:
Xlibris Corporation
1-888-795-4274
www.Xlibris.com
Orders@Xlibris.com
44883

Once again, to my husband James

Acknowledgments

To everyone who helped me in the writing of this book I am extremely grateful. I am especially indebted to my husband James for his photographs of Toscana and Umbria and for his tireless consulting and advising; to my daughter Holly for editing and sustaining encouragement; to Becky Spetz for her thoughtful reading; to Gay Tucker for the oil painting of a field of sunflowers near San Sepolcro which does double duty as the cover image; to Pat Wilson for the author photograph and as always, to my loyal readers who infect me with their enthusiasm and compel me to continue to write about the transforming and enduring power of great art.

1

A Peculiar Occurrence at London's National Gallery

Emma looked in disbelief at the key Mary Hale held in her palm. "And this is the key the copyist dropped as she left?"

"Yes, Miss Darling. I didn't even hear when it fell, much less see it! It must have slid across the floor and stopped at my foot when she folded up her things and left so suddenly. We were standing in front of the *Nativity* by Piero. She was copying nearby."

"I didn't see the key until we began leaving the room. This is the first chance I've had to show you." Mary looked fearful, her face a bundle of apprehension.

Had she done the wrong thing?

"Never mind, Mary. It's all right." Emma spoke calmly to reassure the shy girl whose feelings were so easily wounded. But why was the woman in such a hurry to leave? Was it anything she said? She had been speaking to her students in the National Gallery on the Italian Renaissance artist, Piero della Francesca. There were a few questions from the girls about seeing the Piero paintings in Tuscany and Umbria on the forthcoming class trip, comments about the legendary Piero Trail on the schedule.

Then the unattractive woman with the pout, wearing a dress of an unpleasant shade of yellow, suddenly gathered up her belongings, threw a large cloth over the easel, and clattered away on sky-high heels, dark eyes glowering at them. From the time they'd crowded into the room where she was copying the Piero *Baptism*, she had frowned in an unfriendly way Emma recalled.

Her students, now sitting with her around a table at Fortum and Mason's American Fountain drinking tea, had put down their cups and looked at Mary in amazement.

It was obvious they hadn't noticed the key at her feet.

"I remember she glared at us all while you were speaking as though she willed us to disappear. It was creepy!" Marigold Barry rolled owl-like eyes behind thick lenses.

"Surely not, Marigold," Emma replied. Marigold could be counted upon to view everything through a glaring, unfavorable prism. And yet?

"I know! It's a mystery, isn't it, Miss Darling?" chimed Caroline Turner, a skinny bean pole of a girl, words falling from her lips in staccato like bursts, a halo of brown hair waving like fine wires over her head. "We thought we were going to the National Gallery for a lecture on Piero, and instead we landed a mystery, didn't we?"

A smile spread over the petite face, transforming her.

"We don't have anything to base that on yet, Caroline," Emma answered, knowing she and Mary, best friends, relished devouring mysteries and thrillers. "Let's talk about our trip. What study preparation should you be making?"

Discussion followed. In only three weeks they would be flying to Tuscany for the class trip of London's Celia Drummond School, but Emma found it hard to concentrate on the conversation. Lingering doubts plagued her about the key handed over by Mary. She'd have to telephone the National Gallery to ask if they had an address for the copyist on file. She tucked it away, turning it over in her palm, *Il Giardino* engraved on the back. The Garden. But what garden? Italy? Possibly, but where?

Parting with her students after coffee, Emma retraced her steps toward the Leicester Square Underground while they hurried off for the shops in Oxford and Regent Streets.

She returned to Trafalgar Square, presided over by the imposing National Gallery of Art and also Nelson's thrusting column, flanked by four enormous lion sculptures dominating the vast open space. Tourists were buying sacks of corn from the ever present vendors, and pigeons were swooping down to feed on the treats. It was a crowded, noisy scene, filled with clashing colors, people from dozens of different countries: laughter, foreign phrases floating on the air along with the smell of exhaust fumes borne by traffic moving endlessly around Trafalgar Square.

When Emma and her students had entered the National Gallery from the rear entrance on Orange Street earlier, the sun was making a determined effort to push through sullen clouds over London. It had seemed like spring. But while they were inside, the warmth from the sun vanished, giving way to cooler winds and now the mist was creeping in, Emma thought glumly, as she made her way past the lighthearted scene toward the Underground.

They had gone up to the Early Renaissance galleries she recalled, first stopping at the security check point to leave knapsacks and coats, opening their handbags for inspection. London was jittery; nervous from several terrorist attacks by the IRA, the Irish Republican Army. Everyone knew galleries and museums were favorite targets this troubled year 1975, there was no grumbling about bag searches.

Only last week, a warning had gone out to the Tate Gallery in the form of an anonymous telephone call, and the entire gallery had been emptied of people for two hours before the all clear sounded! Everyone seemed on edge. Emma found herself thinking suspiciously about the strange woman in the gallery, copying one of the masterpieces of Piero della Francesca. Could she somehow be an agent of the IRA? But she discarded this idea immediately. The woman not only looked Italian, she dropped a key with Italian words imprinted on it. Steady on, Emma! Italy, not Ireland!

You are paranoid, she scolded herself, worrying about everything; the Irish Republican Army threat to London was becoming an obsession. Careful, or you'll be like those people you read about in the *Sun* who leap out of a cab the moment the cabbie speaks out in an Irish accent! She smiled. You're twenty three now, you're an American, an art historian employed by the Celia Drummond School and living in London. Don't panic. Grow up!

The following day, when she telephoned the National Gallery to enquire, she was told by the flutey tones on the other end that the copyist, one Anna Cortina, would not be returning to the Gallery. "The easel was in place, but she left without bothering to let us know! She also abandoned her paints for us to cart away. There was no forwarding address." Disapproval crackled through the wires.

"No forwarding address at all?" Emma echoed.

"No. All we have is the name Anna Cortina and her address—Italy. Can you believe it? That was on her application when she signed on! Highly irregular! There should be a London address as well as a *complete* permanent address. I can't think who would accept such an incomplete form, but believe me, I'll find out.

Our rules strictly forbid such sloppiness. She won't be welcomed back to copy again at the National Gallery, you may be sure!"

Emma received the distinct impression staff members were due for a dressing down very soon. She even felt twinges of sympathy for the missing Anna Cortina, landing crosswise with such a dragon.

"She is not a friend of mine," Emma hastily explained, "But should I see her, I'll deliver the message! Many thanks." Slowly she replaced the telephone in its cradle. So the point is, we rattled the copyist, Anna Cortina from Italy who was copying one of the Pieros. But who knows why? Maybe we never will. But in this thought, she was mistaken.

TOSCANA

2

Final Preparations for Following the Piero Trail

The last class before leaving for Italy at the Celia Drummond school brought the students to the classroom for a final look at slides of the paintings of Piero della Francesca who had become the class favorite. Emma brought up a slide of the *Baptism, a* painting they had seen on their recent visit to the National Gallery.

"Tell me what you think," she asked after speaking to them briefly on the life of Piero della Francesca and the history of the painting. At once Lettice raised her hand. Tall, golden haired, Lettice Lygon possessed both beauty and a regal bearing, borne quietly and with grace. She was wildly popular with her classmates.

"The color is amazing. Fresh and bright, it looks like sunlight. Yes, that's what it's meant to be—sunlight." Her brow wrinkled in concentration. "I don't recall ever seeing a specific time of day attempted in paintings of this date, mid-fifteenth century."

"Yes, fifteenth century, or *quattrocento*, as the Italians prefer. You are right, Lettice. It is one of the earliest representations of sunlight in a painting. Remember, Piero studied in Florence under the Venetian, Domenico Veneziano. The Venetians always considered light a primary component of any painting. Think of the water in Venice! All those canals, reflecting the light!"

Emma loved her job as an art lecturer at the Celia Drummond School. Passionate about art, especially Early Renaissance painting, her favorite assignment hardly rose to the level of work for her: she relished taking these girls, studying to be executive secretaries, employees of art galleries, plus a few bound for modeling jobs at famous British fashion houses, on weekly visits to look at London's art treasures.

"The figures seem carefully drawn," Winkie spoke up. "Look at the young man in the middle ground who is taking off his shirt. He might be a life study, don't you think? He doesn't appear to be stiff, like cardboard." Wilhemina, or "Winkie" Taylor-Davies was another of Emma's outstanding students. Her round face shone with fervor. Short, plump, unfailingly good humored, she possessed an intuitive grasp of art which lighted wide-set, intelligent brown eyes.

"Oh yes, Miss Darling," Caroline joined in, wiry hair waving. "Winkie's right. They remind me of those frescoes from Padua you've shown us on slides, the Arena Chapel frescoes by Giotto."

"Good, Caroline. They do remind us of Giotto. You and Winkie are both correct. Remember, Piero is over a hundred years later than Giotto. He's had the advantage of looking back, not only at Giotto's frescoes, but also at the work of Northern artists who have filtered down into Italy by this time. I mean artists from countries we know now as Belgium, Germany, France and Holland. He's learned a lot from them about realism in painting. He has humanized that figure of the young man in the near background, caught in the act of removing his shirt before his turn to be baptized, do you all see?" They craned necks toward the image on the screen, peering earnestly.

"We know as a matter of record that Piero made sketches from life; many of his figures are portraits. This altarpiece contains a donor portrait. Can you guess which one? It is in the face of Jesus, not relegated to a side panel, as were most donor portraits of this date, but rather one of the principal figure of the painting."

"What is a donor portrait, please?" whispered Mary. Before Emma answered, bossy Marigold, something of a trial, blinked owl-like eyes and fired a volley in Mary's direction.

"The one who gave the money for the painting of course, Mary!"

Emma ignored her, beamed a smile at Mary and continued. "Documented records tell us that the face of Jesus was actually the likeness of a grandfather of the man who financed this painting, the donor. Perhaps some of the other faces, John the Baptist particularly, and the young man Winkie pointed out, are not necessarily donors, yet certainly they are portraits, wouldn't you agree, Mary? Each figure, including the group of three highly individualized angels at the left, must be a likeness of a particular person." Mary timidly smiled and nodded her head.

"The bulk of Piero's work remains in Italy, a large chunk of it scattered about in Tuscany and Umbria. Unfortunately, the paintings, probably frescoes, he did in Rome are lost."

"When we take our class trip, will we see all of his paintings? I really like Piero best," said Patricia, pushing flaming red hair out of her eyes. A Scot from Edinburgh, she rolled her "R's" and for this suffered merciless teasing from the others.

"Let's see, there is a dazzling pair of portraits at the Uffizi in Florence of Federigo da Montefeltro and his wife Battista Sforza, the rulers of Urbino. They were Piero's most famous patrons. We'll see those, of course. Most of the other paintings are off the beaten path, in smaller cities and towns. As we follow the Piero Trail we'll catch the most important ones."

"You know the copyist's key, Miss Darling? Well, we think she is bound to be in Italy, maybe where we are going, and we can look for her house, or a hotel named *Il Giardino*." Fiona and Elizabeth spoke together, alternating phrases. Though not sisters, they roomed together, wore kilts of similar plaids and pale twin sets, (jumpers, not sweaters). Their wardrobes seemed to consist exclusively of plaids; their thoughts were programmed, like twins. Emma hadn't yet sorted out their different personalities.

"Don't count on it, girls. Italy is a big country, and we are going to visit only a small area, Tuscany and a bit of Umbria. I was informed only that her nationality is Italian, and her name is Anna Cortina. The National Gallery told me what information they had when I telephoned. She left no forwarding address."

Emma handed out a tentative schedule of the trip, promising a complete itinerary before departure, and they strolled out of the classroom, chattering about Piero and Italy.

3

Word from Aberdeen; an Unexpected Reaction

Emma returned to her flat in Cadogan Square in late afternoon and found a letter from Sam McGregor in Aberdeen had dropped through the letterbox. Her spirits lifted at once as she sank down on the couch and began to read:

> Dearest Emma,
> A quick note while I'm on night duty. I'm missing you so much here I have trouble remembering your face. Why did I ever leave you in London! I've just received wretched news. I can't get down to be Charlie's best man at the wedding. My Registrar said "no" absolutely. I've rung Charlie and he says there isn't a problem, he has a substitute in mind, but I feel rotten that I won't be there to see Jane

and Charlie tie the knot, especially after all our adventures together in Greece and London last summer. I've got to find a job in London, Emma! We need to start planning our wedding, right? I'm slowly losing it, Emma, because of our being apart. I want to hold you, kiss you until you're breathless, see those blue eyes trained on me in adoration! Can you ever forgive me for missing Jane and Charlie's wedding? Must run, my buzzer's going crazy! Please understand.

        Love to my Darling Emma.
            Your Sam.

Frowning, Emma tapped the letter on her knee, hating the fates that conspired to keep them apart. She inspected the lovely garnet and rose diamond ring that belonged to Sam's grandmother, her engagement ring, given to her by Sam after they met in Greece last summer.

Greece. Hot sunshine beating down, scents of rosemary and wild thyme on barren hillsides, remote temple sites, the faint smell of drains at Pensione Anastasia, where they'd stayed in Olympia. Pungent, aromatic coffee, cigarette smoke at *taverna* tables where old men of the village gathered to gossip; fishy smells, salty breezes at the seaside; heat rising from dusty roads; stern-faced mothers clad in black, prodding noisy children toward schoolhouses; white cubes of buildings lining village streets; cerulean blues stroked into cloudless skies of blinding intensity. Sam. Magic. Greece!

Nursing a bad temper, Emma let her displeasure mount. She was on a University of London tour of temple sites when she met him. Now Jane and Charlie, their best friends, were to be married. And where was Sam? Trapped at his hospital in Aberdeen, missing the fun and excitement of Jane and Charlie's wedding! Couldn't he somehow have managed a two-day leave for a best friend's wedding? Irritation close to anger bubbled up as she read the note again.

She opened a second letter from her parents in Virginia, describing the beauty of the Blue Ridge in spring and telling her how much they missed her. Her father, born in England, met her mother when he accepted a teaching post at the University of Virginia. Much later, with Emma, her mother and two younger brothers, the family settled in the village of Crozet, near enough to Charlottesville, but more rural than urban, with the foothills of the Blue Ridge surrounding them. Emma missed her home, especially at upsetting times like this.

Two short rings of the telephone interrupted her thoughts. The head of the Celia Drummond school, Dr Clark, rang to inform her hotel reservations were complete: they'd be staying at the Hotel Contenta in San Sepolcro, then move on four days later to Florence and Hotel Giardino. He had engaged a tour company, Bella Toscana, to meet them in Pisa with a coach and drive them along the Piero Trail, the legendary road covering the most important locales of the paintings of Piero della Francesca, including the towns of Monterchi, Arezzo and Urbino.

"I wanted you to know the reservations are confirmed for San Sepolcro and Florence. Very nicely priced, too, enough to offset the cost of the coach and driver, which will be a great convenience. Once you are away from Florence prices, Emma, things look quite reasonable. And, by the way, Barbara Bone, the physical education instructor, will be accompanying you as co-leader. She speaks Italian. I know you'll conduct a great tour, Emma! I'll give you more details later." He rang off.

Emma took a moment to reflect. She was proud of her qualifications: a degree in art history from the University of Virginia and another year of graduate study at the University of London. She knew she was ready to lead after all those years of preparation. She considered her future. Where would she be this time next year? Would she and Sam have married? Or would a wedding be put off again while they struggled with jobs in different places, straining to keep their feelings for each other intact? Her pique with Sam returned.

She went into the tiny kitchen of her flat, made a cup of coffee essence and ate a sausage roll for her supper. A dismal meal seemed appropriate after the unwelcome news from Sam. Idly, she took up the morning paper, the *Telegraph*, which had rested unread on the table since breakfast. Then tardily she recalled the key still in her coin purse. *Il Giardino*, the name imprinted on the key dropped by the copyist at the National Gallery. So it was also the name of their hotel in Florence, Dr. Clark had said.

Could this key have come from the hotel? Might they see the copyist there? Stranger things happened. Reflecting on the conversation with Dr. Clark, Emma realized she knew very little about the newly-named assistant, Barbara Bone, the physical ed teacher. Short, plump, a black cord and whistle wound around her neck, she appeared daily in spotless white trainers and navy gym uniform. Dark hair pulled back in a careless ponytail completed Emma's stored impressions of Barbara.

She must be around thirty. I wonder what she's really like? She opened the newspaper. The Tories were lambasting the Laborites about Union excesses. The Laborites were protesting the "heartless indifference" to the poor of the nation by the Tories. The spring of 1975 contained the usual political party squabbles. Suddenly her eyes locked on a small story buried among the inside pages.

"Art Thieves Target Provincial Italian Museums." Then, "A well disguised team of art thieves is plundering some of Italy's more remote galleries and provincial museums and churches. San Gimignano, Turin, Pisa and Ravenna have recently been robbed of paintings."

"The Minister of Arts for Italy, Luciano della Porta, has spoken out, warning smaller museums to improve security and do whatever necessary to protect their belongings or risk loss of national funding. Often thieves send a copyist ahead to reproduce their targets before stealing them, substituting the fake painting for the original, thereby gaining valuable time before the loss is discovered."

"In San Gimignano last month, the theft of the painting in the cathedral went undiscovered for several days, long after thieves had fled with a small *Madonna and Child* painting by Renaissance artist Domenico Ghirlandaio. A convincing copy had been inserted into the original frame."

Emma's thoughts winged their way to the copyist Anna Cortina in the National Gallery. Could this unpleasant, sloppy artist be mixed up in such a scheme? Highly doubtful, Emma reasoned. Anna Cortina's work was far too amateurish, would not fool anyone. Moreover, the ring of thieves wouldn't be desperate enough to try to rob the National Gallery in London! Her mind rolled over audacious art thefts she'd read about in the past. What a cheek some of these famous art heists! And she was on her way to the very center of all the trouble, Italy. She absent mindedly twisted a lock of sandy hair while she wished for a calm, untroubled trip, unmarred by art thefts and other unpleasantness on their journey.

~~~

Barbara Bone rang to tell Emma how thrilled she was to be going to Italy. "I know I'll be able to manage. I don't know anything about art, but I do know Italian. My mother came from Italy, you see." She paused.

"Why that's marvelous, Barbara. We can certainly use your help in translating, being our spokeswoman. You know, I was just thinking, you and I haven't gotten to know each other this year, just too busy I suppose." Emma sensed the shyness in Barbara's voice, the hidden longing for a friend.

"I, I didn't think I would be able go when the director first asked me," Barbara admitted. "My mother, well, she's in a wheelchair. I take care of her. That's one of the reasons I don't have much free time to meet other teachers and make friends."

"Oh, I see. Sorry, I didn't realize," Emma murmured. A shame she doesn't have the freedom most people take for granted, time to have fun. Emma resolved to make the trip enjoyable for Barbara, a change of pace from a routine of work and responsibility for an invalid mother.

"My aunt lives in Henley-on-Thames and she's offered to come up and stay with Mother, so everything is arranged. I've never been to Italy before. When I went with my parents on holidays as a child, it was only to Wales or Scotland. My father planned it, you see, and Mother had no living relatives in Italy anymore. She was born in Greve, a small town near Florence."

Emma realized Barbara's knowledge of things Italian as well as language would be a huge help. "What about spending so much time looking at art? Will you enjoy tramping around daily looking at museums and churches? We'll be spending most of our time nosing about sculptures, frescoes and paintings."

"I'd like that. I need to widen my horizons beyond the gym. I'm already making a list of things I need to do to help make the tour more organized."

~~~~

After the excitement of Jane and Charlie's wedding, which was memorable but a little sad without Sam, the days before departure swam by in a twinkling and Emma found herself, complete with fluttering doves in her chest, boarding the Alitalia flight bound for Pisa at Heathrow Airport with Barbara Bone and a covey of eighteen chattering girls.

4

Along the Piero Trail, a Surprise at the Hamlet of Monterchi

Mario, young and darkly handsome, waiting for the group when they emerged from the customs hall at Pisa airport, held up a neatly printed placard complete with flourishes reading "The Celia Drummond School." Neatly dressed in chinos and an immaculately ironed white shirt, Mario's muscles bulged as he loaded the bags onto the coach, sending waves of a perfumed hair dressing around the cluster of girls watching spellbound.

Emma looked out of the corner of her eye as several of the younger girls gazed soulfully at Mario's wavy brown hair and large brown eyes. Hopefully, no trouble with Mario loomed on the horizon. She would not worry unduly, but she knew she must be ever vigilant with her young and impressionable charges, many visiting Italy and the Continent for the first time. Mario seemed businesslike, polite and willing, claiming to understand her every word, but she realized like many of his countrymen, he wanted to please and possibly spoke very little English.

Emma made her way to a single seat at the rear of the coach while Barbara stationed herself across the aisle from the driver and checked off each girl as she boarded. The bags were loaded. Mario hurried into the driver's seat with a *Va Bene!*, and they rolled off.

Barrel-tiled roofs in varying shades of terra cotta capped the farmhouses seen from the window as the coach moved into open countryside. Occasionally the road wound through a village with its tiny church and clutch of small houses, most of them looking festive with early summer flowers blooming in pots clustered around doorways. Emma was struck by the natural sense of harmony displayed in these humble gardening efforts. Italians seemed to possess a love of nature in bloom. They must be born with it, Emma decided.

Carefully tended vines in precise rows were beginning to sprout on terraced hillsides behind the villages. Emma noticed every village had its own wine *cooperativo*, proclaimed in large letters on the sides of barn-like buildings usually located near the outskirts of town. When vineyards no longer dominated the fields, Emma gazed at rows of olive trees racing by the moving coach. Many of the trees had knotted, gnarled trunks, looking as though they had been planted for generations. Italy, a land of tradition, Emma realized, was regulated by climate and the planting cycles.

Monterchi, the first stop along the Piero Trail, displayed a tiny collection of modest, well-tended farm houses and barns off the main road to San Sepolcro. The hamlet of Monterchi was believed to be the birthplace of Piero della Francesca's mother. Surrounded by irregular plots of neatly tilled fields like a patchwork quilt, Monterchi presented a montage of cultivated earth and sun baked walls in pleasing shades of faded amber and barrel-tile roofs of a darker hue. Everyone's mental image of Italy, Emma thought.

The fresco of the *Madonna del Parto*, the Pregnant Madonna, a world-famous icon for Piero lovers, covered one wall of the tiny chapel. Piero had painted it as a tribute to his beloved mother Romana who died before he became famous. Emma, who had seen the fresco on previous trips, knew it would be of the greatest interest to her students, hungry for their first glimpse of Piero's work on the legendary Piero Trail.

Mario guided the coach to a stop beside a small black Italian sports car in the modest parking area. Emma glanced toward the car, where she noticed a dark-haired young woman in the passenger seat. The driver's seat was empty. As Emma's group walked toward the entrance, the woman suddenly left the car and overtook them, gaining the entrance first and disappearing inside. Emma, busy framing the presentation she planned for the students, proceeded thoughtfully toward the tiny ticket office. Suddenly Caroline appeared at her elbow, eyes wide and alert, the halo of wiry hair standing at attention.

"What is it, Caroline?"

"Miss Darling. That woman who dashed past us at the entrance. She's the copyist from the National Gallery, I'm positive!" Nervously she plucked at her handbag.

"Surely not. Couldn't you be mistaken? We're a long way from London."

"I don't think so, Miss Darling. I caught her eye as she went past us and it seemed to upset her. She recognized us, I know she did! Then she hurried inside."

Emma saw the woman in a small room off the chapel, speaking rapid Italian to a young man dressed in a shiny silk suit and wearing dark glasses, no doubt her companion in the sports car. He seemed tentative, not too sure of himself, Emma thought. The woman looked Emma's way, frowned and seemed to become even more agitated. She whispered to her companion and he abruptly turned his back on the attendant and the pair hurried out of the tiny chapel. Emma recognized the woman: she was indeed the copyist from the London gallery. Caroline was right!

"Well, look at that, they're leaving!" Mary Hale whispered at Emma's elbow.

Emma opened her coin purse where the key engraved "Il Giardino" gleamed up at her.

"Maybe I can catch her," she murmured, turning toward the door and hurrying outside.

But she was too late. The car quickly reversed from its parking place, sped off toward the main road. Only the driver Mario remained in the parking area with the empty coach. He was leaning back in the driver's seat, giving every appearance of napping, a newspaper shielding his face from the sun. Emma gazed after the disappearing car churning up plumes of dust, then retraced her steps. Could the sight of them have made the strange woman urge her companion to leave? Or was it the sight of someone else? But only the Blue Bella Toscana coach with Mario at the wheel occupied the parking area. Emma could not figure.

"Aren't you going to talk to us about the Piero fresco, Miss Darling?" Marigold's whine greeted Emma's return to the little chapel. I could dislike that girl very easily Emma thought, cautioning patience to herself before replying.

"Yes indeed I am, Marigold. I've been busy trying to catch the young woman whose key Mary found at the National Gallery. Remember?"

Choruses of "What?" and "Where?" rang out on all sides as she told the girls gathered around her what Caroline had seen.

'The young woman in the sports car appeared to be Anna Cortina, the copyist from the National Gallery. Caroline is to be congratulated for her keen powers of observation."

"But Miss Darling," Lettice asked, "What on earth could she be doing here? This Monterchi seems little more than a hamlet. Isn't it strange she should be here, of all places in Italy?"

But Emma had no answer for that question. Shrugging her shoulders she smiled, *Tutto e`possible*. She looked toward the entrance, hoping to inquire about the purpose of the couple's visit, but the chapel attendant and ticket taker had vanished.

The Piero fresco covered almost the entire surface of one wall; it was certainly not a target for stealing, she thought idly, even if by chance the mysterious Anna Cortina was mixed up in the recent art thefts in Italy she had been reading about. It was far too large. And the little museum seemed to contain no other paintings. She pushed the thoughts to the back of her consciousness and began to speak.

Standing beside the *Madonna del Parto*, Emma described its three figures to her students. "On each side of a towering Madonna stand attendant angels, realistically painted, who draw aside rich brocaded draperies to reveal the Mother of Christ, the simplified forms giving Mary a queenly bearing in the recognizable genre of all of Piero's women. She is obviously awaiting birth of a child. The buttons of her dress are open at the waist and her hand rests on the womb in a dignified manner. Her demeanor and stately bearing inspire the deepest veneration in spite of such a startling, shocking image."

"Many famous museums have offered to pay lavishly in order to borrow this fresco, which was detached from the wall many years ago and is now mounted on a backing. What a draw it would be for special exhibitions all over the world, but officials of Monterchi always have refused." Emma paused.

"They could never risk the wrath of the local women if the fresco were removed, even for a short time, because her miraculous powers are legendary. The fresco, since it was put in place, has been the object of special prayers by young women of the village down through the years who pray before her for the safe arrival of their babies."

"When I saw this fresco for the first time I was told the two angels were holding open the curtains to let us, the spectators, see the miracle of Christ's mother before she gave birth. After seeing it, I realized the curtains were not being opened, they were *being pulled shut* because the time for the birth had actually arrived. What do you think?" The students discussed this possibility at length, clearly impressed with the sight of their first painting on the Piero Trail.

"I hope you find this amazing work of art as compelling as I did the first time I saw it," Emma concluded and indeed, the grandeur yet simplicity of the work seemed to have silenced all whispers. Deeply moved, the students quietly filed outside the little building and made for the coach.

After a short drive, they reached San Sepolcro and Mario maneuvered the coach into a narrow side street alongside the Hotel Contenta, near the center of town. San Sepolcro, a pleasant, small city, owed its fame, and collected ample tourist dollars, as the birthplace of Piero della Francesca. A maze of one-way streets within the walls of the old town discouraged the use of motor cars. A lovely town to walk about in, Emma told the girls, but not before a shower and clean-up for dinner. They have had an extremely long day. After leaving the chapel at Monterchi, they had stopped in a small pizzeria on the outskirts of the village for a slice of pizza and a cool drink, but by now, they felt travel weary and yearned for showers and a proper dinner.

As Mario lifted bags off the coach, Barbara and Emma dispatched room keys. The girls quickly disappeared for unpacking and a short rest. Emma reminded them to reassemble in the hotel's reception room at eight that evening.

The hotel staff were young, pleasant and eager to please. The building itself. designed in the nineteenth century, proved architecturally undistinguished but pleasant, and sported fresh paint on old plaster walls; chairs and sofas recovered in a green and white garden chintz. Reproductions of paintings by the town's most famous resident, Piero, decorated the walls.

Emma unpacked, showered in a curtained-off corner of her room, an ingeniously created space for showering from a small tap. She put on a cotton robe, surveyed her spacious room with its tiny shower in one corner and the most surprising ceiling—a fresco depicting lovers in a beautiful garden. Dante and his beloved Beatrice, Emma decided, noting the medieval style of clothing worn by the two. Created by a naive hand, the fresco looked to be less than a hundred years old, but an antique in its own right, copying a style of the Middle Ages. Emma marveled at her good fortune.

"Only in Italy would there be a frescoed ceiling over a combination bedroom and shower cubicle in a small hotel, catering to student groups," she mused to herself, wishing Sam could be with her in such a delightful country, a country proud of its art and history, her displeasure with him forgotten at that moment.

A timid knock sounded at the door. Probably Barbara, Emma thought, wanting to know if the room she assigned to me was comfortable. Barbara, decidedly helpful, had displayed outstanding organizing skills. She seemed to get on well with the girls. No complaints. Emma was grateful for the few additional moments of quiet to collect her thoughts before she lectured to the students. And Barbara obviously enjoyed traveling in the company of young people. Life with her invalid mother had imposed constraints, but she chose not to complain. Emma admired her for this. The knock sounded again.

"*Pronto*! Come in."

Caroline slid soundlessly into the room followed by Mary. Caroline let out a screech when she saw the charming fresco decorating the ceiling.

"Look! A frescoed ceiling! Miss Darling, you are so lucky! Why, it's above your shower cubicle. How positively divine. Look, is it Dante and his Beatrice?"

Emma nodded. "Aren't I lucky? Your room doesn't have one?"

"No, no. This is the only one we've seen, and we've been inspecting all the rooms." Emma smiled at the unlikely pair, one wired with energy, the other quiet, shy and retiring. Nothing could quell the curiosity of Caroline and Mary. *Niente!*

"Yours is special, Miss Darling." Mary sighed reverently, looking up at the scene.

"Then you must tell all the girls to come and have a look," Emma smiled. "Now, what can I do for you?"

"Well," Caroline began, "You know the woman we saw at Monterchi, the copyist. We've been thinking. It looks like she became upset *only when we pulled up and she recognized us!* Now why would that be? Remember, she was sitting in the car alone. After she had a look at us, that's when she got out, ran past us, hurried inside to talk to the man."

"Hmm, yes, maybe you are right, but why should we upset Anna Cortina? Even if she knew we might remember her from the NG in London, is that a cause for flight?"

"Well," Caroline continued, "We thought they might have been planning to steal something, and being recognized, well, it spoiled her plans. That girl Anna looks so mysterious and sulky, I just know something tricky is underfoot." Caroline frowned, shaking the wire of her hair. Mary nodded, agreeing.

"Now Caroline, steady on! We can't jump to conclusions. Besides, they couldn't remove a fresco like that—it's enormous, even if it already has been detached from the wall. No, if they were after something, it's bound to be something else. Something smaller, something we didn't notice." Emma reflected on the recent visit.

In spite of herself, Emma felt the excitement of the two younger girls. And yet what they suggested must probably be the result of a mushrooming imagination, nourished by reading too many mysteries and suspense novels.

"You see, I read in the paper that art thieves are working in Italy now," Mary spoke softly, "Raiding small churches and museums. That's why, I guess, Caroline and I thought the incident might somehow be important." She sounded apologetic.

"I read that article too, Mary," Emma answered, patting her arm. "It certainly is important that we keep our eyes open. Tell you what, when we go over to Arezzo to look at Piero's greatest fresco cycle, the Legend of the True Cross, we'll stop at Monterchi and have another peek to see if there is anything else of interest in that little chapel. You wouldn't mind seeing the Pregnant Madonna again, would you?" Emma's eyes glinted mischievously. "But remember, I told you our hotel in Florence is *Il Giardino*, the same as Anna's key! We may see her there and have a chance to unravel the mystery."

~~~~

Dinner at the Hotel Contenta was served on an upstairs terrace on the east side of the building, shaded from the strong sunlight of afternoon and delightfully cool by eight o'clock. Other guests dined later, at nine or ten.

"I'm glad we are having dinner early, early for Italy anyway," Winkie Taylor-Davies sipped *aqua minerale*, eying the large platter of pasta brought steaming to the table. "I could eat the whole platter all by myself." Heads bobbed in agreement.

Emma marveled not only at Winkie's appetite, but also that of Lettice and Caroline who were sitting at her table. Willowy those two, not plump like Winkie, but their appetites seemed huge. Nine girls made up her table, nine at the second table with Barbara.

After a first course of pasta, they were served veal *alla scalloppina* followed by *insalate*, a simple green salad dressed with olive oil and vinegar. Dessert arrived, *zabaglione*, a custard of egg yolks, sugar and Madeira wine, followed by fresh fruit. Lavendar and Vanessa entertained the table, showing them how to properly use fruit knives and forks.

San Sepolcro: Statue of Piero della
Francesca in a Little Park

"This is the first time I've ever eaten a banana with a knife and fork," Marigold boasted.

"Smaller slices please, Marigold," Lavendar advised, delighted to have the opportunity to show bossy Marigold how to do something. Usually it seemed the other way 'round.

After dinner Emma suggested a stroll to the *cattedrale* in the piazza, the heart of San Sepolcro. On the way, they came upon a charming small park, dominated by tall trees glowing with tiny white lights. In the center stood a fountain near a large sculpture, the figure of a man.

"Let's see who it is," called Marigold racing ahead as Emma, Barbara and the others followed.

"Oh, Miss Darling!" Winkie cried as she discovered the statue of Piero della Francesca. "Come see!"

The little group clustered around the imposing sculpture towering on a plinth surrounded by a circular path lined with flowers. Hidden in the branches of the trees, cicadas played their blending chorus of violins; townspeople strolled the paths or relaxed on benches while children played tag and catch ball on the tiny lawn. Everyone seemed to relish the cool evening air.

San Sepolcro: The Cattedrale

Piero della Francesca's likeness dominated the little park, a sensitive face, large deep set eyes, a halo of curls framing his head. He wore a pill box hat, typical of the time. Dressed in tunic and hose with soft slippers, a long cloak fell from his shoulders in dignified folds. Around his neck he wore a heavy chain on which a large medal dangled. One hand held a palette, the other several brushes.

"That medal he is wearing would be the official seal of San Sepolcro. Piero served as a councilor in his home city for many years," Emma explained as they admired the figure.

"He wasn't very tall," observed Mary. "But stocky!"

"He lived in a house across the street from here," Emma told them. "The park, by the way, is named for him. Shall we have a closer look at the house?"

They made their way carefully across the narrow one-way street. A facade with an imposing doorway held a plaque stating that the house of the artist Piero della Francesca once stood on the site. The present building contained a library devoted to Piero and offices of various scholarly societies.

"Imagine," Winkie sighed, "Being in this place, absorbing the essence of the man, we can almost sense his presence."

"Watch out, Winkie," Emma smiled at her enthusiasm. "You'll be turning into an art historian if you aren't careful. We'd best move on toward the cathedral. Remember, tomorrow is an early day because we have a long drive to Urbino. But we'll have plenty of time to see Piero's work later, San Sepolcro will be our base for several days." She was rewarded by Winkie's glowing look. Perceptive comments were not unusual among her students Emma reflected with pride, thinking how inspiring the role of teacher could be.

The old cathedral, a stark building with a façade of unadorned stucco, dominated the irregularly-shaped square. Like many ancient churches in *Toscana*, the façade was never finished with a dressing of marble or fine stone. Perhaps the money ran out before it was completed, Emma told the students. But the rough terra cotta looked right somehow, blending with the walls of nearby buildings, a reminder that early Tuscany was ruled by the dei Medici, who honored simplicity and dignity in their architecture and art. The drama of baroque would come later, in the seventeenth century, she told them.

Diners at several outdoor *ristoranti* nearby were enjoying not only food but a splendid view of the ancient buildings surrounding the tastefully lighted piazza. People of all ages strolled in the cool evening air. From a side street, guitar music drifted along with the babble of lyrical Italian which enveloped them as they joined the *spectacolo*.

"They are celebrating a perfect evening," Emma commented. "How beautiful Tuscany is! People know how to enjoy life slowly, like a luscious peach is enjoyed."

Her eyes followed an elderly couple walking, a tiny poodle daintily prancing on the cobblestones before them. The hustle and bustle of misty, rainy London seemed far away. Her thoughts flew to Sam. She pictured a quick vignette: a weary doctor trudging the wards at the hospital in Aberdeen. Feeling guilty about her anger with him, she resolved to write a letter before climbing into bed, describing her first evening in Italy.

After a leisurely promenade around the piazza, the students reluctantly turned back toward the hotel. "I'll go in front, Barbara. You can bring up the rear, in case there are any stragglers," Emma called to Barbara as she moved ahead. In a few minutes they arrived at the side street, then the entrance of Hotel Contenta.

But when Barbara finished tallying, she turned to Emma with a frown. "Two are missing."

"Surely not, we were all together, weren't we?" Emma felt a sting of unease in her breast. She couldn't lose anyone on the first night!

"There are only sixteen of us," Barbara said firmly. "Two girls aren't here." They watched the chattering students move inside and slowly mount the stairs, calling out goodnights. For everyone, the day had been an exhausting one. Emma and Barbara looked at each other, trying to keep calm.

"Caroline Turner and Mary Hale. Room-mates. They are the ones," Barbara whispered. "Oh, Emma, how could they?"

Missing in Toscana

"Don't worry, Barbara, let's don't say anything yet. You wait here to see if they show up, and I'll dash back to the piazza. It's possible they wanted a gelato, got in line, and missed our departure. Or maybe they ran into Mario. I'm sure everything is all right."

She hurried off, remembering Mary and Caroline were the ones so keen on pursuing a mystery; she knew "following clues" would be more important to those two rather than a chance encounter with Mario or a last minute ice cream. *And only minutes ago, I was thinking about how inspiring my job as a teacher was,* Emma thought glumly, wondering where the two could possibly have taken themselves.

The street was still crowded as Emma retraced her steps. The primary streets were well-lighted. *Now if Mary and Caroline used good judgment, and stayed away from dark, twisting side streets,* her thoughts ran. Hurriedly she made a tour of the square. They were nowhere in sight. She inspected each of the outdoor tables at the restaurants. *Non da qui.* The cathedral doors were firmly shut by this time. None of the businesses remained open save the *gelateria* and the several *ristoranti*. But Mary and Caroline were nowhere in the line of people waiting to order a gelato, nor were they at any of the outdoor tables.

Mustn't panic, mustn't panic. There were two of them and they seemed like sensible girls Emma thought, biting her lip as she turned toward the Hotel Contenta, heartsick and with rising concern. If they weren't at the hotel when she returned, she and Barbara would have to question the others. What could have happened? Where were they?

Suddenly the welcome sound of running footsteps reached her ears. Two figures emerged in the soft glow of the hotel lights and she recognized Caroline and Mary. Emma's knees wobbled with relief, thankful she wouldn't be forced to place a call on their first night to Dr. Clark, with the unwelcome news that two Celia Drummond students had disappeared.

"Miss Darling, Miss Darling," they chorused in unison. "You won't believe what happened to us!"

"Your story had better be good," Emma answered, the knot in her abdomen slowly dissolving after first sizing them up, seeing they were unhurt. "Do you know I've been combing the piazza, half-sick with worry? What is the meaning of this? Miss Bone is in the hotel looking for you and she is as upset as I am. What can you be thinking of?"

"Miss Darling," Caroline begged. "Please forgive us, but we saw Anna Cortina again, wearing a blond wig this time, and we just had to see where she went!"

"We recognized her in the ice cream line and couldn't believe it," Mary added breathlessly. "Oh, Miss Darling, it was such an impossible wig she was wearing. She was made up to look much older, and she almost fooled us. But she had on that same awful yellow dress she was wearing at the National Gallery in London."

San Sepolcro: A Back Street with a small Piazza

"And when she saw us, why she bolted. That's when we knew we had to follow her. It was just too suspicious, don't you see?"

Caroline took up the story. "Only she was too quick. She kept going into smaller and smaller streets, some of them barely streets at all, alleys really, and we lost her."

"Then you knocked over the rubbish bin and we had to pick that mess up," Mary recalled, wrinkling her nose. "Of course by then we realized how late it was and how hopeless finding her would be, and we hurried back here."

"Caroline, Mary, whatever am I going to do with you? You simply cannot go running off willy nilly. You must stay with the group. I insist on it, else I'll have to send you home. Do you understand?" Emma assumed her most serious face and used her I'm-in-Charge voice, hoping it would resonate with the truants. Miserably the pair nodded, too embarrassed to reply.

Emma, noting the wilted faces and feeling perhaps she had come down too hard on them, relented a bit. "I understand you thought Anna might be involved in an art theft. But we have not a shred of evidence, not one shred of proof, that Anna has done anything wrong! And more to the point, you are a part of this group, and I must have your loyalty, obedience and responsible behavior at all times. Do you understand?" But as she spoke, the thought occurred to Emma that Anna Cortina might be feeling she was prey to a pack of bloodhounds, a coach full of young, energetic English girls who seemed determined to run her to earth.

"Yes Miss Darling," Mary answered for the two of them, eyes downcast. "We promise."

"And we are really sorry for all the trouble we caused," Caroline finished, pushing at her wiry hair.

"Good. I accept your apology. Now, let's put this behind us and go inside to bed."

5

Terror at the Palazzo of Duke Federigo in Urbino

The following morning after a good night's sleep, everyone's good humor restored, the group breakfasted early and departed, eager to be on the Piero Trail, the coach rumbling in the pearly morning light toward the Mountains of the Moon and Urbino, capital city of the province of Umbria.

Alpe del Lunae, the Mountains of the Moon; Emma poured over her map as the coach journeyed onward. What a romantic name. Romantic, like so much about Italy. With a pang she wished with all her heart she might be seeing these mountains with Sam. She looked out the coach window at views stretching thirty miles of majestic peaks and valleys. Quickly she put aside musings. When they reached the motorway, she moved toward the front of the coach, switched on a hand held microphone and began to speak as they traveled along:

"The Ducal Palace of Federigo da Montefeltro, built circa 1444, in the *quattrocento,* survives as a perfect example of the architecture of the period. Here, in his jewel of a palace, Federigo, a *condottiere,* a hired soldier who earned fame and a great fortune fighting battles for others, retired to live as a respected, fair-minded ruler. Duke Federigo, truly one of the most colorful figures of the period, gathered learned philosophers, teachers, poets and artists, assembling a glittering court which became the envy of all Italy, for he was one of the great universal men of the Italian Renaissance. At the same time his ducal palace became a showplace.

"One of the artists Federigo summoned to help decorate the walls of his sumptuous palace rising in Urbino was Piero della Francesca. He became the Duke's principal artist. Another who answered Federigo's call, who became Piero's good friend, was the architect Leone Battista Alberti, a writer as well, whose books ranged from family life and courtly conduct to how to paint supremely beautiful pictures. His fame, like that of Piero, spread far beyond the boundaries of Italy.

"Piero's double portraits, or diptych, of Duke Federigo and his lovely Duchess Battista is now in the Uffizi gallery in Florence. We'll see it when we arrive in *Firenze* of course. However, two important examples of Piero's art remain in the palazzo at Urbino, now the Museo Nationale of Umbria. One, a small

Flagellation of Christ, the second, a *Madonna and Child of Senigallia*, both seem to me the perfect embodiment of the period. You have seen these works in our slides and art books, and I know you long to stand in front of them and study them, as I do, and to explore the ducal palace designed for Federico by the architect Luciano Laurana, a perfect example of Early Renaissance style."

Higher and higher the coach climbed, as the road switched back and forth before reaching the summit of the Mountains of the Moon. Mario, Emma noted thankfully, was a careful driver on the narrow mountain roads. He did not take chances.

Around eleven they reached the city gates of Urbino. This was as far as Mario could take the coach, for large vehicles were forbidden entry into the beautiful hilltop city within the walls. He dropped them off and arranged to meet them at the same gate at five in the afternoon.

Emma reflected that as yet, Mario had been exemplary as their driver: polite and efficient; he knew his job and didn't overstep.

After disembarking the group meandered along narrow, twisting streets leading upward toward the ducal palace, now maintained by the Province of Umbria. The old city with its beautiful buildings surrounded by walls and battlements seemed remote, self-contained, yet prosperous. The townspeople looked well-to-do, seemed pleasant and well-mannered as they went about their daily business, nimbly dodging throngs of students weighted down with rucksacks.

Missing in Toscana

Emma gave them a brief commentary on the man Federigo da Montefeltro, as they paused at a little green park within the city. "He became an exemplary leader, scrupulous in all of his dealings with his people, a great scholar and patron of the arts, a man created by, and perhaps helping to define, the Renaissance in Italy."

"Honest, fair-minded, compassionate in dealings with his people, he quickly won their loyalty and respect. Noblemen all over Italy rushed to send their sons to Urbino to the court of Duke Federigo to learn not only the martial arts, but the fundamentals of courtly behavior. The court of Urbino became renowned as a model training school for the young, well-grounded, Renaissance man. Federigo's fame spread far beyond the stories of his valor on the battlefield. Artists like Piero who were summoned to his court could hardly believe their good fortune; he was the perfect employer, generous to a fault, encouraging them to take other commissions so long as they accomplished work he required for the ducal palazzo."

Entering the palace and obtaining tickets, Emma and Barbara led the group up a wide marble staircase, sumptuous enough for a king rather than a duke, to the *piano nobile*, the floor where the principal chambers and galleries were located. They entered the first of a series of connecting rooms following along the outside walls, probably designed as audience rooms for the conduct of ducal business in centuries past.

Now almost empty, with clean, whitewashed walls and soaring ceilings, fireplaces in which half a dozen people could comfortably stand, these rooms held minor paintings of forgotten artists and objects of interest from the time of Federigo da Montefeltro.

Many of the stone fireplaces displayed the Montefeltro crest, which Emma pointed out to her students. So many rooms, so few visitors, she thought, as the group made its slow progression, looking at frescoes and panel paintings adorning some of the walls.

Emma was amazed at the number of deserted rooms. Most of them had no attendant on duty at all. When they eventually came upon a guard, he was usually a wizened little man who looked so frail a strong puff of wind might blow him away. Clearly, he had not long to wait before he claimed his pension and retired to a small farm in the Umbrian hills to tend his olives and vines.

"When are we coming to the Pieros, Miss Darling?" Winkie asked "There are so many paintings here I can't keep them straight. Are they important?"

"They are important in that they give us insight into the period when Urbino was the center of a powerful ducal kingdom. They tell us what clothes people wore, how they arranged their hair, how their rooms were furnished, what jewelry and ornaments they preferred, and also, for remember, during this period the Church was the greatest patron of art, how they worshiped. The paintings, however are principally by unknown or forgotten artists."

"As for the Pieros, you can be sure his works will be toward the end of the galleries, and in a very impressive setting, a room of their own. A sense of drama is never lost on the Italians, Winkie. Right Barbara?" She nodded toward Barbara, remembering her Italian heritage, and received Barbara's lovely smile. Barbara was enjoying herself.

"Miss Darling," Vanessa asked, "Lavendar and I haven't seen many warders, or guards about. Have you noticed?"

"Indeed I have, Vanessa, and I have wondered why. I suppose there is just not enough money in the budget to spend on hiring more security warders. Can you imagine what a packet it must cost, just for the upkeep of this palace?"

As if in reply to Emma's words, the lights suddenly flickered, dimmed and went out, then flickered, and came on again. The lights dimmed a second time and stayed off. A little daylight filtered in through the small windows cut into foot-thick outer walls, but it was so dark they could not see the paintings. Suddenly they heard shouts coming from several rooms back.

Quickly Barbara spoke. "It's the guards calling out. They are saying there's something wrong with the electrical circuits. They have notified the main offices and someone will be coming soon to fix it." Thank goodness for Barbara and her fluency in Italian Emma thought, urging calm to the students. She recalled earlier doubts about Barbara. How mistaken she had been. Why already, Barbara had proved her worth.

The lights flickered on again as Emma led the students forward. The exit was marked by an abrupt turn and they found themselves walking down a corridor which had no exhibition rooms on either side, only one or two closed doors. They passed an open door and Emma glimpsed a tiny cubbyhole, hardly more than a closet, containing two ramshackle chairs and a dilapidated table on which stood an electric kettle and a couple of coffee mugs. A sheaf of mops and brooms stood propped in a corner. The cleaners storage room and a place for coffee breaks, Emma thought. The lights flickered and they were once again thrown into darkness.

"Oh no," groaned Winkie. Cries of dismay met Emma on every side. "We won't be able to see the Pieros if this keeps up." And Emma, though she said nothing, was inclined to agree. The lights flickered, came on.

"Hurry along, now, we'd better move smartly and go right to the Pieros," Emma called firmly. "We can spend more time in the secondary rooms on our way out." A younger, more agile guard hurried toward them.

He began speaking in Italian, then realized they were English or American and paused. "*Capisce?*"

"*Capisco*, I understand." Barbara spoke firmly, urged him to continue. In a few short sentences the man explained.

"He says the problem with the electricity may well last the rest of the afternoon. If we want to come back tomorrow they will honor our tickets."

Emma, who had understood most of what the man said, grasped Barbara's arm. "No, Barbara. We cannot leave! We must see the Pieros today. We will be going to Arezzo tomorrow. We have to see those two paintings now. It is our only chance! We must go quickly."

Hurrying along, they met a few visitors walking toward the exit, obviously giving up plans for a visit to the palazzo on this particular day. Soon they entered a splendid room, walls covered in blue damask and furnished with heavy antique *cassone*, the enormous wedding chests often presented in the Renaissance to newly married couples. It was an inner room, there were no windows. Two small paintings stood on easels near the center.

"We have arrived," Emma sighed, relieved. There the two Pieros were, as she had hoped. Without preamble she moved beside the *Flagellation* painting and began to speak.

"From Aldous Huxley, who praised the *Flagellation* in one of his novels, to John Pope-Hennessey, the eminent art historian, who I understand is presently working on a book giving his interpretation of the painting, experts have puzzled over its meaning. Some have called it the most beautiful small painting in the world. But what it is all about still remains a mystery. It is a painting composed of two scenes."

"On the left Christ is bound to a column and is being flogged with a delicate grace by his tormentors in a room as beautifully proportioned as the rooms of this palace. It seems quite possible that Piero painted it as a tribute to his patron's emerging palazzo which as you know became one of the architectural wonders of Italy. In the other scene, time jumps forward to the Renaissance. An unknown young man with the physique of a Greek god wearing toga-like robes, stands on a loggia in the company of two older men dressed in robes of the period."

"What does it all mean? We know very little: who the figures are, for they surely are portraits, where the scenes take place, or the relationship of one scene to the other. If their identities were known in Piero's lifetime, they are now obscured by the mists of time. We do know Piero painted the work for his patron, Federigo da Montefeltro, when he was in residence here in Urbino. We also know Federigo came into his title because of the untimely death, murder some say, of his young nephew, whom he is said to have idolized. Is the nephew the young man being memorialized here? Tempting as it is to speculate, there is no documentary evidence whatsoever to support such a theory."

"We do know is that in this small painting we are looking at the work of an unsurpassed genius: harmonious spatial relationships and perspective merge fluidly with carefully realized figures, an accomplishment worthy of Piero. At the time it was painted, he was nearing the height of his powers."

"Did you know Piero had a consuming interest in mathematics and was writing out his theories in a book later published and dedicated to Duke Federigo? Remember, Piero had befriended Leone Battista Alberti, the architect in residence at the ducal palace. Alberti had written the famous *Delle Pittura*, his book on how to paint the perfect picture. It would certainly have been known to his friend, Piero, and indeed, many of Alberti's instructions for a perfect picture are carried out here."

"As yet, Piero had not been summoned to Rome by the pope; that would come later, but his fame was spreading, and he was an ambitious man. He was keenly aware of the possibilities for advancement that lay ahead. Indeed, it is thought that one of the reasons he never married was because he was far too ambitious, too willing to travel, anywhere, any time in order to enhance his reputation as an artist. Few wives, unless forced by necessity, could have endured that, even in *quattrocento* Tuscany. But then, endurance has often been woman's lot through the ages, hasn't it?" She smiled at her students.

Emma moved to the second painting. "This little jewel was painted much later, toward the end of Piero's painting career, probably the 1470s, before his eyesight began to fail. He died in 1492, you remember. We do not know who the lady is, someone he had met earlier perhaps, before he was in the Duke's service. At any rate, the figure of mother and child is set in a perfect Renaissance space, a domestic setting, sparkling with the calm and order, the perfection of Piero's mature style. The idea of placing the Virgin and Child in a secular, domestic setting originated in the North. Possibly Piero had seen works by the Master of Flemalle, Robert Campin, a Northern artist who delighted in painting the Madonna in homelike surroundings. Actually this work was probably painted in one of the rooms of this palace we are standing in today. Remember, the Duke surrounded his court with a plethora of outstanding artists whose innovative styles would have been carefully studied by Piero."

"The woman is cool, collected, imbued with an inner strength, starkly beautiful in the quiet, compelling manner of all of Piero's women. Think back to the *Nativity* Madonna in the National Gallery or the three angels of the *Baptism*. There is nothing fussy about them, rather all is presence and poise. Of course, the Madonna was the symbolic icon to which every woman of the period aspired. In this work what we see is a very personal and private portrait in the guise of a religious painting. One wonders if Piero had ever been in love with the lady. Certainly affection and personal regard seem to drip from his brush. She and her child are idealized humankind. Magnificent also are the attending angels. Do you remember the androgynous quality of the two angels of the *Madonna del Parto* fresco in Monterchi? Here, in contrast, Piero has given each angel a definite male and female appearance. Note the beauty of the male head, the jewel at his neck. Above all, notice the assured, expressionless yet confident faces of the figures in both paintings."

"Although I admire the eminent Kenneth Clark, the leading senior art historian in Britain today, I cannot forgive him for saying that this painting is an inferior work by Piero, that his powers had begun to decline in old age. If such is the case, then in the *Diana and Actaeon*, in the National Gallery in London, Titian has 'gone off', and Rembrandt, in the ravishing portrait of Hendrijke Stoeffels, also in the NG, is the work of a man in a downward spiral. Completely false, of course. You remember when we looked at both of them, I am sure. I prefer John Pope-Hennessey's words about this particular Piero painting: 'It ranks as one of the loveliest paintings in the world today.'"

Outside San Sepolcro, Looking toward
Mountains of the Moon

"Now, you students have traveled far to see these two masterpieces. Savor the moment!" Cheeks ablaze with the fervor and passion delivered with her words, Emma took a step back and the students burst into a spontaneous round of applause.

"Bravo, Miss Darling, a wonderful talk," Vanessa and Lavendar spoke together, followed by the others.

Somewhat embarrassed, Emma turned aside and Barbara, her eyes praising, leaned close to whisper in her ear. "Splendid, Emma. The girls are thrilled. It's after one o'clock," she added, consulting her watch. "I saw a *trattoria* near the palace called *Trattoria del' Amico*. We might have a bite of lunch there then come back for more viewing if they reopen. Our tickets are good all day. We should be able to find sandwiches of salami and cheese, or pizza and pasta at this place."

"Right on, Barbara. Yes, that will be best. I heard several of the girls' stomachs' rumbling while I was speaking. Would you gather them up and take them? I'll join you in ten minutes, after I've studied these works a bit longer. You see, I've never seen the actual paintings before and I simply must have a few minutes to study them alone. You understand?"

"Of course, Emma. Leave it to me." And as Emma moved back to the *Flagellation* Barbara Bone quietly collected the students and they began retracing their steps toward the palace exit.

Emma stood in front of the *Flagellation* several minutes, then moved to the *Madonna of Senigallia*. What an unforgettable face,

Emma thought, turning her attention to the attending angels. She knew Piero often placed angels in his paintings. She recalled the trio of angels to one side of the *Baptism,* and the musical chorus of five angels in the *Nativity*. They were portraits too. But here in front of her were special portraits. Emma believed Piero felt deeply about the woman. Who was she? Destined for a small church in Senigallia, near Urbino, the face of the Madonna could have been a likeness of someone in Piero's wide circle of acquaintances. Who could the woman have been? And the attendant angels, one male, another female. Whom did they represent? Emma resolved to delve into research on Piero when she returned to London. Surely the British Library could shed some light on the mystery surrounding this painting.

She was dimly aware, examining the two paintings, of being alone in the room. Barbara and the students had left for the *trattoria*. There was no chatter of visitors from the hallway. Emma was engrossed in examining the works, oblivious to the silence, as she summed up her thoughts.

Suddenly from behind, a coarse cloth was dropped over her head. Before she could cry out, a menacing voice hissed in her ear, "Quiet! Stay quiet and you won't be hurt!" Cruel hands grasped her arms in a vise-like grip as the world turned into blackness.

6

Emma Considers Her Options

Emma felt herself perspiring, dizzy, her heart pounding as she was pulled and pushed along. She stumbled uncertainly, blind with the covering over her head, not sure what her footing was, nor where she was being hurried along. Desperately trying to take note of her surroundings, she counted twenty footsteps, then felt something hard underfoot as the hands which grasped her arms shoved her in an abrupt turn to the left. That meant they had left the gallery where the Piero della Francesca's were displayed for the corridor. Her entire body trembled with fright. They were proceeding quickly along the passageway from which Emma and her students entered the Piero room, at least that is what she thought was happening.

The harsh words and rough treatment filled her with near panic; she dared not, nor could she cry out, so paralyzed with terror had she become. *Non voglio moiré,* I don't want to die! A knife in her back or in her side, the horrible prospect flashed in her mind.

Suddenly they halted; she heard the creak of an opening door. Abruptly she was turned around, thrown off balance, and thrust back without warning into a sitting position in a chair, her arms still tightly held. Silently and competently the two mysterious figures bound her to the chair, wrists tied together, legs tied to the chair legs.

Quickly they lifted the cloth from her head, replacing it with a blindfold. She managed only a glimpse of the feet of her captors, nothing else. Enough to focus on a pair of black leather shoes with small tassels at the end of the ties, tassels bound in tiny gold bands. The top of the shoe was finely woven in small strips of a supple leather.

Her eyes were covered, a tape clamped over her mouth and without another word the door slammed and she was left alone, immobilized, unable to cry out. The outrage of what had happened made her furious, in spite of the danger. By what right? How dare they!

She despised her captors who handled her so roughly. Emma knew what was happening. She was an inconvenient witness to the theft of one, or both, of the Piero paintings; what else could be the horror unfolding? She recalled the flickering on and off of the lights, the young attendant smoothly trying to coax everyone out of the palace galleries, suggesting they leave and return the following day when 'everything will be fixed'.

Fixed indeed! Her thoughts raged. It was all a part of a carefully orchestrated scheme. She realized that now. That is why no alarm bells sounded. The electrical system had been disarmed, probably broken. And the aging museum guards, how were they dealt with? Probably drugged, or knocked senseless.

Barbara and the students must have been among the last visitors to exit the building. Then the thieves locked the doors, thinking they were alone. When they found Emma in the room containing the Pieros at the end of the corridor, it must have been an unwelcome discovery, but only a momentary setback. They lost no time in dealing with her, herding her into a suitable hiding place. Where was she? A dungeon? A torture room in the old palace? What would they do with her now? Was she to be taken hostage in their escape? Panic blossomed over her like an unwelcome rash.

Emma did not believe they were planning to kill her, the only witness to the crime. She was thankful for that. Or were they? Surely not, she reasoned, because *I didn't see anything*. Italians had the greatest respect for human life. She read this somewhere quite recently. They adored children, she has witnessed many examples of this affection, and yet? Newspaper headlines of past kidnappings ending in murder leapt into consciousness. Fear again spread over her like an incoming tide washing over a sandy beach.

Her thoughts raced; she blamed herself for failing to anticipate what was happening. Why hadn't she been alert to impending disaster with the flickering of the lights? That is the first thing she should have registered. A child would pick up on that.

And those expensive shoes. Italian shoes. She willed herself to remember everything about those shoes. It might be important. She almost laughed out loud except for her gag, rendered giddy by fear and despair, thinking what Sam would make of those fussy, pricey Italian shoes! One thing she knew, no museum guard had been wearing costly shoes like that. Yet the trouser leg above the shoe had been the dark blue of a museum uniform. An impostor, posing as a warder, had worn those shoes. Emma was certain of it. If only she could remember the face of the young guard who urged them to leave when they were in the corridor. But of course it was impossible, unregistered in her recall of the moment. She had barely looked at him.

Despairing, hands tied together, feet bound to the chair, she bent her head down and bumped against something solid, like the edge of a table. Nudging along she felt first a kettle, then some mugs as she explored with her head. Heavens! she was in the little coffee—break room off the corridor she had glimpsed at the open door when they were hurrying toward the Pieros, the room with mops and brooms standing in the corner. Emma felt a rush of elation: in the vast ducal palace of Urbino, she knew where she was!

As the minutes crept by, Emma tried to keep calm. She strained to hear anyone moving along the corridor. Once she imagined she heard footsteps in the passageway, but when she tried to signal, no sound came from her lips. If only she had seen their faces, glanced at a watch or a ring. Even so, the memory of the fussy shoes with the gold tassels was seared on her brain. Best of all, she was unhurt. She felt grateful for that.

Surely sooner or later someone would find her, or she might discover a way to cut the bonds binding her wrists, then untie her legs, rip the gag and blindfold off. Barbara and the girls would soon raise the alarm. Barbara would convince the police that Emma had to be somewhere inside. Above all, Emma knew she mustn't panic.

Time inched by. She heard bells peal the hour from the steeples of various churches. Two o'clock. Her fingers felt numb. She tried to move them. Hadn't Barbara alerted the police? Could they have ignored Barbara? Surely not. She worked the cords, forcing them to loosen slightly as she applied what twisting pressure she could while her wrists, raw and bleeding, smarted with pain. But she realized she could never stretch the cords enough to untie herself. She must think of some other way to cut them through. But how?

She remembered the kettle. Was there a spoon? Or a knife. Her heart pounded with fresh hope. She nudged the surface of the table with her forehead again, touching something sharp, as though the veneer had been broken away from the edge, leaving a sharp nick. Could she possibly maneuver herself, chair and all, so that she might sever her wrist cords against the sharp edge?

Urbino: The Palazzo Ducale

Slim chance, Emma admitted, but she had nothing else left in the way of hope. Time was important. The sooner the police were notified, the sooner they could begin searching for the missing paintings.

She knew the students and Barbara must now be fearing the worst. Awkwardly, she hitched her chair and it grated on the stone floor, making a high, screeching noise. Would that sound fail to attract attention? Emma gave up trying to free her wrists and began scraping her chair in earnest. But if all of the guards were drugged or knocked out, who would hear her? Surely the police would be arriving soon! Tears of frustration welled in her eyes. She rammed her head over the table top in one great swipe. Metal teakettle and china mugs crashed to the floor. Frustration set in. Her wrists throbbed with pain. She was exhausted.

"Stupid! Cretin!" She admonished herself. "Stop sniveling. Try harder." With a desperate lunge she managed to stand with the chair latched to her back and placed her wrists at the sharp corner of the table. With supreme effort she moved them back and forth but she had no way of knowing what progress, if any, she made. When the pain became unbearable, she stopped, sat down and began scraping the chair across the stone floor. Emma hated the sound of a fingernail scraping on a blackboard, and this sound was so much worse. But she kept struggling to make any sound she could.

Reaching the point of exhaustion, hope almost abandoned, she heard shouting in the corridor. Frantically she made the scraping noise with renewed vigor. A door creaked open and Emma felt the glow of light on her face.

"*Dio Mio!* What have we found! Who has hurt you? Those bloody wrists! Untie her, Roberto! *Presto!*" The voice sounded deep, rich, filled with alarm and concern. It sounded like an American voice.

The blindfold fell from her face to the floor. She blinked toward the strong beam of the flashlight, saw two men, one wearing the uniform of the police. Relief! They leaned over, peering intently down at her.

"What is this? Who did this to you?—Now for the gag at her mouth, but gently, Roberto. Don't hurt her any more than she has been hurt already," the man in charge ordered. Emma gulped in air as the gag was eased off her mouth.

"Are you all right?" The rich, resonant baritone reassured her.

Who was he, this man wearing an old tweed jacket with pockets bagging, a red string tie threaded through a carefully ironed, snowy shirt collar? His eyes gleamed a luminous, rich brown, the color of *caffelatte*. He spoke English with an American accent.

"Perfectly all right," Emma answered, lips tingling from the gag. "But my wrists and feet feel numb."

"I'll bet they do! A little bloody too, those wrists! Hang on! We'll have you up and about in a jiffy." Gently he wrapped a clean pocket handkerchief around her left wrist, the worst of the two.

"You're speaking English! With hardly a trace of an accent." Emma's curiosity triumphed as she blurted out the words. And using American vernacular, she noted silently.

"Lucky I spent a part of my life in California, isn't it?" His smile won Emma over in an instant as his relaxed, good humor beamed her way. In a matter of a few seconds he had transformed into her savior, her liberator.

"I am Inspector Luigi Rovere, Urbino police. This is my sergeant, Roberto Benoso. And who might you be, Miss?"

Quickly and succinctly Emma identified herself, recounting what had happened. "I fear the thieves have escaped with the Pieros," she finished, her voice sad. "Have you been to see if they are missing?"

"We were just on our way when we discovered you," he replied. "Heard you, that is," he amended. "Come on, you might as well go with us. You've pretty well messed up this space with broken tea mugs and a big dent in the teapot." His smile was engaging. "Roberto and I know precious little about art. You can help us spot this Piero fellow's work."

Urbino: The Court of Honor. Palazzo Ducale

Emma rose shakily to her feet and immediately toppled forward. Had not Inspector Rovere been alert, her legs would have buckled to the floor. Suddenly she found herself encircled by strong arms inside the scratchy tweed jacket. Supported by the Inspector, she took a few feeble steps, gradually becoming more sure-footed.

"You'll be all right soon, you just need to get the circulation going. Find your sea legs, I think the expression goes."

Emma nodded grimly and made a heroic effort to stand alone. In a few moments they entered the small room where the Pieros were displayed and the powerful flashlights picked out the two easels. There were paintings on each one, but when Emma approached the *Madonna* painting, she saw at once that it was different. She bit her lip. She must be sure before she spoke out. But there was simply no doubt. The painting by Piero had been exchanged for a poor, inferior copy. Luigi Rovere was watching her closely.

"Is there a problem?"

"This one, I'm afraid, is not the genuine Piero. It is a copy." She moved to the painting of the *Flagellation*. "However, I think this is the real one. It looks like they stole only the *Madonna of Senigallia* by Piero. The museum director can confirm."

"At this moment the director is in no condition to help us sort this out," Inspector Rovere answered thoughtfully. "He is at the *ospedale* nursing a very bad headache caused by being hit on the head with a hard object, we are not yet sure what. When he returned from lunch and found strange men wearing the uniforms of his guards, he protested, was tied up and got a goose egg on the head for his trouble."

She smiled at the words of this genial Italian police officer, but inwardly Emma's heart plummeted. So the *Madonna* painting had been stolen. She would stake her life on it. The colors of the version left on the easel were right, but drafting of the faces and figures was wrong; the soft patina of age, the *gravitas* of Piero's style was missing.

"No doubt about it. It's a fake." Her spirits sank to her shoes at the sound of her voice.

"I'm no art expert myself," Rovere muttered, peering uncertainly at the painting, then at Emma. As Emma observed him she was drawn to the large, expressive brown eyes, filled, she thought, with tenderness and compassion. She segued to the missing painting.

"I'd stake my reputation as an art historian on its being a copy," she answered. "I looked at the genuine painting about one o'clock. I was standing in front of it when a cloth was thrown over my head and I was hustled off to that storeroom, bound and gagged. The thieves took the real one and made off with it, as sure as I am standing here before you."

"Roberto!" thundered Inspector Rovere. "Get Pirelli on the car radio and tell him to get over here with as many men from the lab as he can spare. I want this building searched inch by inch. We won't find the painting, but we may find out how they got it out and who helped them steal it. Hurry!" Roberto ran ahead in the darkened silence of the deserted building toward the police car parked outside.

Luigi turned to Emma. "Now, Miss, I want to take you to headquarters, to hear exactly what happened from the time you entered the palace until we found you."

"Of course, Inspector, but I must let my assistant and my students know I am safe. They will be trying to find me, and our coach is scheduled to leave Urbino for San Sepolcro at five p.m."

"Don't worry. We'll get word to your group. I promise."

They made their way down the staircase and out of the building where the small police car waited. The Inspector turned on the patrol car radio as Roberto eased away from the palazzo and Emma began to feel a lessening of the tension which had tied her stomach in knots the past several hours. But the horror of the disappearance of the painting weighed on Emma like a stone strapped to her back as she recalled her ordeal from the back seat of the police car speeding toward the Urbino *questura*, the police station.

7

A Conversation while Crossing the Mountains of the Moon

"I'm afraid I cannot release you just yet," Inspector Rovere told Emma, seated in a chair in his office, sipping an *espresso*. "Not until the Chief Inspector gives his okay. It shouldn't be long."

Her blue eyes widened with alarm at his words. The students. They shouldn't leave without her. And the drive from Urbino was a long four hours. He noted her agitation.

"Roberto has spoken to your assistant, Miss Darling. He will see that the students return safely to San Sepolcro. In fact, they are most likely already on their way," he said, glancing at his watch. "As soon as the Chief gives his okay, I'll personally drive you over to San Sepolcro. This is an enormous theft, and we are going to do everything we can to get the painting back where it belongs. I promise you I'll see you safely to your hotel well before midnight. We'll start just as soon as we can glean every crumb of information you can supply for us. All right? You did say you and your group won't be returning to Urbino, didn't you?" he reminded Emma.

Glumly, Emma nodded. Then, recalling her joy at being rescued, safe but for a few cuts and scratches on her wrists and legs where she had been tied up, she knew she owed a debt to the kindness of this police officer. She readied herself to go over the experience yet once more. She would do everything in her power to help. She was safe, and she knew she had been extremely lucky.

~~~~

Seated in the small Fiat belonging to the Urbino *questura*, a box of sandwiches on her lap, Emma looked at the road ahead as they left Urbino in the twilight. Darkness came swiftly in the mountains although the days of high summer were fast approaching. Luigi Rovere guided the little car skillfully up and around the switchbacks of the Mountains of the Moon in the fast-fading light. She was returning to the hotel in San Sepolcro, unharmed, but would she ever release from memory the harrowing experience in Urbino?

Emma, exhausted, had no desire to sleep as the car sped along; she was overcome by feelings of lethargy, emptiness and frustration at the turn of events on what she had hoped would be a highlight of their trip, a happy, carefree day in Urbino.

Urbino: Looking down from the
Palazzo of Duke Federigo

Uppermost in her mind was the horror of the stolen *Senigallia Madonna* by Piero. She was present when it happened, yet unable to prevent it. Filled with a sadness that held twinges of bitterness, she wished now that fear had not kept her from screaming out for help before she was bound and gagged. But the risk was too great, she feared for her life, not knowing what deadly weapons her abductors carried.

Looking back with regret was of no value to anyone now Emma knew. But recall was needed: recall of any detail, any forgotten impression to pass on to Inspector Rovere to expedite finding the missing Madonna and capturing of the thieves. Even though I've already told him every thing I've remembered she reasoned. But Emma knew, having heard it often enough from her friend Charlie St. Cyr of Scotland Yard, a witness can recall some seemingly unimportant detail days, even weeks later, a routine incident which might possibly crack open a case.

Earlier, at the police station with the Inspector and his assistant Roberto, she told everything, from previous encounters with a suspicious copyist Anna Cortina in London to the glimpse of her abductors' shoes as they tied on the blindfold. She carefully described the expensive, black, woven leather shoes worn by one of the men. Anything might prove helpful.

Throughout the interview Luigi Rovere was sympathetic, considerate, anxious not to overtire her after her ordeal. If only police everywhere could be so perceptive, Emma thought, secretly studying his profile as he competently guided the car around mountain switchbacks. The information she gave seemed like precious little, but, as he told her, everything she could remember would be useful. His optimism boosted her flagging spirits. He displayed a firm conviction they would soon recover the painting.

"We'll find it soon, Emma," he reassured her as they sped along. "Police all over Italy will be inflamed, just as I am, at the audacity of this theft. Lifting secondary works from small museums is bad enough, but to steal a painting by one of our most famous masters . . ." He sighed in frustration.

Emma recalled his gentle touch, his voice when he found her and bound up her bleeding wrist. How he supported her when she stumbled on numbed legs and almost fell after Roberto cut her bonds. And although he was not an expert on art, she knew he felt deep outrage at the theft. A portion of every Italian's heritage had been plundered. No, the world's heritage, she amended. Piero was universal. Her thoughts continued to roam.

Emma admitted to herself she admired Inspector Rovere. He talked about his life as the little car sped over the mountains. He returned to Urbino from California with his sweetheart Linda a few years back, planning to introduce her to his family, announce their engagement and his future plans to return to Italy with Linda as a bride. But as things turned out, Linda wanted no part of Italy: life moved too slowly, there was too much emphasis on the past. She broke off the engagement after only a few days.

He seemed lonely, Emma mused as they moved swiftly onward, toward San Sepolcro, enveloped by the velvet night.

Her thoughts turned to Sam, who probably was lonely in Aberdeen at this moment, missing her. Caught up in the drama and tumultuous happenings of the day, she had not given Sam a thought. Guiltily, she attempted to redirect her reverie. But she was unsuccessful, and found herself secretly thinking of the police officer sitting beside her, wondering if he was around thirty five or nearer forty, watching his profile as he skillfully guided the car on mountain slopes.

Someday, if Sam chose to remain in Scotland, she might be forced to decide whether or not she could adjust to a very different life there, like Linda, Luigi's former sweetheart. Such a dour, cold country, Scotland seemed to Emma, but how could anyone fail to love a country like Italy, she wondered. *Or a brave inspector like Luigi.* Unbidden, the renegade thought brazenly presented itself and Emma felt at once disloyal.

Her mind traveled back to Urbino earlier that afternoon. What a nightmare her disappearance must have created for Barbara when she failed to appear at the *trattoria*. Should she notify police at once or wait and see? What turmoil she must have felt when Emma failed to show up. But hearing Barbara's account would have to wait. For the moment her thoughts swiveled back repeatedly like a swinging metronome to the compelling man seated beside her who had assumed the mantle of hero, her rescuer.

"And have you recovered from the disappointment of a broken engagement?" Emma asked, longing to learn more about him.

"I suppose so," he replied, a small smile breaking over his face, eyes glued on the road ahead. "One does overcome these things. I decided to return for good to Italy where my people live. It was a good decision, I like my work, but I can tell you, Emma, I miss America!"

"So that is your plan now, to stay? No unfulfilled yearnings to go back to the United States?"

"*Certamente*, there are many things I like about America," he reflected as they came down out of the mountains onto the straight stretch of road. "Things run on time normally for a start," he laughed. "Yep. *Normale* is what I like!"

"This country, Emma, can be painfully frustrating in so many ways. But I've also gained an appreciation of Italy I never really had before. People are focused on living, feeling with intensity all the little moments of their lives. These things would seem ordinary to most: admiring a sunset, a pretty girl, a flower, are daily occurrences deepening life's journey, making it richer, more meaningful."

Emma thought a minute before speaking. "So you'll marry, settle down here one day?"

"If I find the right girl." Emma drank in the words and eagerly awaited his next remarks.

But in this she was disappointed, for Luigi, thinking it had been too long since his lunch of one small *panino*, suggested

Emma open the box of sandwiches. The afternoon had vanished with no thought or time for food and he was hungry. Now that they were safely out of the Mountains of the Moon, heading on the straight stretch toward San Sepolcro, he suggested food. So Emma shared a ham and cheese sandwich with him and continued to listen with interest to the man beside her.

~~~~

When Barbara had returned with the group to the palace shortly after two p.m. and found the gates locked, she panicked and hurriedly made her way to the Urbino *questura* to report Emma missing.

By that time the Inspector and his officer had already answered a call for help from the director, stunned by a blow to the head when he challenged strange guards he encountered in a corridor. Obviously the thieves hadn't expected him to regain consciousness so soon; they did not even tie him up. The officers Luigi left behind to see that the director was treated at the *ospedale,* joked among themselves that the director's thick head of hair almost obscuring his facial features must have dulled the blow!

When Barbara arrived at the *questura,* the police knew a famous painting had been stolen, but a missing American *signorina* at the palace of Duke Federigo? Details given by Barbara were carefully taken down, but no information was given out. They simply assured her they would investigate Emma's disappearance.

Missing in Toscana

At four o'clock when bells began to chime in churches all over Urbino, Barbara gathered up the students to proceed to the east gate, to meet the coach and Mario. Barbara informed the police what she was doing, giving them the hotel telephone number in San Sepolcro where she could be reached. She was resigned to the fact the best course of action must be to return the students to their hotel to await news of Emma. The enormity of her disappearance was sinking into all their minds by this time, and spirits of the little group were at a low point. Only Mario seemed relaxed, quietly standing by as they boarded, ready to get underway quickly with his usual efficiency.

But as they began boarding the coach a police car sped into view. A young policeman got out of the car and hurried to Barbara, speaking in rapid Italian, telling her Emma was safe at the *questura*, helping the police learn as much as possible about the theft. He added that Inspector Rovere promised "*La Signorina Inglese, Signorina Barbara,*" that *"Signorina Emma"* would be safely brought back to her hotel in San Sepolcro later that night. Barbara took the welcome news calmly, feeling a surge of relief that Emma was unharmed.

The coach trip back to San Sepolcro would take around four hours; they should arrive around eight-thirty. Barbara told the students Emma was safe, and would join them shortly after they finished dinner. News that their leader was unhurt brought whoops of delight from the girls. Barbara, looking at the excited faces around her, dismissed any thoughts of a quiet ride back to San Sepolcro. With Emma's dramatic disappearance to be revealed and the theft of a Piero painting to speculate on, the students were bound to chatter all the way back to the hotel. Barbara closed her eyes and leaned back. Relief that Emma was safe made her feel giddy; had she not been found, well, she dared not think about that. They would hear the full story soon, from Emma herself. She dozed off, thankful not only that Emma was safe, but so were she and all of the students, with a responsible driver like Mario at the wheel. "Let Mario take charge now, "she thought, closing her eyes. "He'll get us safely to the hotel."

~~~~

Lettice and Patricia quickly made plans to invite everyone for hot chocolate in their room after dinner to celebrate Emma's arrival, and to hear her account of what happened. The girls kept up the chatter all during dinner about "Miss Darling's Adventure".

Their high spirits had been somewhat subdued earlier when the enormity of the theft of the Piero and their leader missing had sunk in, and a spell of gloom descended over them. But with a party to celebrate Emma's return, things looked brighter.

Emma, arriving at the hotel, gathered her thoughts and prepared to meet with the students. She gave a brief farewell to Luigi who would set out after a coffee at the San Sepolcro police station on the long drive back to Urbino, hoping to salvage a few hours sleep in his bed before the daily grind resumed. With admiration in her eyes, she followed the little car out of sight.

She quickly turned to Barbara and the students, waiting for her in the hotel's reception room. She was moved by their warm welcome. The least she could do was to share with them what happened, no matter how weary she was going over and over everything with the police. She put aside nagging worries about the missing painting. Inspector Rovere would find it, she was certain!

Emma took a few minutes to freshen up, then joined the others in Lettice and Patricia's room. The waiter arrived soon after, wheeling in a cart bearing pitchers of hot chocolate and dishes of *biscotti*. Lettice and Patricia had pooled their spending money to provide a memorable homecoming for Emma. This rallied the girls, determined to show their appreciation to the hostesses by their enthusiasm. Emma felt her spirits revive and her mood lightened.

"You two are the best party organizers," Winkie said. "We don't even have to bring our toothbrush glasses to drink from as we usually do on these impromptu occasions. You've thought of everything. Look at these darling little chocolate pots with lids to keep the cocoa hot!"

Lettice served hot chocolate to Emma and Barbara, who occupied places of honor, sitting in the room's two chairs. The others arranged themselves on the beds and the carpet at Emma's feet while Patricia handed around *biscotti*.

"I know you want to know the sequence of events when you left me at the palace," Emma began.

Alice Heard Williams

The students' eyes widened as she told them she was bound and gagged after the shock of a cloth suddenly dropped over her head. They looked at her bandaged wrists in dismay as she described the place where her captors hid her, her efforts to free herself, the eventual arrival of the two policemen. She told them of the missing Piero Madonna, and the poor copy left in its place. She described her stay at the Urbino *questura*, how she repeatedly went over her experience with Inspector Rovere.

"I believe the police will do everything possible to find the missing picture," she said in conclusion, keeping her personal admiration for the Urbino inspector to herself.

"Did they take fingerprints, Miss Darling?" Vanessa's brown eyes were open wide with the excitement of Emma's adventure.

"Of course, Vanessa. More police were called in. They covered every inch of the room where the Piero paintings were as well as the entire palace."

"I wonder, do they think there was cooperation from someone inside the gallery?" Winkie frowned, tossing the single, dark blonde braid which hung down her back.

"That's a possibility. I am sure by this time the police have asked a lot of questions of the guards. They found the director dazed and recovering from a blow to the head, I do know that."

"And did the police tell you to carry on with our tour?" Marigold asked anxiously.

"*Certamente,* Marigold. They did indeed. I gave them a copy of our itinerary and they asked me to keep in touch if we discovered anything to report. Inspector Rovere may ring tomorrow morning, before we leave for Arezzo, to report any progress in the case."

"Speaking of Arezzo, I think because it is so late now, we should have a free morning in San Sepolcro tomorrow so we can catch up on sleep. We'll depart for Arezzo at one o'clock. It's only a short drive. We all need a bit of time to relax and recover from an unexpectedly dramatic day." Heads bobbed in agreement.

"If you get up early, you can visit the cathedral on your own, or do some shopping at the open air market in the street behind the cathedral square. You might have a leisurely lunch at one of the restaurants. Those of you who fancy it might enjoy a picnic in the little Piero park we visited the other night. There is an *alimentari* behind the park; they make delicious sandwiches and sell coca cola. We will board the coach promptly at one. How does that sound?" The response was enthusiastic, several girls expressing a wish to visit the shops. Emma sounded a final note of caution.

"Just a reminder: you need to be rested and relaxed before we look at the most important of all Piero's work, frescoes of *the Legend of the True Cross*. It's a complicated story Piero has to tell, and I want you to be able to enjoy it."

Emma smiled as she rose from her chair. "*Buonasera, mille grazie, Signorine*" she said, thanking the hostesses and wishing everyone goodnight, knowing tomorrow would come too soon. Caroline and Mary paused beside Emma as she unlocked her door.

"Miss Darling," Caroline asked, "May we come in, just for a minute?"

Emma nodded. "Of course, Caroline, if it is only for a moment Frankly, I am exhausted." She opened the door and they hurried inside.

"We thought we should tell you, even though as you say, it may have nothing to do with the theft of the Piero." Mary began, looking at Caroline, hoping she would speak up.

"While you were being held in the palace," Caroline began, pacing nervously in front of Emma, "We took a walk right after we finished our sandwiches at the *trattoria*. Miss Bone gave us permission as we were just passing time, waiting for you. We promised her we'd be back in thirty minutes. Anyway, we walked a little along the ramparts. We saw a Fina station down below us, on the circular road that winds below the city walls. Then we noticed a black Alfa Romeo drive in to be refueled. It was the motor Anna Cortina was riding in when we saw her at the chapel in Monterchi, the very same!"

"Now, Caroline, there must be a lot of black Alfa sports models in Italy," Emma smiled at the girl.

"But Miss Darling, Anna got out of the car!" Caroline's eyes held Emma's.

"We saw her, really we did." Mary's voice was firm. "She got out of the driver's seat. We couldn't see anybody else. I really believe she was alone. She was driving, that's for certain. And she had on the same blond wig we saw her wearing at the gelato shop on the square in San Sepolcro. Caroline and I remember the station is along the west wall of Urbino, below the west wall I mean."

"Did you get the registration number?"

"No, that is the great disappointment," Caroline sighed. "We were too far away. But we are sure it was Anna. She was wearing a black dress and sunglasses. We can't be mistaken, we'd never forget that blond wig. Remember? We told you about it." Emma nodded.

"Well, this certainly places her not far from the palace," Emma said, thinking aloud.

"What time would you say it was?"

"Not quite two o'clock." Mary answered. "I know because I remember looking at my watch. We were keeping close track of the time because we knew we only had thirty minutes until we were due back. We, we didn't want to be late!" She lowered her eyes, remembering the night before when they turned up late.

"We were really worried about you, Miss Darling. We were hoping you'd have been found by the time we got back,"

Caroline added. Emma's thoughts raced ahead. She should notify Inspector Rovere, but it would have to wait until morning. She was exhausted, and she knew he'd hardly had time to arrive back in Urbino. Anna's constant appearance on the scene was becoming more than a coincidence. She thanked the two girls, promising to report the information to the Urbino *questura*, then wished them goodnight, closing the door and quickly preparing for sleep. She would call Inspector Rovere first thing in the morning.

~~~~

After a breakfast in her room of coffee, *pane Toscana* and jam, Emma dialed the number of the Urbino *questura*.

"Rovere," the clipped voice answered on the first ring.

"Inspector, this is Emma Darling in San Sepolcro." Emma experienced a moment of uncertainty, shy about calling him first. She edited out the thought. This is not personal. I am merely reporting information that will help.

"*Ciao* Emma! Is everything all right?" She heard no irritation or impatience, only concern.

"Perfectly fine, Inspector. A good night's sleep worked its magic. I've learned a bit of news which may prove helpful. While walking about Urbino around two o'clock yesterday, two of my students spotted Anna Cortina in the black Alfa Romeo sports car, refueling at a Fina station below the west wall of the city.

This is the same car she was seen in with an unknown man at Monterchi a few days ago. Remember? I told you about that. I cannot verify the car's make, but the girls seem sure of it. She was wearing a blond wig, a black dress and sunglasses. The girls are certain it was Anna. They had seen her before in the wig. She was alone."

"I see," he answered, pausing a long minute. "Registration number?"

"Unfortunately, no," Emma replied. "They weren't close enough to make it out."

"Never mind. This places her in the right place at the right time. Possibly she could have been driving the escape car. I know that Fina station. I'll go around and have a chat with the attendant. Good work, Emma."

"I hated to disturb you but I thought it might be important."

"It could be very important. Call me again if you hear anything else, any time. And be careful, will you? Don't get yourself in hot water again! You've had enough drama and excitement to last you the trip, Miss Emma Darling!"

"Right, Inspector," Emma said softly placing the telephone in its cradle, telling herself the inspector was only expressing the friendly courtesy of *un' uomo Mediterraneo*, the Mediterranean male.

Alice Heard Williams

~~~~

Emma sipped an *espresso* at the sidewalk cafe opposite the cathedral in San Sepolcro and let the sun warm her back as she watched a flock of pigeons flutter onto the cobblestones at the foot of the *cattedrale* steps. So pigeons have behaved for time immortal she mused as she watched the birds jostle for position. She admired their dun colored feathers against the earth tinted stucco of the church. Being on her own for just a bit in a public place where she knew she was safe was a small pleasure she could not resist. One of the most difficult aspects of being a tour leader was constantly being surrounded by students bombarding her with questions. Flattering, but wearing. Just a little time alone to go over events of the past day was precious.

She reviewed the theft of the Piero painting. The morning newspapers carried headlines of the outrage but scant information. Did Anna Cortina really play a part in the plan, or was her appearance in Urbino at the time of the theft merely coincidence? The papers revealed nothing of course about suspects, but Emma felt more links to Anna would be uncovered as the police probed, links which might draw her closer into the theft.

Hopefully Hotel *Il Giardno* in Florence where they would be staying would yield valuable information. Anna just might live there or have a connection to the hotel. Inspector Rovere told her earlier he planned to go to *Firenze* as soon as he could get away to check it out. Her fingers rubbed the key tucked in her pocket. She had meant to leave it with him, but forgot in the excitement of yesterday. She would have do that when she saw him again. A smile crept to the corners of her mouth at this possibility in spite of the clamp she had placed on her feelings. Upset as she was with Sam for missing Jane and Charlie's wedding, she was still in possession of her engagement ring, although she was not wearing it. And she still intended to marry Sam, of course she did.

The pigeons decamped suddenly with a whirring of wings. Time to move, time to explore the town even though most of the students had chosen to sleep late before the departure for Arezzo. Emma stood up, leaving coins on top of her bill and strolled out of the piazza, deciding to follow a different street, away from the road leading to the little Piero park and the Hotel Contenta.

This must be a very old part of town, she decided, noting the weathered stucco of the buildings lining the narrow street. The houses, built with common walls; had no space in front for gardens, their facades met the cobblestones. Colorful window boxes blossomed with amazing results. She came upon a tiny neighborhood church named for Saint Agostino. Its stone facade looked even more ancient than the cathedral.

She pushed open massive doors, beautifully carved, to inspect the interior. There was a small nave with a central aisle, cane bottom chairs placed in neat rows on either side, and a simple altar at the front. The pristine altar cloth gleamed, snowy white, impeccably ironed. A clear glass vase held an arrangement of the most beautiful lilies she had ever seen; she was nearly overwhelmed by their sweet, heady fragrance. Everything about the little place of worship seemed lovingly respected and cared for. Modest windows of clear glass sparkled, letting in a rush of sunlight.

She sat down for a moment to meditate in the deserted sanctuary and to enjoy the beauty of the plain surroundings. A *vecchia,* an old woman bent with age, shuffled about, flicking a cloth lightly over any imaginary dust motes which earlier may have escaped her notice. The custodian, Emma realized, and said a few words to her, praising the sanctuary, the loveliness of the lilies.

The woman's face brightened as she answered, proud that she was responsible for the cleaning of the church. She told Emma that the flowers came from '*il giardino*'. Emma, supposing she meant her own garden, smiled her thanks and departed. Leaving the church, continuing on her walk, she saw remains of the ancient city walls ahead. The street would end at the walls, she realized.

The final house sat alone with its own ground behind a high wall over which flowering vines trailed. Shrubs, showing green above the burnt orange walls flourished. Through gaps in the delicate tracery of the wrought iron gate Emma peered in, glimpsing a faded but enchanting old house, almost hidden by the same flowering vines which clambered about the walls in attractive profusion.

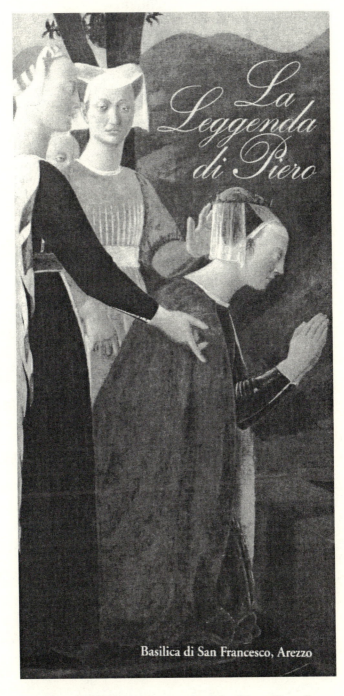

Arezzo: Piero's "Legend of the True Cross" frescoes, Church of San Francesco

Alice Heard Williams

What looked to be a carefully tended garden rose up on one side of the house, while on the other, a lean-to of sorts, roofed with rushes, stood with doors ajar. Emma made out a large, mounded form in the lean-to. Looking more closely, she saw it was a a car tucked away. The shed must be a tiny garage. Emma leaned forward, pushing aside foliage on the wall to get a better view through the narrow line of vision the gap in the gate permitted. Her left hand touched raised letters on the solid wall. Underneath clinging tendrils she pushed aside, she found a graceful wrought iron script spelling out *Il Giardino*, obviously the name of the house and grounds.

With a start Emma grasped the enormity of what she had stumbled upon. She had assumed the key in her pocket was a hotel key where perhaps Anna Cortina lived in Florence. Here was another *Il Giardino* much nearer where Anna had been seen, in San Sepolcro! She groped for the key in her pocket and thrust it into the keyhole. A small click of release sounded as she turned the key. The gate slowly opened. The scent of lilies coming from the garden engulfed her.

Elated, she quickly slipped inside, stepping back into the shadow of the wall. What next? She knew she must keep out of sight. She was trespassing and wondered fleetingly if perhaps she should have left all to Inspector Rovere. Before she could move, however, a fierce looking gardener rounded the corner of the house, trundling a barrow toward the lean-to. He saw Emma immediately. There was nowhere to hide.

She stepped bravely forward and said in her best Italian, "I'm looking for my friend Anna. I have something to return to her."

"Nobody here. Nobody here. You go away. Now!" The man frowned menacingly but Emma held her ground. The gardener looked middle-aged with thick gray hair and work-roughened hands, a large straw hat pulled down, obscuring part of his face.

"But I see her car," she protested, pointing to the small black sports model in the lean-to. "I'm sure she is here, and would want to see me."

When she pointed to the car, the man became agitated. Sounding, Emma thought, as though I caught him out in a falsehood. He took a step closer, forcing her to retreat quickly out of the open gate and into the street. The gate slammed shut with a clang.

"*Vada via!*" "Go away!"

So much for that encounter, Emma reflected bitterly on the outside, looking in.

She felt frustrated. She had not even advanced enough to see the car registration number, or to confirm it was the car Anna was driving in Urbino.

As she began retracing her steps, she recalled her earlier visit to the church of Saint Agostino. The cleaning lady had said the flowers came from the garden. Did she mean her own garden? Or could she have meant the lilies came from *Il Giardino*, the house? Emma walked rapidly toward Saint Agostino. The first thing she noticed when she entered was that the floors were wet.

"*Prego, Signorina,*" the cleaning woman approached smiling sweetly. Emma noticed that she was older than she first thought, and seemed to be wearing house slippers. The church indeed felt home-like and comfortable. Maybe more people would come, if all churches encouraged worshipers to wear comfortable slippers, she mused.

"I have just finished with the mop. You cannot go in just yet." The woman smiled in a friendly way.

Emma quickly explained the reason for her return in halting Italian. Could she tell her if the beautiful lilies came from the house nearby, *Il Giardino*?

"Indeed yes," replied the woman. "Maddalena picks them for the altar almost every day. She is cook there."

"I see," Emma replied. "And do you think she might let me look at the garden? I, I love flowers, especially lilies." True enough, she thought, remembering her mother's garden in Virginia.

"*Certamente*, she will be pleased. If you like, I will take you to her now. I have finished my work and am on my way to the market." She gathered up her shopping bag bulging with the bundle of altar linen to be washed, and the two left Saint Agostino together.

Emma reminded herself that this time she must not fail as they approached the gates of the house. She must get the registration number! Her companion from the little church called out in a musical voice at the gates.

Arezzo: The Church of San Francesco, Bookshop

"It is Giovanna! Giovanna here! Are you there, Maddalena?" Emma was careful to keep some distance behind Giovanna, hoping the gardener would not see her.

Short and stout with rosy cheeks and a welcoming smile, Maddalena appeared, hurrying as fast as she could propel her generous bulk. She opened the gate, inviting them inside.

Beaming with pleasure at the interruption to her usual routine, she seemed to dance on the tiniest of feet. She wore a wide skirt of red stripes and a simple white blouse. She greeted them effusively as she was charmingly introduced by Giovanna to "*La Signorina Inglese*," who had discovered the church of Saint Agostino on her walk around San Sepolcro and who wished to inspect the marvelous lilies of the garden.

Bobbing and smiling, dancing in her tiny slippers, Maddalena ushered them toward the lilies. But the gardener, alerted by their voices, sprang out from the lean-to like a menacing jack-in-the-box, startling them. His face was a thundercloud.

He sprayed a rapid-fire barrage of Italian, complete with shakings of the head and waving of arms, the meaning of which was perfectly clear to the three women. *Il Signor Cortina* had ordered no one was to be admitted at the gate! Emma took note of the name Cortina and that the orders came from 'Il *Signor*'. Anna's father? Brother? Husband? The gardener repeated the declaration of her previous visit, that no one was at home.

Emma took his tirade calmly, edging marginally closer to the lean-to, close enough to see the car's registration plate. She had expected the gardener might discover them. But the cook Maddalena was humiliated that a guest, such an important guest, a *Signorina Inglese,* had been turned away. Embarrassment turned her face beet red. The three of them moved swiftly toward the gate, Maddalena and Giovanna mumbling apologies.

Emma pressed Maddalena's arm when she saw the tears welling in her eyes.

"Do not fret, Maddalena. I will come another day." And Emma and Giovanna began walking toward the market. Emma parted with her new friend as they arrived at the cathedral steps now turned into a gala fete with the market bounty heaped everywhere. She thanked Giovanna for taking her to the house.

Her plan to confront Anna had failed, but perhaps that was not a bad thing. The important fact was that she succeeded in her main objective, to obtain the car's registration number, which she had branded in her mind. Also, the name of the family in residence was the Cortina family; she had found the genuine *Il Giardino*! Not a a hotel in Florence, but a house in San Sepolcro! She hurried to ring Inspector Rovere with the news.

8

A Difficult Assignment in Arezzo

Emma was speaking to her students in front of the Piero della Francesca frescoes in the apse of the Church of San Francesco in Arezzo.

"The Franciscan church, built early in the fourteen hundreds, was fairly new at the time Piero took over the painting of the frescoes around 1452-1456. A simple, even an austere church, but the richness of the paintings in the apse lifts the interior into the realm of the sublime."

"The Franciscan movement swept across Italy like wild fire in the years immediately following the death of Saint Francis of Assisi in 1226. Other religious orders active in Italy at this time envied the swelling ranks of the Franciscans and the endless streams of gold flowing into their coffers, enabling them to hire the finest artists in Italy to decorate their austere churches."

"The fresco cycle of the Legend of the True Cross was given to Piero when the first artist to receive the commission, Bicci di Lorenzo, died suddenly from a fall off the scaffolding. This unhappy occurrence indeed proved fortuitous in the history of art, for this fresco cycle is the backbone on which the fame of Piero della Francesca mainly rests." Emma paused. Were they paying attention? Yes, the magic of Piero and following the Piero Trail had rendered them spellbound.

"Piero's powerful intellect was brought to bear on this tangled legend. Spanning centuries, obscure in meaning, it derives from *The Golden Legend* by Jacopo Voragine, a popular book of the middle ages. Difficult, tedious, but richly rewarding, given Piero's genius for clarity, order, and geometry combined with a love of simplicity and *gravitas* in all of his figures. Arezzo indeed is the highlight of traveling the Piero Trail. It is important for you to understand that the theme, the Legend of the True Cross, was not a Renaissance subject: it was outmoded by the 1400s, largely a motif for The Middle Ages. However, this did not trouble Piero, whose primary aim was to please his patrons, the Franciscans, who requested it."

"The entire cycle comprises ten episodes, legends if you will, about the wood of the cross on which Christ died. And Piero took this complex and bewildering account turning it into twenty panels filled with logic and reason. It begins with the death of Adam. The tree soon to sprout over his grave will

Arezzo: Church near the Piazza Grande

provide the wood for Jesus's cross far into the future." The girls studied the fresco silently, absorbing the style, the rhythm of Piero's effort.

Stopping for a fifteen minute break in her lecture to give the students time to relax and look more closely at the panels of the convoluted story, Emma hurried to a telephone kiosk outside the church and rang Inspector Rovere. She quickly gave him the registration number of the car, told him at the same time she had located the house *Il Giardino,* that her key fit the gate, the key found earlier in London at the National Gallery, *the key dropped by Anna Cortina!*

As Emma revealed her findings, Luigi let out a low whistle. His progress on the case, working in Urbino, had been disappointing. He told Emma the attendant at the Fina station verified the presence the afternoon of the theft of a woman driving a black Alfa Romeo into his station, but he noticed little about her. Emma's news gave the police something to sink their teeth into! He told her he would drive immediately to San Sepolcro and together with the San Sepolcro police, question the occupants of the house, searching the car, the house and grounds for the painting and confirming ownership of the car.

"This brings us closer than ever to finding the painting, Cara." He rang off, promising to keep her informed of further progress.

Emma felt a blush come to her cheeks at the word "Cara". Dear, it meant. Of course it was a general term used for friends, relatives, even casual acquaintances, but also an endearment for someone special, the unruly thought crept into her consciousness. She hastily remembered she was an engaged woman, and this turned her thoughts guiltily toward Sam.

Emma left the telephone kiosk and returned to the fresco inside the church, thoughts going back in time to her first visit to Arezzo. What an impact the frescoes had on her as a young art history student from the University of Virginia. She wanted the visit to be equally meaningful to her students.

"In the episodes in the central panel we see two women in separate scenes who occupy important, yet divergent time periods in history: the Queen of Sheba and Helena, the mother of the first Christian emperor, Constantine. The Queen of Sheba, the wisest and most beautiful woman of the ancient world, is en route to visit King Solomon. Her gift of perception reveals that the wood of the little bridge over the river Siloam she is about to cross with her retinue of ladies in waiting, grooms and horses, has been built from wood from which the cross will be built far into the future, the cross on which misguided people will crucify Christ, the promised Messiah."

"Remember, this is an Old Testament woman, alive long before Christ's birth. But she is famous not only for her beauty, but also as a prophet. She refuses to step on the bridge, and hurries by another route to tell King Solomon this unwelcome news, begging him to have the bridge removed, buried deep in the ground, hoping to circumvent its intended use."

"In the companion panel the story has moved forward many centuries. Jesus' crucifixion has taken place. Helena, the emperor Constantine's mother, is on a mission to locate the holy wood of Christ's cross, lost for many years after the Crucifixion. Remember, Constantine was the first emperor to become a Christian. It is fitting he play a role in this important fresco. Helena is led to a certain spot; her workers begin to dig and find not one, but three crosses, one belonging to Jesus of course, the others to the two thieves who were crucified beside him on that fateful day. But which of the three crosses is the true cross? It is identified when, in turn, each cross is held high over the body of a dead man whose funeral procession is conveniently passing."

"Note the scene is taking place in front of a charming little Renaissance style church, one of the earliest representations of Renaissance architecture in painting. Remember Piero, with connections to the leading architect Alberti, also in residence at Duke Federigo's palazzo in Urbino, plus other outstanding painters and sculptors, was in the forefront of developments in the all the arts of Renaissance Italy. The true cross is revealed when it is held over the corpse, because the dead man rises up, restored to life. A miracle has occurred."

"Can you just imagine how Piero felt when he was given such a complicated assignment as this fresco, filled with many different figures and time periods? Yet he did not waver, and the end result is a wonder of order, precision and clarity." Emma noted the emotional looks on the faces of the students as she moved along describing the panels.

"Piero also created two great battle scenes, one a battle between Constantine and Chosroes, the pagan ruler. Incorporating principles of geometry and his knowledge of Renaissance architecture, Piero painted a sculptural fresco, unrivaled at its date in realism, depicting two great battles in all of their brutality, passion and intensity."

"Here is keen observation of suffering, both of animals and humans in both battle scenes. Horses rear and snort. Men cry out in fear as the death blows are struck, or they kneel holding their heads as though making one last appeal to God for salvation. We observe the fear of men who realize they are about to die; we sense panic in the eyes of their horses. A limpid, atmospheric quality unifies all panels of the fresco. Now look at this small night scene where we see the Dream of Constantine." She points.

"The spatial composition of this little gem in which Constantine learns he will be victorious if he leads his troops into battle holding high the Cross, shows us cubist volumes very close to those of some well-known late nineteenth century artists. It is not surprising that Piero was the Renaissance artist whom Paul Cezanne and Georges Seurat, French Post-Impressionists, admired more than any other. Without question, Piero has become the most popular Early Renaissance artist today."

"You have now been traveling along the Piero Trail for three days. But before we depart for Florence and the Uffizi where the double portraits of the Duke and Duchess of Urbino await you, we will see the final link, the astounding painting of the *Resurrection* by Piero at the San Sepolcro *Museo Civico*. His *Madonna of the Misericordia* is also hanging in the excellent little city museum. I have purposely waited until tomorrow, our final day in San Sepolcro, to take you to see them."

"After studying this primary body of Piero's work while following the Piero Trail, you will be ready to view other great artists of the period in the context of the emerging Renaissance whose work we shall examine in Florence: the Giotto frescoes at the Church of Santa Croce, Fra Angelico at the monastery of San Marco, Botticelli and Domenico Veneziano, Piero's teacher, at the Uffizi. Then you should be ready to put Piero in his proper place in the history of Renaissance art."

Her presentation finished, Emma knew the girls had been moved by the *brio* and conviction of Piero's work. Caroline and Mary approached her, reminding her of the promise to stop by Monterchi for another look in the small chapel there on the return journey to San Sepolcro.

"Oh, dear," Emma answered in dismay. "I'd forgotten, and we haven't yet visited the Duomo, the cathedral. There is a painting by Piero of Saint Mary Magdalene." Quickly she summoned Barbara and they began the ascending walk toward the cathedral. But by this time the students were tired and lagged behind.

At last they reached the summit where the cathedral commanded a fine view over surrounding countryside with a small park on one side of the piazza. The church's pride, a beautiful Romanesque campanile, flanked the opposite side of the square along with other imposing buildings. Once inside in the dark gloom of the cathedral, the group had difficulty locating the Piero painting, a standing figure of Saint Mary Magdalene.

"Poor Mary Magdalene is not considered important enough to have a good light," Winkie joked. "These people don't realize what a treasure they have." And in short order the girls, whom Emma realized had reached saturation point, inspected the painting of the saint and left the church in barely disguised haste to make their way downward toward the coach.

Midway down the hill, they came upon a beautiful Renaissance square, visible on a side street, the Piazza Grande, filled with outdoor cafes, colorful umbrellas and the sounds of strumming guitar music floating on the air. Overlooked on their upward climb, they paused, taking in the scene, a longing in their eyes Emma could not ignore.

"Miss Darling, you simply must let us stop for *spumoni*," Lettice begged, bluebell eyes imploring. Emma looked over the exhausted little band. All of them, even Mary and Caroline, echoed the plea. They look like slumping rag dolls she thought. She knew if they did not stop, it could turn into an unfulfilled memory long after the trip ended. She too was weary, and her left shoe was cruelly pinching her big toe. Also, they were up very late the night before, all of them.

Emma smiled, signaling approval, and in a rush the girls swooped down into chairs under the colorful umbrellas and began ordering *spumoni*, the special ice cream in multi flavors studded with fruit. Emma informed them this famous square, the Piazza Grande, was the very place where Piero lived during his residence in Arezzo when he created the frescoes. Ever mindful of his status as an artist, Piero chose a prestigious address for his rooms, she told them, taking a suite in a faded palazzo on the Piazza Grande.

"So our stop here is an important one in the light of Piero's most famous fresco. We need to feast our eyes on the beauty of this square and the buildings, many of which Piero would have seen and admired," Fiona chirped as she sat spooning ice cream next to Elizabeth.

"Right you are, Fiona," Emma replied, wondering if some of the others, not just Winkie, might turn into future art historians. Her eyes rested on Lettice and Winkie at her table, who as usual, were putting away great quantities of *spumoni*.

By the time they reached the coach it was past five o'clock; Emma was fearful the chapel at Monterchi would be closed. And in fact, they found the chapel doors firmly *chiuso* when they arrived in the little town, and Mario expertly swung the coach around and headed back toward the main highway and San Sepolcro.

~~~~

Inspector Luigi Rovere arrived at the Hotel Contenta during the last course of dinner, cheese and biscuits. Quickly

Emma left for the reception area where he waited, inviting him to join her and Barbara for an *espresso* in the little salon off the dining room as soon as they finished. Graciously he accepted, saying it should provide just the relaxing moment he needed after a busy day before he made the long drive back to Urbino.

Emma noticed that Barbara showed a positive reaction to the handsome, debonair inspector. On this night she had let her hair hang loose from the ponytail in a pretty page boy roll, and she had changed for dinner into a becoming navy blue dress with white collar which flattered her. She looked attractive, Emma thought, beginning to see Barbara in a new light, minus gym shoes and whistle on a cord.

Luigi stretched long legs under the tiny table on which small coffee cups rested and began to unwind from what had been an exhausting day. He sipped the fragrant coffee and Emma was aware that he looked now and then at Barbara with approving glances. When he discovered Barbara's mother was born in Greve, a small town south of Florence, her approval ratings shot even higher she observed.

"So you are the lady who drove my desk sergeant to distraction the other afternoon in Urbino, urging him to waste no time locating Emma." His tone was playful and the wrinkles around his eyes deepened with good humor. Barbara blushed becomingly and lowered her eyes.

Wouldn't it be wonderful if Barbara could find someone while we are on this trip, Emma mused, while at the same time in her innermost thoughts she wished Luigi might pay more attention to her. What an unworthy feeling, Emma, she thought, the sepia image of a tired Sam making rounds at the hospital in Aberdeen looming up in her mind. She felt guilty for disloyal thoughts.

"You see, we all were so worried, Inspector. I came as near to panic as I ever have when Emma didn't show up at the *trattoria*." Barbara lowered her eyes again. Emma watched as Luigi took note of the flutter of dark lashes. Out of her gym clothes Barbara was indeed a very different person. A few more pleasantries were exchanged, then Barbara, sensing that the Inspector wished to speak to Emma in confidence, tactfully wished them goodnight and left.

"I know you are wondering what we found out today," Luigi began.

Emma quickly nodded, watching Barbara in the hallway as she led some of the students out of the hotel for a stroll around the piazza.

"First of all, the car was registered in the name of Pietro Cortina. Everything about the registration is correct, as far as we can tell. Pietro's sister, Anna, is indeed a copyist, and recently returned from London where she worked on her paintings for several weeks in various galleries in and around London. She told us she sold them to collectors for modest prices. But why would she go all the way to London to make copies, when the whole of Italy is one enormous closet bulging with art?" Luigi was clearly bewildered.

"Pietro and Anna receive money from their father, and apparently little work is expected of them. The father is quite wealthy. "Fiesole wealthy", you know, that millionaires' roost above Florence where the pricey villas are located."

Emma nodded. She had heard of the sumptuous villas belonging to Florentines and others of great wealth from all over the world who occupy them. Like green velvet strewn with jewels, she was told, these fabled villas blanketing the small town of Fiesole high in the hills.

"Anna admits she was in Urbino yesterday. She says she was visiting friends. But what friends? Where? Her brother says he was in San Sepolcro all day, that he did not go to Urbino with his sister. Unfortunately we cannot substantiate either alibi with witnesses aside from his gardener who says he saw Pietro in and out of the house during various unspecified times of the day. Neither can Anna give us names and addresses of her friends in Urbino. Says they were casual friends, students passing through and they are gone now. Pretty flimsy we think. The brother and sister were polite, but cool, until the time came to search the house. That fussed them."

"What a disappointment! I just knew Pietro was the one wearing the expensive shoes with the tassels."

"It's quite possible both of them are lying." Luigi paused and took a sip of coffee. "I have a hunch he was right there, one of your abductors. But I've got to prove it! *Molto dificile*, very difficult. Clearly, we will make a return visit to extract a bit more."

"In the end they had to let us conduct a search and Luca, one of my colleague here in San Sepolcro, went over the house carefully while I looked through the car and we turned up nothing. If we missed anything, it's well hidden. So not much has been learned." He gave a sigh of disappointment.

"However, there is one thing: they appeared very nervous when we questioned them about others in collaboration with the theft. I feel strongly there is a partner involved, that this pair is not running the show alone. But who?"

"We also need to find out just how much young Pietro has lost in his gambling. As for Anna, she cannot make much money selling those sloppy works. Her paintings are just not that good. The ones in her studio look very amateurish, even to someone knowing zero about art, like me. So what do you make of all this?" He leaned back, draining the last of his *espresso* from the cup.

"I don't suppose you took away any of her work?" Emma asked, drawing circles on the white cloth of the table with a finger.

"Why no, we didn't, although I suppose we could take some paintings in. Why?" he asked, brows marching like patrolling ships above worried eyes.

"It's just that I feel Anna may be hiding something, that the insipid copies she produces are a front for something else, something more important. But I have no idea what. It's just a hunch," Together they drifted slowly out of the little café.

"So now we take all the little bits and pieces we have collected, let them whirl around *sotto sopra*, topsy turvey, in our brains. We wait. Something is bound to turn up." Luigi took her arm and they walked toward the front of the hotel.

"So tell me more about yourself, Emma," the thoughtful brown eyes regarding her drew her like a magnet; her heart thumping. She gave him a brief biography as they paused in the hotel's lobby, but she carefully edited out any mention of Sam in a brief summary of her life. Why? She asked herself, not wanting the answer.

She knew she felt powerfully attracted to this relaxed, informal inspector with the casual, easy demeanor of an American and the old world courtesy of the Italian male. She had never met anyone like him before. She admitted that she saw him as her knight on a white charger, her rescuer, the man who saved her. And Sam? She refused to think of Sam, not tonight, anyway. Scotland seemed so far away, another planet, on this warm, seductive Italian night and Sam, well Sam's image had turned into an old photograph drained of color, blurred and indistinct.

Luigi departed with a *Buonasera, Signorina Emma,* and Barbara rejoined Emma, asking for more details about Luigi as they climbed the stairs to their rooms. Emma replied that he had lived several years in California with an aunt and uncle, returned to Italy with his American girl friend whom he intended to marry. But Linda had ideas of her own, preferred to be in California rather than move to a faraway place lacking in the latest modern conveniences, where people spoke a language she didn't comprehend and life inched along. The engagement was called off and she decamped to California while Luigi decided to return for good to Urbino, where he now lived with his parents.

Barbara gave Emma a blushing smile, admitting that she found Luigi appealing as she said goodnight and disappeared into her room.

It was clear to Emma her assistant was smitten by the charming detective. Feelings of jealousy ignited in Emma before they could be tamped down. How could I, when I have Sam, to whom I am already engaged, hoping we'll be together soon, married, in fact! But is that what she really wanted? She felt puzzled, unsettled by the conflicting thoughts doing battle in her mind.

As she prepared for sleep, Emma thought of Sam and how disappointed she had been when he failed to get down to London before she left for Italy. She had not realized until this moment just how important that reunion which did not happen at Jane and Charlie's wedding might have meant to her future, with someone else appearing so unexpectedly who now was occupying her thoughts, every waking moment it seemed.

The following morning, Emma stayed in her room after breakfast, going over notes for her talk at the picture gallery of San Sepolcro. The telephone rang.

"*Buon Giorno,* it's Luigi here," he greeted her. "I've been thinking of our talk last night and I wanted you to know I am coming back over to San Sepolcro today. I am bringing Anna in for questioning at the San Sepolcro *questura*. We'll see how her story holds up when I get her away from her brother. I didn't press her hard enough yesterday. She will have more to say today, you can count on it. She and Pietro are bound to be protecting someone. Concealing a partner could prove a very foolish path for Anna and her brother to take and I am going to be certain she knows it. I'll point that out to her when she is alone and more vulnerable."

"I've been puzzling over the case most of the night," Emma confessed. "I agree with you, Luigi. Their statements of non-involvement just don't work. There are too many incidents linking the pair to the theft, and I doubt they could have done it without help from someone else. I also wonder about the visit they made to Monterchi. Anna's ill-concealed haste to get away, her saying she went to Urbino only to visit friends, unidentifiable friends. By the way, you checked out Pietro's shoes, didn't you?"

Luigi answered with a laugh. "You bet I did. But they were mostly brown sandals in his closet. No black woven leather with gold banded tassels. No, there were not any shoes like that in the house. We searched carefully. Another hope dashed; if not Pietro Cortina's shoes, then whose? Who could afford such shoes, certainly not one of the guards?"

"Well, the father up in Fiesole certainly could," Emma mused.

"Far-fetched, Emma, but I suppose it's a possibility in this crazy case." He rang off, anxious to be on the road for the long drive, saying he would drop by to see her before her late afternoon departure for Florence, if he could finish up in time.

The visit to San Sepolcro's *Museo Civico* signaled the end to following the Piero Trail. Only the artist's double portraits in the Uffizi in Florence of Federigo da Montefeltro and his wife Battista remained for them to see.

In viewing the San Sepolcro paintings and frescoes, Emma had given considerable thought to the time sequence. They began their study seeing the beginning of the earthly Jesus in the Pregnant Madonna of Monterchi, and they would finish on the Piero Trail in San Sepolcro by looking at the Resurrection, Piero's magnificent work expressing his most deeply held religious beliefs.

She knew the startling image of the hollow-eyed Christ, climbing from the tomb, so powerful and profound, would be a memorable experience her students would not likely forget.

Moving inside the small art gallery filled with paintings by provincial artists, Emma led the students directly to the Piero which shone with a convincing mastery of execution and intellectual brilliance. Emma and the students were joined by a few tourists in their wake who wished to piggy-back on her commentary. In front of the *Resurrection* fresco, the most important work, Emma told them Piero chose the moment for his painting when Christ rose defiantly out of the sarcophagus, one bare foot planted firmly on the ledge. The hum of girlish chatter died down as the students viewed the work for the first time.

"Did you know that in Piero's century, the medium of fresco was considered by far the most exacting and difficult method a painter could adopt? Wits of the period joked that easel painting was fine for young girls, old women and monks to admire, but the real masters of painting excelled in fresco." Emma skillfully captured their attention as the group around her expanded.

"As you have learned in our class, fresco was the technique of painting on freshly spread moist lime plaster with water based pigments. Because the fresco had to be worked quickly in *wet* plaster, this meant that only *one* day's plaster, the *giornata*, could be applied in the space of a day. This forced the artist to work inventively and quickly, sketching in broadly, speedily before the plaster got too dry. Not surprisingly, the best artists loved the rapidity and inventiveness fresco allowed. Early on, artists relied on the *sinopia*, a drawing made of the rich red earth from Sinope, the Greek city in Asia Minor, which had to be applied *from memory on the wet plaster which covered up the preliminary drawing.*"

"Later, cartoons, or patterns were commonly used, the exact tracing of the day's work outlined in needle sized holes and dusted over with chalk before the wet plaster had covered up the wall sketch; this meant an exact rendering could be achieved, and a large measure of creativity went out of the process. With the pattern, or *cartone,* in place, assistants could take over. But the cartoons came later than this work. Remember the Raphael cartoons we studied in the Victoria and Albert Museum in London? You could easily see the tiny holes along the outlines where the chalk had been dusted through." She paused a minute before continuing.

"Occasionally, colors the artist wished to apply would fade out of the wet plaster, and the artist would resort to restoring the color on dry plaster, or *fresco secco.* Most of the time this resulted in disaster as the color dried and soon after began peeling away. You see, it needed the wet lime to lock it in. Questions girls?"

"But if it was so important, why did it die out as a medium of expression in later years, Miss Darling?" Winkie twisted her fat braid thoughtfully.

"Great question, Winkie. There were a number of reasons. First off, reading became more general as use of the newly invented printing press became more widespread. You see, the medium of fresco, perfectly suited to tell a story in pictures in consecutive panels, like a comic strip, lost some of its power to instruct. People could read for themselves in Bibles as the printed word became accessible to the masses." Emma paused.

Arezzo: Rescue Ambulance,
Society of the Misericordia

"Most importantly, however, fresco became outdated because of the difficulty of the exacting medium, and the high rate of failure. Remember, many artists simply did not possess the arsenal of skills needed to succeed in painting fresco that would endure, pass the tests of time. Even Michelangelo, when he began the Sistine Ceiling frescoes in the early 1500s, lost the first portion of his work because the stucco refused to dry properly and mold sprouted all over the surface."

After a brief discussion of Piero's *Madonna of the Misericordia* hanging nearby Emma reminded her audience that today, in San Sepolcro and all over *Toscana,* the organization of the Misericordia still flourished, driving ambulances and emergency vehicles to care for the sick and injured. Emma brought her talk to a conclusion and gave the girls free time to look about on their own in the charming little gallery.

After the visit to the San Sepolcro *Museo Civico,* the girls planned to pack, have lunch on their own, and spend the remaining free time left in San Sepolcro as they wished, a final look around Piero's birthplace. The coach would depart in late afternoon for Florence arriving at the hotel in plenty of time for showers and unpacking before dinner.

Barbara confided to Emma as they enjoyed a quick lunch at the hotel's little cafe that she wished she could see Inspector Rovere before leaving. Would he return to Urbino soon? Or perhaps follow them to Florence? Emma understood Barbara's longing, but she could only tell her she had no idea of Luigi's plans; he might possibly be free to see them off, or he might not.

Emma had finished packing and was going over the final leg of their journey along the Piero Trail. Surprised by a knock on the door around mid-afternoon, she opened it to find Luigi Rovere. Previously their meetings had been in the public rooms of the hotel. When Emma saw him standing at her door, she became flustered.

"I have just finished talking with Anna, and I have things to tell you no one must overhear," he explained as he entered. Emma motioned him to a chair.

"As I suspected, she told me a lot more when I pointed out the evidence we have against her. Here's what really happened: She drove her brother to Urbino, dropped him off at the palace, collected him later and drove him home again. He was dressed in a uniform and took over as one of the palace guards. But she was adamant that she did not participate in the theft, and that the picture did not leave Urbino with them."

"She insists that there is a man called Matteo who gives her brother orders. He planned the theft. Pietro owes him money and Matteo has threatened to reveal everything about his gambling excesses to Pietro's father if he won't cooperate. Now Pietro depends on his father for money. Anna too. Naturally, they are sick with worry the father will find out about their involvement and Pietro's gambling debts." Luigi shook his head. "What messes people get themselves into."

"Also Anna insists she doesn't know Matteo's last name or where he lives. I asked her if she gambled. She said no, but that she loves her brother and wants to help him out of his trouble. And, old softie that I am, I believe her. I can't be sure she is leveling with us on everything, however. And of course, she is deeply involved, whether she likes it or not."

"So what about her painting? Why was her copy of Piero's *Madonna and Child* left on the easel?" Emma looked puzzled. She could not be quite as trusting of Anna as Luigi.

"Just a delaying action, apparently, thinking the theft might go unnoticed a bit longer. Fat chance of that! It stuck out like a sore thumb! She admitted it is her painting but denied any part in putting it in place of the real Piero. She said Matteo believed it might keep the police from discovering the theft immediately. She knows, by the way, that she is not a good painter, but she keeps trying. She was humble in the extreme about that. But I am not entirely convinced the brother and sister aren't masterminds of the entire operation. We simply do not know at this point."

"By the way," Luigi added, "The San Sepolcro police are going out to search the house again this evening. They will bring in some of her paintings to test them in the lab, to see if they can learn anything."

"Good. It may be they find something hidden underneath. It was only a feeling I had. Where do you think this Matteo is hiding?" Emma studied his earnest face. A wayward thought intruded: How could that California girl have left him and returned home?

Firenze: River Arno with Goldsmith's Bridge

"It's anybody's guess where he is. I've had word from Urbino that a tourist at the museum who happened to have a Brownie camera got a good shot of one of the men apparently masquerading as a guard. The tourist was an American, naturally, and didn't realize its importance until yesterday when he read the papers. It seems the guard was good looking, according to his sixteen year old daughter, and she wanted a picture of him, which he proceeded to shoot with her Brownie." Emma pictured a quick vignette: a pretty sixteen year old cajoling an indulgent father into taking a photo of the "cool" guard.

"Of course," Luigi continued, "It could be a picture of Pietro instead of Matteo. But he's on the scrawny side, and no muscles at all. His hair is already thinning too. If it's this Matteo, maybe our ship has come in at last. When I leave you, I'm paying a visit to Paolo the father at his palazzo in Fiesole. I want to find out if *he* knows about Matteo. I learned much more when I talked to the brother and sister separately."

"You must have worked every minute since I saw you last, to come up with so much," Emma responded admiringly, at the same time wondering for what possible reason they failed to interrogate brother and sister separately the first time. But she only added, "When do you ever find the time to rest?"

"I don't get much sleep when I'm in the middle of a case. Now that I have to trundle between Urbino and San Sepolcro, even less. Still, I manage. So many pieces of the puzzle won't fit. Maybe some will never fit, like Anna's labored copies of famous paintings. That brother and sister are deeply involved, however, I'm sure of it." He grinned engagingly at her.

"Probing, probing, probing. Never satisfied. Single-minded, I am, Emma, like that young surgeon of yours. Sam, is it?"

Emma felt her cheeks burn. She had mentioned Sam casually, as a friend, in the statements she made after her abduction in Urbino. Luigi sensed that he was special to her. He spoke before she could frame a reply.

"I'd like to think that perhaps, just perhaps, you have special feelings for me too, Emma," his voice so soft she barely heard. Soundlessly, he had glided closer and quickly covered both of her hands in his.

Startled, Emma drew back. Guiltily she thought of Sam, aware that she had given free rein to repeated romantic thoughts of Luigi Rovere and his magnetism, and now things were heading in the wrong direction. Observing her in the privacy of her room, Luigi had sensed her unspoken approval.

This sort of scene had no business being played out. What about Barbara, who had shared with me her feelings for Luigi? She was the one he should be flirting with, not me! And Sam. Whatever would Sam think now? What about my students? Luigi shouldn't even be in my room! But the unruly imp inside her whined in her ear: *Move closer, not farther away!* Thoughts whirled confusingly in Emma's brain as she struggled for composure.

Inching closer, Luigi wrapped his arms around her and before she could retreat, planted a kiss on her lips. Emma pushed awkwardly away, indignant.

"You shouldn't have done that." Her voice was harsh, a verbal slap.

"Ah, Cara. I cannot help myself. You are irresistible." His eyes and his words teased her, his smile was merry.

"You distract me," he went on, "I'm accustomed to working with that ugly face of Roberto in Urbino and well, *Cara*, my emotions have run wild and now look where we are!" The brown eyes narrowed and wrinkles around them deepened with good humor.

He's making fun of me, she thought wildly. Frustrated, she felt powerless because Luigi was so debonair, so charming and obviously an experienced flirt. Feelings of desire and frustration mingled, whirled about. Finding herself at a loss for words, she moved toward the door, jerked it open with shaking hands.

"I think you should go now," she spoke stiffly, sounding petulant and prudish, not self-possessed and calm. She could not help herself, as thoughts and images of Sam and Barbara paraded through her head. Her brain drummed on, 'What about Sam? What about Barbara? What sort of a person am I?'

"Oh my, surely you are not going to banish me forever?" Luigi's voice mocked as he nonchalantly ambled on long legs toward the door, perfectly at ease. "We have made such progress on the case, surely you are not going to force me to solve it alone and spoil our partnership." His serious words belied the smile hovering about his lips, his eyes twinkled, making Emma feel both foolish and fussy. He is laughing at me, she thought, feeling a flush cover her face.

"Please, do not let this happen again," she spoke in her most severe voice, usually reserved for wayward students. "Of course I hope you will continue to keep me informed," she added, aware her voice was rising and falling, predictable, like the rhythm of a syncopated fountain. "Certainly I will report to you if I find out any more information. Now, I really must finish packing." Emma felt empty, deflated, like a Victorian heroine's worst nightmare, party to a love scene she both longed for and at the same time rejected.

Luigi glanced at the closed suitcase and then at the room, bare of all of her personal belongings. Clearly the packing was finished. "Ah, yes, your packing, Emma." Giving the smallest of good natured nods he moved toward the door. "*Ciao*, Emma." And he was gone, leaving her feeling empty and close to tears.

What was going on here, Emma wondered, her eyes boring into the closed door. This outrageous man has flipped everything *sotto sopra*. And Sam? But when she tried to bring Sam's face into focus, the upturned mouth and white teeth of Luigi Rovere marched before her. Involuntarily, her wayward fingers strayed to her lips, as she remembered the kiss. What was happening?

Emma felt fear of a new kind, as if she walked toward the edge of a precipice, but was bent on edging closer. Unable or unwilling to banish the image of a tall, elegant police inspector who had become her protector and her ideal, she inhabited a limbo of her own creating.

9

A Punctured Tire, A Startling Revelation

Barbara glanced nervously up and down the busy street in front of the hotel Contenta as she helped the girls hand over their cases to Mario to load onto the coach. Emma knew Barbara was hoping Luigi would appear like some dazzling Prince Charming driving an Urbino police car rather than riding a white horse, willing him to appear to see them off.

Guiltily Emma kept silence wound around her like a tight cord. Her dilemma was weighing heavily. Whatever was wrong? Why couldn't she banish Luigi from her mind? And put Sam in his place, where he should be, a small inner voice whispered.

Mario good-naturedly teased the girls about how much heavier their cases were becoming as he lifted them into compartments at the side of the coach.

"Too many souvenirs, no?" he asked in simplistic English of the covey of admirers circled around him.

As far as Emma could tell, Mario had maintained a discreet distance from the girls. Emma was glad for his good judgment. His demeanor spoke well for him. An alert and careful driver, quiet, yet watchful, simply but neatly dressed. Today he wore dark trousers, blue chambray shirt; brown trainers. No, Mario presented no problem, but Luigi. Her thoughts flew like an arrow to him.

As the coach moved toward *Firenze*, Emma's thoughts, soared like an airborne glider, spiraling out of control in a fickle wind. She needed to rein in her feelings. To date, except for witnessing the theft of a priceless painting and being abducted for a few hours, everything on the trip had run predictably. Each day had proceeded as planned. The girls were participating with enthusiasm. Barbara's presence was proving to be a godsend. The coach driver was reliable and kept to his duties. They had seen the Urbino paintings, the Pregnant Madonna, the Arezzo and San Sepolcro paintings along the Piero Trail.

I must pay attention, keep everything humming along. Should I let a silly infatuation with a handsome policeman, years older than I, upset everything? Her thoughts raced along passing all the road signs of predictable logic. I have met someone who challenges my love for Sam and threatens our chances for a happy life together. I must not let anyone destroy that.

Emma could put her finger on the problem, yet she was unable to act. A strange torpor imprisoned her, left her powerless to banish feelings she had for Luigi, however much she wished it; it was the heart causing all the trouble. It was as though behind her closed eyes, a mocking, smiling Luigi Rovere taunted her, dared her.

Barbara. Guileless Barbara, inexperienced in attracting an admirer, but someone who admired Luigi. Barbara trusted me with her feelings, Worse yet, I have betrayed her trust, indulging in romantic dreams about a man she has found attractive. *Luigi is free but I am not.* I've accepted an engagement ring from someone else!

She took a grip on her feelings. Steady on! Drop this fantasy. Forget him! But as she looked out at spring twilight falling over the beautiful, rounded Tuscan hills gathering purple tones in the deepening shadows, she wondered if she could stop herself? Surely this Italian countryside was the most achingly beautiful of any she had ever seen. Idyllic. Poetic.

Her thoughts were interrupted by a loud hissing noise followed by sinister vibrations and shudders of the coach. In seconds Mario had eased the coach to a stop on the narrow verge of the road.

"What is it, Mario?" Emma hurried toward the front.

"A puncture," Mario answered, swinging down from his seat and opening the door. Emma cautioned the others to stay seated for the moment as she followed him. Dismayed, she saw the front tire was indeed flattened. Mario mumbled something unintelligible and hurried to one of the storage compartments on the side of the coach. Light was failing and Emma knew darkness would soon be upon them. The road was narrow, winding and unlighted, a bad spot for a breakdown.

"Barbara and I will hold a torch for you, Mario," Emma offered, as he opened the compartment, quickly taking out a jack and a wrench.

"Okay. I manage in a hurry. You look for torch there." He pointed to the open compartment then turned his attention toward the spare tire, rolling it briskly along at his side.

"*Prego, grazie*" he called back as an afterthought. Waves of scented air billowed in his wake, the ever present hair dressing, Emma thought absently as she strained in the fading light to see the torch somewhere in the compartment.

Her groping soon turned up the flashlight. Grasping it triumphantly, she flicked it on and was about to turn to Barbara who had appeared at her side when she saw something small, gleaming in the strong beam of the torch, partly hidden by the tool box in the luggage compartment beneath the coach. She leaned closer for a better look.

Tiny gold bands shone around black leather tassels on a pair of black, woven leather shoes. Those shoes! She had seen them before. Never, in a hundred years could she forget the shoes worn by her abductor in the palace at Urbino!

At the same time, the forgotten scent of hair dressing she had smelled when she was captured permeated the night air, exploding into her consciousness. The same, the identical woodsy smell! The memory had languished, buried in her mind until now. Suppressed information surfacing at this moment in her brain! The sort of revelation police everywhere hoped would emerge during endless reconstructions and recollections of crimes.

In a split second she recalled her experience: bound and gagged, a cloth thrown over her head. And yes, the *same* scent of hair dressing, worn by one of her abductors. Quickly she turned away and, keeping her countenance blank, hurried toward Mario, Barbara following behind her.

Mario had removed the tire and was tightening the replacement. Silently she handed Barbara the gleaming torch. In a few minutes the bolts would be secured and they would resume their journey. But things looked different now. Her mind raced to process what she had discovered.

Mario! The one who bound and gagged her in such an efficient way! Owning those shoes! Could it be possible? What was he doing, driving their coach? *Mario, Matteo,* they sounded a lot alike. *His* hair dressing. Now she clearly associated the scent with that fateful afternoon in Urbino. A *frisson* of fear gripped Emma. The scent of the hair dressing, the shoes! In a matter of seconds the fear and horror of her capture loomed afresh. She felt nauseous, frightened.

Disguised as a palace guard, had he been the thief? Mario? Those shoes were impossibly expensive for a mere museum guard to own. Or a coach driver, come to that! Of course she had not seen his face, only felt his muscular strength as he pushed and pulled her along the palace corridor. She had *smelled the scent!* The men who tied her up were strong. Pietro Cortina was one. Was Mario the other?

Emma climbed quickly aboard, heart hammering, reassuring the students the tire had been changed; in a moment they would be on their way. Her knees turned to jelly as she sank into her seat. Would Mario realize she had glimpsed the shoes? The black fear she felt at the time of her capture clung to her again, making her hands feel wet and clam-like.

Silently she turned events over in her mind as the coach gathered speed. What part did he play in the theft of the stolen Madonna? *Mario, Matteo.* If he were the one, he was a consummate actor, playing faultlessly the dual roles of thief and the competent, not too intelligent coach driver for a bus load of tourists. Heavens! The stolen painting could have been riding beneath them in the coach ever since its disappearance in Urbino! Hunted world wide, was the Piero Madonna actually underneath them at this moment?

One thing Emma knew for certain: She must contact Inspector Rovere as soon as she reached Florence, whether she wished to or not. In spite of herself, her heart flipped in a joyful leap in the silence of the darkened coach. Had she stumbled upon the real mastermind of the plot to steal a priceless painting? Possibly, and she must inform Luigi!

~~~~

When Emma telephoned the Urbino police station from her hotel room in Florence, she was told that Inspector Rovere was unavailable. No, they did not know where he could be reached nor when he would return. Emma felt the female voice speaking rapid Italian on the other end of the line was taking enormous pleasure in delivering this unsatisfactory message to an unknown female voice speaking in simplistic Italian with an American accent. Frustrated, Emma told the woman she had important information and wished him to return her call, no matter how late the hour.

Earlier. when the group reached *Firenze* and checked into the hotel *Il Giardino*, there was a letter from Sam in her mailbox. In the rush of assigning rooms, unpacking and hurrying to dinner, Emma had been unable to open it. Alone at last, she stretched out in the room's comfortable chair and began to read.

Firenze: Hotel Il Giardino

Alice Heard Williams

Aberdeen, 18 May

Dear Emma,

    So much has happened the last few days I hardly know where to begin. On the day you left London for Italy, I received a telephone call from my old Registrar at Guy's Hospital. Remember him? The one who wanted me to go to Cambridge and hole up in the Wren Library for two weeks instead of going to Greece? Well, he offered me a post in London at Guy's, beginning next fall! Assistant to the number one specialist on hand surgery, at a very generous starting salary. Naturally, I accepted. This is what we have dreamed about, Emma! Now I have to make plans to extricate myself from Aberdeen. They have made vague suggestions of my staying on at various times, but nothing definite has been proposed, so I feel free to accept the London offer. Emma, I'm coming back to London! We'll have the rest of the summer to make wedding plans together! I have been missing you so much!

    Next—there's more—I received a call from Charlie, on his honeymoon in Paris. He and Jane are leaving tomorrow for . . . *Toscana*! They have been invited to his aunt's villa there for several weeks, and they want us to spend a week with them. They were not sure of your address in Italy, so Charlie phoned me to issue the invitation. I gave Charlie your phone number in *Firenze*. He'll ring you soon.

Missing in Toscana

The villa is old and crumbling according to Charlie, but he told me 'Emma and Jane will think it's a sublime ruin, with a romantic garden.' It's outside a little village called Castellina-in-Chianti, in the heart of the Chiant country, near *Firenze* as I said. It belongs to Charlie's Aunt Olive who's widowed, an eccentric lady who paints wildly-colored landscapes. She'll serve as a chaperone if you think we need one! And of course, the old, married St. Cyrs will be in residence to keep us on a virtuous path.

I still can't believe those two really have tied the knot! They've known about the possibility of staying in the villa for some time, but didn't mention it to you at the wedding because they wanted their whereabouts kept a surprise. Now it's a *fait accompli!* Pardon the French, but I don't know the Italian phrase for a done deal!

If you can arrange to put your girls on the plane for London with your Barbara in charge and remain in Florence, I'll join you there and we can motor down to the villa together. It sounds like a wee bit of heaven, doesn't it? Write me quickly, or better yet, telephone so we can make our plans.

When can you be ready for another wedding? Our wedding! We can set the date!

Emma, I hope you are as thrilled as I am about this news. It has been too long since we were together, and if I ever get the chance, I'll not make the same mistake of leaving you.

At this moment I am seeing you just as you were when we were at Glyndebourne last summer, strolling about the gardens. I'll never forget how beautiful you looked in that floating long dress, and how happy you were when I placed Gran's rose diamond and garnet ring on your finger. Let me know if you can manage to stay on in Florence and travel with me to the villa.

All love to my Darling Emma along with passionate kisses and scandalous embraces,

Sam

Emma let the letter fall to her lap as a tear rolled forlornly down her cheek, recalling the magical evening of Mozart's Magic Flute at Glyndebourne's summer opera when Sam asked her to be his wife and placed the ring on her finger. The little bower covered in honeysuckle blossoms where he proposed during the intermission slid into consciousness. What a muddle life had suddenly become! Two short rings of the telephone interrupted her reverie.

"I hope I haven't awakened you. I've just checked in with my office." Luigi. That deep, soft Italian voice, sounding so full of hidden meaning, Emma thought, as all her good intentions began dissolving. Emma put the letter down and gave full attention.

"No, not at all. I wasn't sure you would receive my message." She deliberately kept her words cool and impersonal.

"What a day it has been for me. I've been with Pietro Cortina for hours and I have learned a great deal." Luigi sounded debonair, as usual, no smoldering resentment from the earlier encounter in her room in San Sepolcro. Emma noted this with an unbidden tinge of—could it be disappointment? She felt a quick stab of frustration because apparently she could not predict, nor could she subdue feelings bubbling up.

"Before you bring me up to date, I must let you know what I've learned." Emma kept her voice calm. She told him of the discovery of Mario's shoes in the compartment under the coach which triggered her recall of the scent of hair dressing worn by her abductor. The shoes and the scent matched.

Excitement deepened Luigi's voice. "Did he realize you saw the shoes?"

"I don't think so," Emma answered. "He was changing the tire and asked me to get the torch. I discovered the shoes back in the storage compartment as I searched for the flashlight. I'm certain they are the same shoes; he may *think* I saw them and recognized them, but he cannot be sure. He probably didn't know I saw them at all in the palace. My eyes were uncovered only a few seconds. And the scent of his hair dressing I suddenly realized was an unmistakable part of that dreadful experience."

"The man could be very dangerous, Emma, if indeed he is Matteo, and he thinks you are a threat to him. You should be on your guard. I learned enough from Pietro Cortina today to know that Matteo is ruthless, experienced in the underworld and not tolerant of any interference with his plans. Pietro clearly is scared to death of him, but Pietro knows he has to help the police by telling everything or he'll be left holding the bag on his shoulders alone." Emma smiled at the jumbled metaphors.

"If it is Mario, or Matteo who is the ringleader, where is he hiding the picture? Surely Pietro must have some idea," she said. In spite of herself, Emma found she was yearning to be sitting face to face with the inspector.

"That's a good question. Pietro swore he knew nothing about where Matteo lived, what sort of work he did, nor the whereabouts of the picture. But I am not sure he's telling the truth. He also claimed to know nothing of what Matteo planned to do with the painting. Says his assignment was to help pull off the job at the palace, nothing more. Says he's not going to receive any of the profits when it's sold. Matteo forced him to cooperate by downplaying his involvement and threatening to expose his gambling debts to his father. The parental allowance is small, he told me, and Pietro tried to increase his cash flow by gambling, as have numberless fools since time began." Emma imagined Luigi's brows raised in contempt.

"So Matteo actually took the painting away sometime, somewhere after they finished at the museum. Did Pietro say anything about how Matteo made his money?"

"Yes. and here's what makes everything fit like a glove! Aside from what he gleans by petty and not so petty extortion, he operates a travel business of sorts. He has a coach and hauls tourists, mostly foreigners, around. The company is called "Bella Toscana."

"So it ties up beautifully," Emma's voice was jubilant. "He is one and the same person as our driver. I'd been wondering, what if those shoes don't fit Mario?"

"Oh, they'll fit all right. Like a glove. Remember the American who took a photo of a young guard for his daughter on her Brownie camera? Pietro confirmed today the photo is of Matteo. I want you to take a look at it, Emma, then we'll be double sure. We need absolute proof the two are one and the same. With what you've just told me, there shouldn't be a shred of doubt. I'll bring the photograph when I come over to *Firenze*. We need your help!"

"You know I'll be willing to do what I can." Emma felt a little defensive. Surely he could see personal feelings wouldn't keep her from cooperating. More than anything, she wanted the Piero Madonna back where it belonged, at the palace in Urbino.

"And how does Pietro Cortina get in touch with Matteo if he swears he doesn't know where he lives?"

"We've got the telephone number for the travel business Pietro gave us. He says it's the only way he has to contact him. Pietro only knows he lives somewhere in Florence. The number is always answered by a woman Matteo hires to take messages. Probably an older woman, with time on her hands. She tells them he will return their calls. We can hardly ask him to call the police when we ring his number!"

"The phone company has promised to give us the location of the phone, but in this country, Emma, you will learn if you haven't already, that everything inches along very slowly. Sometimes I could die of frustration." Emma smiled, the image of a nail-biting Luigi looming.

He was right. Things were certainly slower than in America. Living in England, even years back when she spent summers in Haslemere, Surrey with her English grandmother Matilda, she found herself impatient. But in Italy, *certamente,* living must not be rushed!

"Well, you can see him and talk to him tomorrow, in the morning at ten o'clock, if you want."

"What do you mean?"

"I mean that he is dropping all of us off at the Uffizi entrance at ten in the morning. Give us time to get off the coach and into the building. Then you can arrest him. That's how it's done in the movies, isn't it?"

Her response was pert, but Luigi's thoughts went galloping ahead. "Matteo is picking up you and your girls and driving you to the Uffizi? I don't like it, not one bit, even if it's only a few streets away from your hotel! The man is a criminal, Emma, and criminals do desperate things when they are pushed. I don't like it!"

"Our coach is discreet and nondescript," Emma continued. "You wouldn't notice it; on the other hand, if you're looking for it, you can't miss it."

Luigi sighed audibly. "Don't worry, I'll see it. But I'll have to be there at your hotel. I won't let you leave with that guy driving you and your group unless I'm following close behind. The pickup is nine-thirty you say? *Dio Mio!*, I can see myself going back and forth to Florence every day now. And it's even further away than San Sepolcro." A moan slid over the wires.

"Look at it this way. Mario might lead you right to the missing Madonna. If I see you at the hotel, I'll pretend you're invisible. Goodnight, Luigi."

"*Buonasera*, Emma. And whatever you do, be careful. Keep your girls together, and don't go off alone, any of you! I'll be there tomorrow."

She put the telephone in its cradle and prepared for bed. It was after midnight and she longed for the oblivion of sleep. The day for her had been an emotional tug of war. First Luigi's expression of his feelings. Then discovery on the coach of Mario's true identity. Finally, the arrival of Sam's letter. Tomorrow with the Uffizi and the Pitti Palace on the schedule would be one of her busiest days fighting the crowds and shepherding her group through two of the world's most popular museums. Her thoughts balked at the prospect.

"I simply can't deal with any more tonight," Emma announced to the tired face in the washstand mirror. "I'm exhausted. Drained." Lying in bed, she twisted the garnet and rose diamond ring around her finger until dropping off into a fitful sleep.

~~~~

Emma cautioned the girls the next morning in the hotel lobby not to leave any of their belongings on the coach. Mario would not be able to wait at the Uffizi and planned to return to the Pitti Palace only in late afternoon to collect them. If indeed the police planned to arrest Mario and impound the coach, who knew when they might retrieve their belongings, but Emma kept this possibility to herself.

Emma knew she could not breathe a word about Mario. The fewer who knew the better, until it was all over. There would be no arrest until the girls had vacated the coach and were safely inside the Uffizi. Luigi's secret escort from the hotel would be an extra precaution, and she was grateful for it. No one would guess he was protecting them.

When the coach pulled up to collect them, she greeted Mario with *Buongiorno*, cheerful but impersonal. He seemed the same as always, polite and reserved. Nervously she stood outside as the girls and Barbara boarded. No Luigi in sight. What had happened? Was the car so well hidden she had missed it? With no reason for further delay she climbed aboard, her thoughts in disarray. What could have happened ?

As the coach approached the Uffizi in the jungle of Florentine traffic enhanced by creative arias of motor car horns, Emma's nerves hovered on a tightrope. Had Luigi been in a car crash? A change of plans was more likely she cautioned herself.

She saw the entrance to the great Renaissance palace come into view. Recalling its history produced a calming effect. Designed by Vasari in 1574 for the dei Medici business offices, the fabled museum had never seemed so welcoming. Knees wobbling, she urged the students off the coach quickly, reminding Mario of the time for the afternoon pickup at the Pitti Palace across the river, a pickup she doubted would occur. She could detect nothing unusual in his demeanor.

On an earlier visit to Florence with her parents, she had learned about the Vasari Corridor, the enclosed passageway connecting the Uffizi with the Pitti Palace on the other side of the River Arno, a corridor running above the goldsmith shops of the famous bridge, the Ponte Vecchio. This corridor, the most precious collection of self-portraits ever assembled anywhere in the world, contained examples by Rembrandt, Raphael, Rubens and Titian, as well as the luminaries of Florentine painting and representatives of the French school such as Ingres, David, Delacroix, and Corot. And it all began with the dei Medici rulers!

Firenze: Brunelleschi's Dome,
Santa Maria Dei Fiori

What a wealth of beauty they had assembled for the world, Emma thought, wishing time would permit her students a peek at these treasures. Perhaps on another visit she thought, beginning to breathe normally now that they all were safely inside. Something must have gone wrong, and Inspector Rovere was unable to contact her. She walked toward the gallery without a backward glance, aware of a thumping heart beating under her jacket as she led the students. Whatever happened was now out of her purview. She cleared her thoughts; she began to speak. She was consumed by curiosity to know if any arrest was taking place outside, but she forced herself to be calm and carry on with her talk.

After a brief introduction she led the students upstairs to the *quattrocento* galleries and stopped before *The Battle of San Romano* by Uccello, one of three giant paintings, a triptych, now separated, with one section in London at the National Gallery, a second in Paris at the Louvre and the third hanging in front of them.

"Don't you think it is especially poignant when works of art are divided up and scattered all over the world?" she asked. "You saw the painting in London which belongs with this one. Hopefully you will someday see the third panel, the middle scene, now in Paris.

"We are looking at the right hand section of a triptych. But perhaps never in our lifetimes will the three panels be reunited, shown as a continuous unit, as Uccello intended."

They moved on to look at *The Coronation of the Virgin* by Fra Angelico. "Tomorrow we will visit San Marco, the monastery where Angelico lived which is now preserved as a museum," Emma reminded them, giving a brief history of the gentle monk and his paintings. She promised more about Angelico when they visited San Marco.

The group moved to the diptych by Piero della Francesca of Federigo da Montefeltro and his wife, Battista Sforza, daughter of the ruling family of Milan. The girls had seen the portraits in art books and in slide lectures, and had arrived in Florence fresh from a visit to the couple's palace in Urbino, but they lingered many minutes in front of the pair of rulers, studying Federigo's broken nose and strong chin, drinking in the luster and sheen of Battista's pearls, her high forehead.

"Doesn't Battista look peculiar with such a high forehead? Didn't you tell us she was reputed to be a great beauty, Miss Darling?" Winkie gazed doubtfully at the blond haired Duchess of Urbino.

"You have to remember, Winkie, styles of beauty change through the ages. In Piero's time, one of the supreme attributes of feminine beauty was to have the highest forehead possible. Battista, and most of her contemporaries, achieved this by plucking out unwanted hairs."

"Ugh!" Marigold spoke up. "I'd rather have a low forehead than do that!" She squinted at the image, her owl-like gaze disapproving.

Missing in Toscana

Patricia questioned the profile views of both of the sitters.

"Good question, Patricia. Profile portraits were popular a short time only in Italy, about twenty years, from around 1450," Emma told them. "It was a style destined to be short-lived. Obviously, it is less revealing than a full, frontal view, but perfect for a diptych, a two paneled work such as this."

They continued through the gallery to the room where Sandro Botticelli's *Birth of Venus* and his *Primavera* hung. Both paintings were wildly popular and the space in front of them was clogged with viewers, many of them students like the British group. Emma and her girls waited their turn to admire Flora, the willowy figure of spring, and the modestly posed nude figure of Venus standing in a sea shell.

By one o'clock the girls had absorbed all they could without a break. Emma and Barbara led them out into the sunshine to the Ponte Vecchio and they leisurely walked over the old bridge across the River Arno, stopping to admire displays in the windows of the goldsmith shops lining the bridge.

On the other side stood the Pitti Palace, built to the plan of the architect Brunelleschi. They broke ranks and crossed over the busy street and disappeared into several small cafe and pizza shops to buy snacks for an impromptu picnic in the Bobboli Gardens behind the palace. Pizza, sold by the slice, was the overwhelming choice. Emma chose a small *panino* for herself. Toasted in its own little mold, the sandwich had become her favorite.

They settled on benches near the delightful Buonalenti Grotto with shell-studded walls and ceiling making a splendid backdrop for lifelike sculptures of animals and sea creatures. A statue of Venus by Giovanni da Bologna dominated the interior.

Emma told the girls about her first visit to the Bobboli Gardens when she was a student at London University. The young art historian, the group leader, brought them by coach from Lucca where they were based, only to discover the gardens closed, with a small hand lettered sign on the gate explaining that due to a special neighborhood election in the area the *giardino e chiuso*. The lecturer was undone, almost in tears, and was forced to declare a free afternoon for them to look about on their own.

"Italian museums are often filled with surprises," Emma smiled as she rose, brushed crumbs from her skirt. "Impromptu closings being about the most frustrating pitfall a lecturer can experience."

"Can't we please have a couple of hours off, Miss Darling?" Marigold begged. "We've really been concentrating hard and it would be nice to relax a little by having a ramble around Florence on our own."

"Well, I suppose you would like that," Emma reflected. "What do you think, Barbara?"

"It seems to me they have earned it. They have been scrupulous in paying attention, not lagging behind."

"And what about the Pitti Palace? Today is our only chance to visit as full as our schedule is," Emma reminded them.

"We could be back by three-thirty sharp. That would give us time to explore Florence a bit. Then we could see the Pitti." Caroline said, consulting her watch.

"Agreed then," Emma replied briskly. "But be sure to take your maps, don't go off alone and don't be a second late getting back. When we meet again in the Pitti Palace, go straight to the Palatine Room. It is filled with High Renaissance paintings and contains eleven Raphaels and twelve Titians. If anything can bowl you over by late afternoon, the sight of that room can do it."

Whooping with joy, led by Lettice and Winkie, they disappeared in a matter of seconds, leaving Barbara and Emma standing alone in front of the Grotto. Barbara wished to shop for presents for her mother and aunt on Via Tournabuoni. Emma yearned to see the Masaccio frescoes again. They decided to go separate ways and meet at the Pitti Palace.

Emma walked along Via Santo Spirito toward the church of Santa Maria del Carmine, a church she had visited on previous trips to Florence, to look at the famous frescoes by Masaccio. It was in a poor neighborhood of *Firenze*, which she had not remembered from previous visits, not at all like the fashionable section of Via Tournabuoni where Barbara was shopping, but Emma enjoyed inspecting the more humble neighborhoods of cities. She knew that one could glimpse everyday life of ordinary people away from expensive shopping streets. And there were plenty of people about, she felt safe as she walked on toward the church. The Masaccio frescoes were a popular tourist destination.

The sunshine beat down, warm and inviting, and she welcomed the walk which was helping her relax. She relished the loveliness of old stucco walls stained a rich, mottled ochre and barrel tile roofs in shades of rust, brown and burnt orange. As she walked she savored the sounds of Florence, the hum of the *vespas*, motorbikes, the ever present hiss of *espresso* machines coming from open doorways of tiny bars on street corners. She remembered walking along this street in other times, when she was a student, eager to pay homage to Masaccio, one of the creators of the new Renaissance style of painting in Florence. She had hoped to show the frescoes to her students, but a shortage of time had robbed them of the opportunity. The students needed a little leisure, so Masaccio would have to wait until another trip, Emma thought as she strolled along.

Firenze, in contrast to San Sepolcro, was bursting with noisy city life. Young mothers she passed looked like Madonnas in Uffizi paintings as they carried plump, attractive babies in their arms. Men were darkly handsome. No wonder *quattrocento* painters in Italy glorified the human face and figure. Even today, many of the men and women had an idealized look, so perfect were their features.

"Why are you not with your students, Signorina Darling?"

Emma spun around at the sound of a voice behind her. "Mario!"

She drew in a quick breath trying to keep surprise out of her voice as she wondered why the police had somehow failed to arrest Mario according to Luigi's plan. Had she misunderstood? Mario should be in custody now. Did Mario know she glimpsed his fancy shoes in the palace in Urbino and again underneath the coach in a storage compartment? How much did he know that she knew? She struggled to appear calm yet already her palms felt damp as questions crowded her thoughts.

"We finished at the Uffizi gallery and my students are sightseeing and shopping. I am meeting them in a few minutes at the Church of the Carmine along this street to look at some frescoes before we go to the Pitti Palace." She kept her voice even and matter of fact, hoping the meeting she had invented would serve as a kind of protection. I warned the girls not to go off alone, she recalled tardily. And I have done just that!

A black robed priest passed. Should she call for help? No, Emma decided. She should not exhibit fear to Mario. Better act in a casual, normal way. Surely Mario did not realize she knew he was one of the thieves. But silently she bemoaned her carelessness, recalling Luigi's warning too late that Mario could be dangerous.

"The Church of the Carmine," he repeated. "But that is a very poor church. You should visit our Duomo, the cathedral. It is a rich church. More to your liking, I am sure, Signorina." There was a heavy dose of irony in his words which disturbed Emma. A little leap of fear shot through her like an electric charge, but she forced herself to speak evenly. She mustn't show fear, Emma knew, her heart beating a tattoo.

"Perhaps you are right, Mario. I will go check out the Duomo instead." Rapidly she reversed course and struck out in the opposite direction. But she was not quick enough to avoid Mario's iron-like grip on her arm.

Just like the abductor in the Urbino Palace, she realized fleetingly as he turned her brusquely around and marched her along, holding her arm tightly in a vise-like grip that seemed to Emma horribly déjà vu. She noticed there no longer seemed to be people about. No open corner bars with hissing *espresso* machines and the hum of talk and laughter inside, no tiny news agent's shops. No buzzing *vespas*. Only tightly closed doors and shuttered windows.

"Come quickly, Signorina. I have something to show you that you will wish to see."

Why wasn't he in custody? Why did Luigi change plans without telling me? Mario was pushing her along the deserted street when suddenly he veered into a narrow alley. From inside a nearby building she heard the sound of a power saw, probably some artisan's workshop, effectively drowning out all street noise, or a cry for help, she thought grimly.

This cannot be happening, Emma raged inwardly as they turned again, this time into a small, bare courtyard used for parking, and she saw the familiar blue coach. Mario was taking her to his place. Am I to go meekly, like a lamb to the slaughter?

"Stop, Mario!" she cried out in a loud voice. "Let me go at once!" She might have been addressing Michelangelo's marble David, for Mario paid no attention whatsoever; her voice came out faintly, unable to rise above the hum of the machinery. Quickly he stepped up, unlocked a dilapidated door to the shabby two story house facing the courtyard and shoved her inside.

An old woman enveloped in black from head to toe, hair bound in a limp turban of sorts, stuck her head out of the kitchen. Mario shouted angrily at her, telling her that her work was finished for the day. She scurried to the door as he yelled, vanishing like a frightened rabbit. Emma, in spite of her fear, marveled at how quickly the old woman moved.

The room in which she found herself was oppressively dark with heavy curtains effectively blocking most of the daylight from two small windows on either side of the front door. Only a few escaping rays of sunlight cast a light inside dancing with dust motes. Wallpaper, fatigued and shredding at the edges, patterned with faint outlines of stripes and garlands, hung in tatters, long faded into tiredness.

She made out the dim outline of an old horsehair sofa, seat collapsed and sprouting its stuffing. A table stood in the middle of the room with a half-emptied cooking pot and the end of a loaf of bread which had been torn in pieces. The old woman obviously had made a meal. Emma's eyes rested on a telephone on the table, but Mario intercepted her glance and quickly moved it out of reach. A chair was drawn up and Mario quickly pushed her into it. On another chair a covered package was propped against the chair back.

"Sit down, Signorina. All will be well, all will be well." She hated the patronizing tone in his voice, but knew she had best play dumb. She said nothing.

"Look," he said, moving quickly to the package and throwing off the cover. As her eyes became accustomed to the dim light, she recognized the outlines of the Piero Madonna.

"Oh, the Piero Madonna!" Mixed feelings of relief and despair competed in her voice. The picture had not left the country. It was still in Mario's hands.

She had found the painting, but was held a prisoner in an obscure house off an alley on a poor street in an even poorer part of Florence, prisoner of a clever, scheming man whom she realized would not tolerate anything or anyone who got in his way. *I must use my wits if I am to stay alive!* She felt the dampness on her palms, the thump of her heartbeat.

From where she sat, the painting looked convincing. She believed she was looking at the genuine Madonna of Senigallia by Piero della Francesca. If it was a copy, it was a very, very good copy. She stood up, preparing to move closer, but Mario motioned her to sit down.

"I assure you, Signorina, this is the genuine painting by Piero della Francesca, my ticket to get out of the Genoa slums, once and for all. It is a marvel, Signorina, isn't it? But you are not really surprised, are you? You stumbled upon my shoes in the compartment of the coach last night, shoes I had been wearing in Urbino, didn't you? You knew then that I was the person who tied you up."

Emma's face presented a study in calm, but she was stunned. *So he knew I might connect the shoes with him!* This man was no amateur. He possessed the full blown mind of a criminal.

"Well, Signorina, that painting has been under your nose, well, not exactly your nose, since it left the *museo* in Urbino." Emma watched as he puffed up like a rooster, amused at his little joke. Conceited man!

"That painting has been in the coach, behind the storage bin where the shoes were stowed. You have been sitting above it all these days! After the tire blew I realized you probably had seen the shoes. I decided to bring you here today and show it to you. But how could I manage to do that? It was a puzzle. And wonder of wonders, as I am racking my brain how to get you here, you come walking along, almost to my doorway! It is a miracle." He preened at his cleverness.

As Mario spoke Emma realized his command of English was much better than he had pretended. Not the poor, broken English he faked earlier. Clever of him, as he could pick up information when others spoke thinking he did not understand,

and at the same time, he gave nothing away. Anger melted away Emma's caution.

"Why on earth do you want to show the painting to me? I am outraged by its theft! That painting belongs to the world. You have no right to steal it! Why do you want to show it off? To make me think how smart you are, to have nicked it?" The words tumbled from her mouth, and she knew, as she perched on the edge of the rickety chair, that Mario was preparing to tell her. She readied herself to listen, bargaining for time.

10

Mario's (Matteo's) Journey from the Slums of Genoa

"I come from the slums of Genoa where life is hard," he began. "My parents had ten children. Work, work, work. When my father died it was much worse. We were always hungry. Cold in winter, sweltering in summer. My uncle took me aside one day and told me I should leave. Go somewhere and work, send money home. He said it was my only chance."

"That's what I did. I sailed off on a ship from Genoa when I was only twelve. Four years later I'd worked up to ship's mate. There was money, not much, but enough to send a little home. I had plenty to eat and could save a bit."

"One of my mates told me I could make more money if I helped him. We were especially nice to passengers on the ship, did little favors for them, gained their trust. It was a freighter and there weren't many passengers on board, but the ones there were mostly rich and wanted to experience a different kind of travel. Just before the ship docked, if a few things were missing, they didn't even notice, their luggage was already packed. Only when they reached home did they discover a missing ring or a watch. By then we were sailing off in another direction. We never took enough to arouse suspicion from our captain. After the voyage, if anything was reported missing, he thought the passenger had probably forgotten to bring the item, left it at home before boarding ship."

"I learned how certain information, if used right, could be valuable. If a man had something to hide, a debt, a mistress, a murder, some secret, he would pay to have it kept quiet." Here Emma's thoughts flew instantly to Pietro Cortina and his weakness for gambling. He must have been an obvious target for Mario. She gave a small nod of understanding in spite of herself.

"By now I had settled down in Florence with the coach I'd bought with money I'd put by. I hauled rich tourists around, but it wasn't making me as much money as I'd planned. I wanted more, lots more. So I decided to go for something bigger. I asked a girl I know who copies art masterpieces to copy the Madonna in Urbino for me. I knew she would do it, she liked me. But the result was a disappointment. I honestly think I could have done a better job myself! Nobody would have been fooled into thinking it was the real picture, nobody would want to buy it."

Missing in Toscana

Emma filed away a nugget of information: Anna, the inept copier, and also a deceiving, scheming woman, had found Mario—Matteo—attractive? Or had it been a ruse, to make him think she would cooperate in exchange for his silence about her brother Pietro's gambling debts? Would Anna and her weaker brother stand quietly by and let such a prize as the Piero painting slip through their fingers? Emma doubted this. Matteo continued with his story as she pondered the possibility.

"I realized that if I wanted to make real money, it would not be selling miserable fake copies as the real thing. I'd have to nick the actual picture, and so I set out to make my plans. About that time I got a phone call from a swell-sounding nob in London who runs a fancy girl's school. He wanted me to haul around some rich kids on an art tour, your school, Signorina. Are you in the picture now?" Emma gave a small nod of understanding.

"Best of all, a teacher was coming with them! Here was somebody who might help me find a buyer for a genuine Piero della Francesca! An art teacher from London, no less. She would surely know a lot about paintings I figured, and she would know a lot of rich people in the art world. Maybe she could help me find a buyer." Emma kept silent. She knew it was useless to point out that neither she nor her students were rich, only middle class. Mario would never believe it.

"So that is where we are at this moment, Signorina. I have the painting. Will you help me find a buyer? There is a lot of money in it for you if you will cooperate."

Emma knew the danger of her predicament. If she cried out in outrage, which was what she felt, she could be "taken care of" by Mario as efficiently as an altar boy snuffed out a candle.

Everything in her makeup rebelled at the horror of what Mario had done. In her mind, art theft ranked right up along with murder and mayhem. Of course she felt sorry for him, his unspeakable childhood of poverty and hunger, but surely the world was peppered with escapees from the slums of Genoa, Naples, Rome, wherever, who had not sunk to bribery, theft, and the unforgivable, such as stealing one of the world's great paintings.

Mario was evil. Was he capable of murder? She feared that he was. These reflections tempered her response. She decided to be agreeable for as long as she could, hoping she might play for time and find a way to escape.

"Who did you have in mind to sell it to, Mario?" she asked, encouraging him to talk some more.

"Maybe some rich art collector who buys stolen art. I know London is crawling with types like that," he finished belligerently as though daring her to challenge him.

Emma sat all at attention, but did not reply. She knew it was useless to try to change him. Her look was thoughtful, encouraging him to go on.

"Or maybe there would be some rich guy in London from the Middle East, a prince or a sheik or something, who had enough oil money to buy a painting by Piero della Francesca."

"Have you thought about the problem of getting the painting to London?" Emma asked. "Customs would be on the lookout for it, you may be sure."

"No problem. My old friend from the freighter could get it ashore. He knows the ropes. Nobody would expect it to be on a freighter, in a poor seaman's foot locker. But I would need help from you when it arrived." He surprised Emma with his depth of planning. He had a clear idea of just how things would go forward. She knew she faced a clever, dangerous and desperate man.

"Why did you go for just one Piero painting in the Palace, Mario? There are two, you know."

His face went quickly on guard. "What do you mean?" Emma saw he was unaware of the other Piero painting, the *Flagellation*, in the same room.

"The other one is small," she answered casually. "Of no importance." His face relaxed. He trusts me, she thought. That was good. It also meant to her that the Cortinas were probably the ones in charge.

"And is your real name Matteo or Mario?" She knew she should try to calm him down, stall for time. And she knew she must flatter his ego.

He grinned at her engagingly. "Which do *you* like? I use five or six names at once."

No wonder the police couldn't trace him; he was slippery, like quicksilver. Emma's mind raced. What should she do? How long could she keep playing along until the police discovered her and the painting? But Luigi had no idea she was missing! Could she make a dash for the door and try to break free? Neither prospect looked very hopeful.

He saw her eyes on the door. "I wouldn't try to run, Cara," he said softly. "I can overtake you in an instant and let me assure you, I do not like my guests to depart suddenly. I would hate to break your pretty arm, but believe me, I could snap it like a twig."

Emma shivered. Everything seemed hopeless. Why did Luigi fail to go through with the plan to arrest Mario? Why didn't he get word to her? And here I am, failing my girls into the bargain. What will they do when I don't show up?

"Mario, what about my students? They will be alarmed if I don't show at the Church of the Carmine, as arranged." She hoped he might fear they would raise the alarm if she did not show up.

"That depends on you. If you agree to cooperate, all will go as planned and nobody will be the wiser. If you do not?" he threw up his hands delicately questioning.

"Isn't it a pity how some tourists in Italy disappear and meet violent, unexplained deaths? Have you noticed? Some are run over by lorries, some step into water over their heads and drown. There are strange accidents you would not believe!" His voice was barely audible, his words spoken in a humorous tone, but Mario did not smile.

Silence in the room became unbearable. Emma, sick with fear, could not agree to his wicked plan, if only to save herself. How could she, she who passionately believed the loss of the Madonna was the world's loss, an outrage not to be tolerated?

The stressful gloom of silence lengthened in the dingy room. As though born of her anger and despair, the doleful quiet was unexpectedly shattered by a deafening thud, some object crashing on the floor above them, like a meteor falling through the roof. Instantly Mario was on his feet, running toward the staircase. The next moment, a great force struck the curtained windows in the downstairs room, sending a shower of glass near Emma. The door burst open followed by two men wearing uniforms of the police and carrying guns. As Emma cowered she hoped they realized she was the captive.

Behind armed policemen she saw the familiar dark hair, the furrowed brow and tall, rangy form of Inspector Luigi Rovere. With a cry that sounded more like a croak Emma bolted, hurling herself toward him. Burying her face in the rough tweed of his jacket she collapsed sobbing as her knees gave way. She wanted never to leave the safety of those encircling arms.

A struggle of the greatest intensity was underway at the foot of the stairs. Two policemen who had jumped through a window upstairs pounced on Mario. They grappled with him, trying to fasten handcuffs as he fought like a tiger. With the aid of the two policemen who stormed the front door, they eventually subdued him and fastened the handcuffs. Mario's curses rained down like physical blows on everyone in the room. Emma was glad her knowledge of Italian stopped short of translation.

At last, the four policemen pulled and pushed Mario toward a police car in the alley. Luigi gently disengaged Emma, picked up the painting, and guided her outside to a second waiting police car.

"I must go to the Pitti Palace, Luigi," Emma said. "My girls surely have arrived there and are wondering where I am." Emma, nerves on edge, could think only of the students waiting for her.

"Don't worry. Barbara is meeting them at the Pitti and they will be fine. She will show them the Palatine Room with the Titians and Raphaels. Then they'll take cabs and be at the hotel when they've finished looking at the paintings. I'm taking you to the hotel now. You need to rest. We'll get you some tea in that downstairs lounge while you tell me what happened. How did Mario find you?"

"But I don't want to rest! Besides, how did you know where I was?" Emma could not understand. How had he known where she would be going after they left the Uffizi? Surely he hadn't purposely let her walk into a trap of Mario's. She could not believe that.

"Barbara told me," he answered quickly. "I met her by accident after lunch on Via Tournabuoni where she was shopping. She was not sure where you were, somewhere looking at frescoes in a church on Via Santo Spirito she thought. Earlier, we followed Mario and the coach, and he went to the house, leaving it parked in the courtyard. As I talked to Barbara I realized the house was near the church where you were headed. My men were never far away, Emma. They were looking out for you from the minute you showed up with Mario. We were listening before we broke in."

"And the plan to capture Mario when the coach dropped us off this morning at the Uffizi? What happened to that plan? Remember, you were going to secretly follow us as Mario drove to the museum." Emma's feelings of resentment rose as she recalled the ordeal she had just been through. Apparently everyone knew the plan, everyone but her.

"Well, ah, there was a change of plans. I'll tell you about it when we get to the hotel and you are drinking a nice cup of tea. That's what you would like, tea, isn't it?" He smiled, looking embarrassed. But Emma was uninterested in joking about trivial things, nor was she captive any longer to his charm. She had been through too much.

11

One of the Students Reveals Some Secrets

The tea Emma drank was surprisingly good, strong and bracing. Have I become so Anglicized I believe the only sensible answer to a problem is a good cup of tea? She accepted another cup of the faintly smoky lapsang souchong which Luigi poured from a steaming pot.

Luigi sat facing her in an arm chair beside the sofa in a small room off the lobby of the hotel. He waited, giving her time to calm down before reviewing events of the trial Emma had been through.

It was an attractive room, slip covers and draperies of silk blooming with irises of a pale blue. Somewhere she had read that the iris was the official floral emblem of Florence, so as a motif, it was appropriate. A clock ticked in the center of the mantelpiece, flanked by charming plates of Italian *majolica* which looked genuinely old. How odd, sitting here in mid-afternoon, when I should be with my girls, Emma reflected. Except for the two of them the room was deserted.

"I rang the police in Florence as soon as I talked to you last night, Emma. I think the man I spoke with must have been asleep on the job. Anyway he sounded crabby and kept asking me if it couldn't wait until morning. When I finally persuaded him I needed to speak to the *Commissario*, he came to his senses and became quite reasonable. He got in touch with him and he called me right back.

"One thing the *Commissario* was dead certain about from the beginning: We would not pick up Mario until we had shadowed him, hoping he would lead us to the missing picture first. The plan he proposed was to follow him, not arrest him at the Uffizi." Luigi paused.

"I should have rung you immediately, but it was so late, and you sounded tired when we spoke earlier, so I decided to wait until I drove early to Florence the following morning. Then, driving from Urbino, the car overheated taking those switchbacks over the Mountains of the Moon. That made me late arriving. When I drove into *Firenze*, I came straight to your hotel, but the coach had already left. I am sorry Emma I didn't get word to you. You know I would not have put you in any danger for the world. I feel terrible. Just remember though, we were watching every movement of Mario. I knew the minute he arrived at his house with you." Emma saw that Luigi indeed looked miserable.

"It is nothing," she said quietly. "Go on."

"Well, the plan of course was to follow him wherever he went after leaving the Uffizi. It was a surprise when he drove the coach right to his house, but we decided to wait and watch before bursting in, hoping that somebody else would show up, the Cortinas, or possibly some unknown members of a gang."

"After watching all morning, I took an early break for lunch but what I badly needed was sleep. I had been up half of the night driving from Urbino. So I got in my car, found a space on the Via Tournabuoni, parked, put my hat over my eyes for a quiet doze. The car radio came on to say Mario was leaving the house on foot but he was being followed, so it was all right. My men said they would continue to shadow him; we'd have the showdown when he returned to the house."

"That's when Barbara saw me. She was on that street shopping. She tapped on the car window. I found out from her your plan was to meet up with the girls at three-thirty in the Pitti Palace. You two and the students would look around for an hour in the Palatine Room and Mario would pick everyone up in the coach. She said she left you to shop, and that you wanted to look at the Masaccio frescoes at the Carmine church on the Via Santo Spirito. As soon as she said that, I realized the church was in the same area, near the street where Mario lived."

"As if that weren't enough, the car radio came on then saying Mario was returning to the house, and there was a woman with him they described as tall, blond, pretty face, dressed like a Brit or an American. That woke me up, I can tell you. I knew it had to be you, Emma. Quickly I told Barbara, who luckily hadn't heard the radio because she was standing outside the car, to go on to the Pitti as planned, and to be prepared to get the girls into cabs and to the hotel if you didn't show up by the time they finished."

"She accepted it all without question. Amazing woman, Barbara." Here Luigi was thoughtful, obviously reflecting that Barbara was the kind of person who let the man do the thinking. Uncomplicated, certainly reserved and submissive. Emma could imagine how his thoughts ran.

"Then I hurried off to Mario's house as fast as I could make my way. What a madhouse *Firenze* can be during the noontime rush! I could have walked there quicker than move in the car! When I finally arrived, Mario and the woman had disappeared inside. I told my men we must go in quickly before the woman was hurt. You know the rest, Emma." He rested a weary hand on his brow. He was still exhausted, Emma thought, and at this moment he looked his age.

The storming of the house actually seemed more real to her now than it had earlier. Emma blinked. She knew she should not blame Luigi and yet, if she had known Mario was walking around the neighborhood where she was headed, would she have gone off on her own to that same area? Or been so surprised when he appeared?

Surely the encounter with Mario had been an unlucky accident, nothing more. I happened to be at the wrong place at the wrong time and anyway, I never carry a grudge. It is not my way to blame others. I'd rather pick up and move forward. She looked at Luigi.

"So what about Mario," she asked wearily. "What will happen next?"

"Mario is being questioned at the police station, charged with the theft of a very valuable painting. He will also be charged with abduction and whatever else they can throw at him. He will not be leaving the station, I can assure you."

Emma gave a sigh. Relief. Satisfaction. She did not know which. She only knew the recovery of the painting was at last a reality.

"Where is the painting?" She wanted it to be returned to the Ducal Palace in Urbino as soon as possible.

"I'll ring Urbino in a few minutes in case the station here in Florence hasn't called the director. My guess is that he has already been informed and that a convoy is on the way as I speak, hurrying down from Urbino to return the painting to the palace conservator's laboratory where it will be gone over with a fine-toothed comb to verify it is unharmed, and that it's the real one, of course." But there weren't any doubts in Emma's mind. The painting she saw in Mario's house looked genuine.

"So it is finally over," Emma said softly, her voice empty. She felt drained, with an overwhelming desire to take to her bed and sleep for a month. Sleep, blessed sleep. And not having to deal with that other pressing problem in her life, her feelings.

Was there some other reason Luigi failed to tell her of the change in plans? His excuses, the delay, the car overheating, the lateness of the hour the night before, did all that put her in real danger? In spite of herself, she began to harbor small doubts about Luigi. Had she misjudged his feelings for her? More importantly, had she misjudged her feelings for him?

As she sipped tea and regarded the iris in the curtain fabric, she fidgeted. Finishing, she begged to be excused to go to her room. Parting came as a relief to both of them; she felt weak, tired; she saw Luigi was anxious to get back to the police station. Their goodbyes were brief. They both suffered from exhaustion of spirit as well as of the body.

~~~~

Dinner had been long and noisy. The hotel was full and the serving staff shorthanded. The girls hardly noticed, they were so excited by the revelations concerning Mario, the discovery that he was one of the thieves who stole the painting! And it had been hidden it in their coach all this time! There was jubilation, now that the Piero had been recovered. But there was also sadness, because Mario had become a great favorite. Emma did not fail to note this, and she puzzled over the anxious glances, the sly looks toward one end of her table. Animated discussions whirled around her, but she could not discern all that was being said. She still felt numb, in a dreamlike state, still in shock after the trauma of the afternoon. And she failed to observe the pain on the face of one of the persons at her table.

As the interminable dinner hour drew to an end and goodnights were said, Emma was denied her rest by a slight tapping at the door. She opened it to a stricken Lettice Lygon whose cornflower blue eyes were brimming with tears.

"Oh, Miss Darling, will you please let me speak with you?"

Emma put her arm around the girl and gently drew her into the room.

"Lettice, my dear, whatever is the matter?"

"Miss Darling, this is the hardest thing I've ever had to confess in my entire life." Lettice rubbed at her eyes with her handkerchief as Emma guided her to a chair. Her voice faltered as she struggled for composure.

"I've been, well, meeting with the man who drives our coach, Mario, on the sly, the man the police have arrested. We have become sweethearts. Is he really a criminal? Oh, Miss Darling!" And she burst into tears a second time, groping for another fresh handkerchief in her pocket.

Emma took her hand and tried to comfort the sobbing girl. How could this have happened? She had watched Mario so carefully. Not once had she seen him flirting. Not once. Barbara had scrupulously counted them all in every night. Emma had insisted on it, remembering Mr. Clark's account of an earlier class trip to Italy which ended in disaster. But somehow, in spite of all precautions, the romance had occurred.

"When did this develop, Lettice? When would you have had a chance to see Mario alone?"

"By sneaking out after we were all checked in for the night, I'm afraid. I am so ashamed! It was mainly my fault, Miss Darling. You see, I'd never had a real beau before, only sons of my parents' friends, and they seemed so young, only pals, really. They were dull, predictable boys. I'd never been talked to like this before, courted I suppose is the word for it. How Mario talked! He rained down wonderful compliments on me, made me feel like someone precious. You know how he looks, dark hair and eyes, well, I was simply overwhelmed by his attentions. But Miss Darling, I led him on. It was not all his fault! Even his accent appealed to me." She cast her eyes down.

"There, Lettice don't cry. You aren't the only girl in the world to fall prey to the blandishments of Mediterranean charm!" Emma had the grace to blush at her words, so truthfully was she describing her reaction to Luigi Rovere.

"Of course you did not lead him on, Lettice. Mario is a con man, pure and simple. He is experienced and smooth in his dealings with people. He manipulates them. You didn't lead him anywhere. I am certain he had you picked out as the person he wanted to attract. He is the one who set out to lure you. But when did he manage to get you alone to tell you these things?"

"This is the hardest part, Miss Darling. Oh, I wish I could take it all back! I wish it had never happened!" And two fresh tears overflowed, finding their way down her cheeks. What was she going to say next, Emma thought, fearing the worst.

"Remember the first night in San Sepolcro, the night Mary and Caroline were late, tracking down Anna Cortina?" Emma nodded.

"Well, after the excitement was over and we all settled down in our rooms, there was a knock on the door. But when we answered it, there was nobody there. Only a small bit of folded paper with my name on it. It was a short note from Mario, asking me to meet him in ten minutes at the *espresso* bar across the street from the hotel."

"I was flabbergasted. I hardly knew him. But Miss Darling, do you know what I did? I told Patricia I needed to go downstairs for a few minutes. I put on my skirt and sweater, and marched right out of the room! Why did I do it? Oh, why?" And the tears flowed again.

"There, there, Lettice. I understand. Then what happened?"

"Nothing, really. But it meant everything to me." she looked defiant as Emma prepared herself for the next revelation.

"We had coffee at the little bar, he told me wonderful things I was longing to hear, that I was pretty, the prettiest girl he had ever seen, that he liked my voice, the way I walked, my smile.

Oh, Miss Darling, it was all so trite, so ordinary, but you see, I'd never heard those words spoken to me before, and the warm night, and the moon, and, I don't know, just being in Italy, I guess, with someone who made me feel beautiful." She looked at Emma, amazement suffusing her face.

"Please, Lettice, try to see this for what it was. Mario is experienced in persuasion, in such talk. He is a con man, a professional, and a criminal. And I do believe most Italian men, the ones I've met anyway, enjoy, well, flirting. It's probably born in them!" Emma silently marveled at the similarity in her response toward Luigi and the response of the girl sitting in front of her. Was it just Italy? The romance of the country? The moon? Emma, regarding another victim of Italian magic sitting in front of her was rewarded by a small smile on Lettice's unhappy face as she dried her eyes.

"How many more times did you meet him?"

"Only twice more, in the evening, after we were supposed to be in for the night. And only in *espresso* bars, we never left to go anywhere else. The meetings lasted about thirty minutes, no more." Her sigh shouldered the weight of the world, but Emma, on the other hand, gave an inward sigh of relief that things had apparently not gone farther.

"The girls found out about it, of course. Patricia figured it out first, when he handed her a note to pass to me once when we were boarding the coach."

Mario was so slick I never even suspected, Emma thought. He was very careful not to act any differently around me, or to anyone in our group, for that matter. Clever? Certainly. Not to raise a hint of suspicion from Barbara or me. Emma learned from a miserable Lettice that Mario made ardent declarations of love to her when they met. But, here Lettice was emphatic: that was definitely as far as things went.

Lettice, who seemed so poised and self-assured, was the most unlikely of her students Emma would have expected to succumb to Mario's rather obvious charms. However, as she thought again, Emma realized, the girl possessed an intensely romantic nature, and, even though she seemed sophisticated, was only seventeen, barely accustomed to living alone in London, away from her home in rural Worcestershire, to say nothing of a foreign country.

At this moment, Emma painfully reminded herself, who would have thought I'd go to the very brink of making a fool of myself over an Italian policeman almost twice my age? The attractions people developed for one another were unfathomable. And Lettice, for all her poise, had led a sheltered life in an English village. For all the love and care lavished on her by adoring parents, she had been in London too short a time to acquire even a thin veneer of the assurance that came from living independently in a city. And she had never been outside England before. For all her seeming poise, she was naive in many ways.

Why Mario settled his affections on Lettice was no mystery at all. She was the undisputed beauty of the group, and her parents were indeed rich. She did not flaunt it of course, her tastes were conservative. But the simple sweaters were cashmere, the pearls genuine, the handbags and loafers came from Gucci in Bond Street. A calculating Mario would have picked up on that affluence in a twinkling Emma knew, thinking of his expensive shoes with the tiny tassels bound in gold, obvious symbols of his upward ascent into the world of the wealthy.

As Lettice told her story she became calmer, dried her eyes and pocketed her handkerchief. Reminded by Emma she should be grateful for her escape because Mario was among other things an extortionist, Lettice began to realize she was indeed lucky, after all. He might have tried to extract money from her or worse still, threatened her parents.

Lettice began to see that Mario's arrest, although painful, may have saved her from a real catastrophe. After all, he was a thief who twice abducted her teacher and had stolen one of Italy's most famous paintings. Reality was taking hold, Emma observed thankfully.

Lettice showed Emma notes from Mario which should be turned over to the police, but she lacked the courage to do this herself. She begged Emma to help her, and Emma promised to give them to Inspector Rovere. All of her life Lettice had been treated like a princess by her parents. This venture into the real world hit hard.

So this explained the sly glances among her girls Emma had noticed when the news of Mario's arrest was revealed at dinner.

Emma knew Lettice was one of the most popular students in the group; they would treat her with sympathy, loyalty and understanding, which was no small thing.

"I have been very foolish, Miss Darling. I am so sorry that I deceived you, and brought you all this trouble."

"Apology accepted, Lettice. You will overcome this. I know it hurts now, but believe me, everything will come right. Just remember how lucky it is that neither you, nor your family, were harmed by this man. I will see that the police get the notes. There is no reason for any further discussion by anyone. I certainly will keep silent," Emma promised.

Lettice revealed Mario had even talked to her about an elopement. Emma shuddered. A lucky escape! When after an hour Lettice had poured out her deepest feelings to Emma, she began to see the episode in its true perspective: a lapse of judgment in which no irrevocable harm had been done. Emma accompanied her to her room where Patricia lay in bed slumbering. Softly whispering goodnight, Emma embraced the girl and returned to her room.

Maybe I'll have a chance to sleep now, she thought wearily, returning to her own bed and gratefully climbing in. She drowsily took a moment to reflect on what surprising occurrences had come to light on this trip. Teaching and leading a group of students was what it meant to be *in loco parentis* she thought sleepily. To act like an adult in all circumstances.

She had almost drifted into sleep when another tap sounded on her door. She forced herself to get up and opened the door to Barbara, whose eye make-up looked suspiciously smudged as though from crying.

"May I come in a minute?"

With sinking heart Emma invited her inside. She was certain Barbara wished to talk about Luigi. She wondered what encouragement she could give her. Emma soon learned Barbara came to confide in her she was unhappy because Luigi seemed unaware of her feelings for him.

"It might make a difference, I mean if he knew how I felt, he might feel differently about me. And now it's probably too late. We're almost ready to go back to England! Isn't it funny Emma, how you plod along, thinking love has passed you by, and suddenly you are hit by a lightening bolt and love comes into your life?"

"Well, yes," Emma agreed, thinking, whatever I say, I mustn't tell her about Luigi coming to me to declare a romantic intent. That would be a dreadful mistake. Why make Barbara more unhappy? She remained silent. Emma herself had received a healthy dose of reality in the past few hours. She was beginning to readjust her own opinion of Luigi, at least where her feelings were concerned.

"Listen, Barbara," Emma tried to keep fatigue out of her voice. "We have a few days left in Italy. I'm betting Luigi will come to see us at least once more, if only to say goodbye. You might suggest a farewell coffee together to give him a chance to speak first, wouldn't that be best? I believe he is the type of man who likes being the pursuer. Why not give him the opportunity before you declare your feelings?"

It was the only plan Emma could think of, short of suggesting Barbara ring him in Urbino, and she knew Barbara would never be that brazen. Barbara soon returned to her room with a few crumbs of hope in her heart and Emma dropped off to sleep at last.

~~~~

"Fra Angelico, called the 'Blessed Angelico' by his peers at the Monastery of San Marco, belonged to the Dominican order and took his vows very seriously, dedicating his life to painting scenes of his faith with moving conviction and purity. In Angelico's world, everything is a delight from the pristine air his figures breathe to the flora and fauna surrounding them." Emma was speaking to her girls at the Monastery of San Marco, now a museum, as they stood at the stairway looking up at the beautiful *Annunciation* painting hanging on the landing.

"Beato Angelico, or Blessed Angelico as he was called, possessed an extremely kind and humble nature and was loved by all. Obedience to the laws of God and his Order were paramount. Indeed, a charming story handed down through the ages tells us that Angelico declined to eat meat when he was invited to dine with Pope Nicholas V in Rome. It seems that his Prior in Florence had not granted permission, and the Holy Father's ultimate authority in these matters did not occur to the devout monk!"

Standing before her students in the monastery after a good night's sleep, Emma felt restored. She reveled in returning to San Marco, one of the most precious memories of her first visit to Florence as a student at London University.

Transportation presented no problem without Mario and the coach. Barbara studied the city transportation guide at breakfast and confidently led students to the nearest bus stop. The bus deposited them almost at the monastery gates for a fare of a few lira.

"Note how competently Angelico defined space in the painting," Emma continued. "Notice the lovely architectural elements of the loggia where the *Annunciation* is taking place, the gentleness and grace of Mary, the submissive reverence of the kneeling angel. There is a lyrical tenderness present in all of Angelico's work. We are standing in front of the work above a staircase which the monks traversed many times each day, and in doing so, their eyes focused on this painting."

"The inscription reads, 'As you venerate while passing before it, this figure of the intact Virgin, beware lest you omit to say a Hail Mary'." Here Emma paused to let the students view the work with renewed appreciation.

"The museum of San Marco which we will visit before we leave the grounds contains several famous altarpieces by Angelico, including the famous San Marco Altarpiece, the *Descent from the Cross*. However, I believe the most poignant and moving examples of his work are the cell paintings in the tiny cubicles where the monks actually passed their days and nights. These images of contemplation are simple and at the same time profound. The *Annunciation, Transfiguration, Adoration of the Magi, Christ Scourged,* and other examples are stark, simplified and moving in their own way as you will see."

"I suggest we visit the cells in silence. We can discuss them later, when we leave the monastery. I believe as you look you will understand the role they must have played in the lives of the monks. You have seen religion powerfully expressed in Piero della Francesca's works. Here the expression of the Christian faith is taken to a more personal level by an earlier gifted artist, Fra Angelico, who exalted his faith in every movement of his brush."

"Remember, and I have told you this several times, were it not for the patronage of the Catholic church during this period, we would be much the poorer in our world treasury of art. Let us now with reverence, visit the cells."

Emma looked silently with the others, as they moved from cell to cell. Suddenly a new thought presented itself as she looked at a different version of the *Annunciation* in one of the cells. In this work, the face of the Virgin Annunciate reminded her of her friend, Jane Hale, now Jane St. Cyr.

An open, sincere face with honest grey eyes like Jane's looked out at Emma, reminding her that Jane was indeed dependable and straightforward. Her rational common sense had helped Emma the past summer in Greece to curb an impetuous spirit and to think before taking action. Jane's face, which she saw in the deeply compassionate features of the Madonna, seemed to be saying, "How could you think of choosing anyone but Sam, who possesses all the qualities you admire most in a human being?"

Emma experienced a moment of gratitude remembering that she indeed had chosen Sam. She chose *him*. Sam, serious, responsible, dependable.

These recollections took her thoughts back to her family roots. Emma, the child of a British father and an American mother who settled in the small mountain town of Crozet, Virginia, determined to raise their children in the pure, fresh air near Charlottesville, about as bedrock an American community as could be found anywhere. She smiled to herself, grateful for the love and care of such parents.

Not living for the moment but living for the calculated plan, the long haul, following the messages sent by the mind as well as the heart. That is the sort of person I want to be, and this unspoken desire gave Emma peace. She looked over at Lettice and met the clear gaze of those wonderful blue eyes. How could she ever have thought of acting irresponsibly, when she knew she was a role model not only for Lettice, but all the others in her care as well?

Fleetingly, she wondered if her frightening experience with Mario the day before and Luigi's failure to let her know of a change in plans precipitated this sudden analysis of feelings occurring in the cell while looking at an *Annunciation* painting. Possibly, she acknowledged, but only in her subconscious. She would take Luigi at his word. His mistake, if indeed it had been a mistake, was accidental. She would not admit it could have been anything but chance.

Relief flooded over her and she knew she could cope with Luigi, whatever happened in the time before Sam's arrival. When she returned to the hotel, she would go straight to the little box by her bedside and take out the garnet and rose diamond ring. *I should have been wearing it every minute!* she realized guiltily. *I won't take it off, ever again!* A buoyancy enveloped her and she quickly guided the girls to the little gallery on the grounds of the monastery, knowing that should a confrontation with Luigi arise she was calm, certain, and prepared.

~~~~

"Angelico was called to Rome by the pope in 1446 to decorate a chapel in the Vatican, the chapel of Pope Nicholas V, which survives today. Later, he returned to Rome to decorate a second chapel which is now destroyed. In a number of the altarpieces in this room, you will see the Madonna surrounded by various saints in conversation together. This is known in art history parlance as the *Sacra Conversazione,* popular with many *quattrocento* artists. Giovanni Bellini and Andrea Mantegna spring immediately to mind as artists especially drawn to the genre. Angelico used it also."

"Angelico's most important pupil was Benozzo Gozzoli whose famous painting of the dei Medici rulers as the Three Magi still hangs in the Medici Palace. It is a painting in which the three Wise Men are transformed into actual portraits of the powerful dei Medici rulers. The disguised portraits of important Florentines during this period would make a fascinating study, or perhaps a thesis subject if some of you carry out your intention of becoming art historians at some university in future."

When the visit ended, she chatted happily with the girls as they walked from the monastery to the bus stop. They expressed elation that the Piero Madonna portrait would soon be returning to its rightful home. Only Caroline and Mary held doubts about the outcome of the investigation. They believed Anna Cortina had played a much greater role in the operation and that many of her actions were as yet unexplained.

"Just look at it this way, Miss Darling," Caroline reasoned. "If she had nothing to hide, why was she so jumpy whenever we saw her, at Monterchi, and at the *gelateria* in San Sepolcro?"

"And the other times when we ran into her," Mary added.

"And why did she go to the trouble of trying to disguise herself with that wig, if she wasn't hiding something important?" Caroline asked.

"We never did go back to that chapel in Monterchi to see the *Madonna del Parto*," Mary said wistfully.

"Well I did try, you remember," Emma replied guiltily, "and it was closed by the time we arrived. As for Anna, maybe she is just being capricious. Maybe she likes wearing the wig."

"Some people just had to have their gelato in Arezzo so we couldn't get to the Pregnant Madonna in time," Marigold spoke up spitefully, having been busy eavesdropping.

"Not fair!" rang out a chorus of voices.

"I remember seeing you noshing down too, Marigold!" Winkie spoke up. "We all wanted to stop for *spumoni*."

Emma hid a smile. It had been good to share this trip with them, drinking in their enthusiasms. hearing their reactions as they experienced new things, noting how they were touched by the great paintings and sculpture they had seen, and, refreshingly, how scrupulously honest they were in their judgments of each other.

~~~~

Luigi Rovere, seated in the little reception room off the main lobby of the hotel, regarded the pale blue of the irises on the slip covers without really seeing them as Emma stepped within his line of vision, holding a note from him she had been given at the reception desk.

Barbara and some of the girls were visiting the famous Straw Market of Florence looking for leather handbags, and Emma planed to join them after changing into more comfortable shoes.

Now that the search for the stolen painting was over, she planned to celebrate its recovery in a lighthearted shopping excursion. Apparently, however, a meeting with Luigi would take precedence.

He quickly stood when she appeared, the lines around his eyes deepened as he smiled at her.

"I'm just leaving for Urbino, and I needed to talk with you."

"I am glad you didn't leave without saying goodbye," Emma said lightly, determined to control the tenor of the encounter and make it as pleasant as possible.

"So that's it, goodbye." He sat down opposite her and crossed long legs, peered intently into her eyes. "I had hoped you might have reconsidered."

I won't be swayed, Emma thought, no matter what he said. She twisted the rose diamond and garnet ring on her finger before speaking. "Luigi, my friend Sam is coming from London to meet me as soon as the tour is finished. I am wearing his ring, you see." She held up her hand, showing the circlet of rose diamonds surrounding a single garnet which she had put on minutes before. "We are to be married."

"I see. His impending arrival is a recent development which I had not heard. Nor had you mentioned an engagement."

"Well, yes. He is beginning a new job in London soon. He is leaving Aberdeen, and in order to take his holiday, he has decided to do it now, and come to Italy. We will be staying at a villa in Tuscany with friends."

"Ah, yes, at a villa. Where else?" His words were a statement, not a question, weighted with sarcasm. "And are you happy about this?"

"Very happy."

"Then I see it is over with us before it ever began, Cara."

His words moved her, but she took a deep breath and repeated his words with conviction.

"Over before it began, Luigi. But I shall always remember how we worked together to solve the mystery of the missing painting by Piero. I won't forget."

Angrily he struck the arm of his chair with his fist and Emma sat up straight, alarmed. His eyes gleamed, ablaze with resentment. "Spare me the posturing please, Miss Jane Austen, making your pretty little eighteenth century speech! Just remember that you threw away, like a used candy wrapper, someone who would have loved you, really loved you, and would have shown you the joy of living in Italy when you are in love."

He stood up and shrugged his shoulders as though shaking off the bitter words, moving quickly toward the door. His real feelings, his pride, always deeply hidden and protected, were revealed, Emma realized, cloaked in a film of bravado until this moment. She was sorry if her words had wounded him.

"*Ciao*, Emma. Tell *Signorina* Barbara goodbye for me, won't you?"

"Wait, Luigi," Emma rose and walked toward him placing her hand on his arm, and looking into his eyes. "You rescued me twice from a very dangerous fugitive and I will always thank you for that. I, I may have misled you in expressing my gratitude, for you became my hero, my protector. Please forgive me if I overstepped. And there is something else, Luigi, You know, don't you, that Barbara Bone is in love with you?" She surprised herself by saying it. But it must be said. If Luigi did not wish to hear it, then at least she had informed him.

"Ah, Miss Austen," he said, shaking off her hand, "Always putting things to rights. As you wish. Emma. You think you are doing me a great favor, sharing this bit of information? You are a carbon copy of all those greedy American girls I once knew. Wanting to control every little thing, whether it concerned them or not!"

Emma felt her cheeks redden. Now he had hurt her with cruel words.

"Maybe I deserve your scorn, Luigi," she answered, "but Barbara doesn't!"

She watched as he walked quickly out of sight, wishing their parting could have been different.

12

Marigold's Defining Moment in the Church of Santa Croce

Emma sat in the arm chair of her room looking out onto the street, beginning to come to life in early morning as the neon signs flickered off and she marveled at the tinges of pink appearing in the dawn sky. A gift to the day. A baker's boy in white apron and cap staggered into the hotel bearing a huge basket of freshly baked croissants for the breakfasts; a small boy on a bicycle delivered a stack of newspapers. A few early workers began passing along the sidewalk below her.

Now that the painting had been returned to the palace in Urbino, she could begin to relax and enjoy the final hours of the tour. There would be a free afternoon tomorrow before the farewell banquet, but before that, she must make overseas calls, to Dr. Clark at the Celia Drummond school, asking him if it would be possible for her to stay on in Florence and not accompany Barbara and the students to Heathrow airport, and to Sam. How she hoped she could wait for Sam in Florence and journey with him to Castellina-in-Chianti. Surely, with Barbara in charge her presence wouldn't be necessary on the return flight.

Today's schedule must be revised, to include visits to several churches, notably Santa Croce, San Lorenzo and the Duomo in the morning in order that the early part of the afternoon would allow time for rehearsal of the evening's entertainment after dinner.

Emma felt it was important for the students, some of whom might never again visit *Firenze,* to experience the pleasure of walking about the city, enjoying the outdoor cafes, shopping for small gifts and mementos. She was reviewing her notes on the church of Santa Croce when the telephone rang in the short staccato bursts. Who could be calling before breakfast?

"Emma Darling here."

"*Buongiorno,* Emma, it's Luigi in Urbino. Please pardon the hour. I knew you would be getting an early start on your last day but one in Florence." He sounded relaxed and cheery, as though the angry scene in the hotel had never taken place.

"Ah yes," Emma answered cautiously, hoping he wasn't planning to propose another meeting alone with her. "I was just looking over my notes."

"So sorry to interrupt, but I felt sure you would want to know: the painting we removed from Mario's house is not the genuine Piero."

"What?" Emma screeched into the phone in disbelief.

"It is a very, very good copy, Emma. But the chief conservator at the palazzo in Urbino has subjected it to every conceivable test. He claims it was painted within the year. He also says it is one of the best forgeries he has ever seen."

Emma felt dizzy. "So just where does that leave us? What about the investigation? And when did someone steal the original from Mario?"

"Number one, I found out the Cortinas, not Mario, left the palazzo with the painting. Anna picked up Pietro after they tied you up and the pair drove away with the painting. They were to meet Mario later, at a secluded spot, away from Urbino, give him the painting then go their separate ways" he answered wearily. "They probably switched pictures before meeting Mario."

"And here's something else: according to the Florence police report just in, Mario swears the three of them, Anna, Pietro, Matteo were equal partners in the whole operation. So much for my thinking about the Cortina brother and sister not being so involved." Luigi sighed.

"I'm leaving for San Sepolcro in a few minutes, going to go straight to the house and question the pair once more."

Poor Luigi, Emma thought. His hard work on the investigation seemed to be unraveling before his very eyes. He deserved better, in spite of yesterday's disaster. But who could have made such a convincing copy of the Piero? Anna? Surely not! But who?

"Why don't you have another look in Anna's studio when you get there?" she asked. "It's possible you might turn up something useful. By the way, did the police lab in San Sepolcro ever check out Anna's pictures they brought in when they first searched her house? I mean, did they search *under* them? A second canvas could be slipped in quite easily."

"You're right, it could," Luigi admitted, sounding a little embarrassed. "You know when the investigation is moving in another direction, the pressure goes off and a new lead grabs all the attention. Frankly, it slipped my mind. I'll check on it when I go to the station."

"It may not be important," Emma replied quickly. "Then again, it might. It's just a thought."

"And a good one, Emma," he said. "You have been right on target during the whole investigation. I'd have done better to follow your leads rather than mine."

"Nonsense," Emma answered briskly, realizing he possibly was leading up to more personal talk and she was determined to head him off. "You're just a little discouraged at the moment. You'll find the real Piero soon, probably before Barbara and I leave Florence!" Maybe the mention of Barbara would jog his thoughts in her direction she hoped.

San Gimignano: City of Towers

"Ah, Emma, you are good for the morale. I'll keep in touch and, by the way, give my regards to *Signorina* Barbara." He rang off.

A glimmer of hope coursed through Emma. In her opinion Barbara had a heart as big as Florence Cathedral, a tremendous capacity for affection. Maybe my unwelcome advice to Luigi yesterday did some good after all. But the Piero was still missing! Her spirits slumped as she consulted her watch. It was still too early to place calls to England and Scotland. Better wait until nearer lunch time.

The shocking news that the Piero in Mario's possession was a fake weighed like a stone. When she first saw it at Mario's house, she hadn't been close enough to examine it thoroughly, yet it certainly looked genuine. But the light was poor, the windows covered. *Had she made a mistake?* Was it the sloppy work of Anna Cortina? Apparently so.

The police needed to press on with their investigation. Time was of the greatest importance in finding the authentic Piero before it was smuggled out of Italy. At last the arrows of suspicion were aimed straight toward Anna Cortina and her brother Pietro. They held the key. She was sure of that.

San Gimignano: Near the Cathedral

Missing in Toscana

~~~

When at breakfast Winkie asked why she looked so worried, Emma realized that try as she might, she could not blot out the missing painting from her mind. Somehow her feelings had become involved, even though her brain signaled her there was very little she could do at this point to carry the investigation forward. San Sepolcro was the center of questioning, rather than Florence.

She told Winkie and the others the disappointing news learned from Inspector Rovere: Mario's version of the Piero had turned out to be a copy, albeit a very good one. Emma observed the communal look of surprise and disbelief on the faces of the girls as she told them the genuine Piero, had apparently eluded the authorities once again. What they had on their hands was another copy.

Emma studied the startled faces as she dealt with a barrage of questions. Yes, Inspector Rovere telephoned just this morning from Urbino with the news. Emma glimpsed the unspoken question in Barbara's eyes.

"He rang before breakfast and will be on his way to San Sepolcro by now to question Anna and Pietro once again. The Cortinas are the prime suspects, and Mario/Matteo, is not believed to be the ring leader any more."

"Then how did it happen that Mario had the fake Madonna in his possession?" Caroline asked amidst buzzing murmurs.

San Gimignano: Hotel Cisterna
near the Cathedral

"It was probably switched with the real one soon after the theft, given to him for safekeeping by Anna and Pietro, to throw him off track, while they kept the genuine Piero for themselves. This way they could let Mario think he was in control. They are very, very tricky, you see. In reality, it is only a copy, but a very good copy."

"So if it is a very good copy, it couldn't be Anna's work, could it?" Mary asked thoughtfully, twisting her napkin into a ball.

This very possibility was nagging at Emma. "Now I'm not so sure, Mary, that Anna *did not* paint it. I think she is a very clever woman, our Anna. She has convinced us all that she is a very bad painter when in reality, she may be a very skilled painter." Emma's eyes held Mary's.

"I knew it, I knew it. Anna Cortina is the key to it all." Caroline brought her hand down on the table with a slap.

"Yes. Caroline," Emma answered. "I have come to believe, for what it is worth, she is capable of doing much better work than she lets on. And I further believe she, not her brother Pietro or Mario, is the ringleader." She folded the napkin at her place and rose from the table amid the hum of speculation her words brought on.

~~~

"Santa Croce, the Church of the Holy Cross, is a Franciscan church possessing two priceless fresco cycles by Giotto in two adjoining chapels, the Bardi Chapel and the Peruzzi Chapel, named for the two most important banking families in Florence of the *trecento* when Giotto painted them, in the 1320s." Emma began the morning session after a quick journey on public transport with the students to the historic church of Santa Croce.

"The Peruzzi Chapel was decorated by Giotto with scenes from the lives of St. John the Baptist and St. John the Evangelist." Emma moved beyond the group of girls and entered the Bardi Chapel. "Today, however, we'll concentrate on St. Francis in the Bardi chapel." The students crowded into the small space as Emma gave them background information on the frescoes, based on scenes from the life of Saint Francis.

"The gradual humanization of religious figures in the twelve hundreds by Italian artists was enhanced by the stirring example of Saint Francis, one of their own, a young nobleman of Tuscany, who gave up all that he had to follow Christ. This humanization subsequently reached its climax in the work of Giotto. Remember, Giotto was a precursor of Piero della Francesca. Piero was without doubt greatly influenced by Giotto. And of course, Piero's great fresco, the Legend of the True Cross, is in a Franciscan Church, San Francesco in Arezzo." She led them closer.

"In the fresco of *Saint Francis Undergoing Trial by Fire before the Sultan*, notice how the ruler sits grandly on his throne, his right arm crossing his body, his head turning slightly to the left. The important thing to note here is the body twist, the *contra posto*, more natural, less icon-like than we have seen in earlier examples."

"On the right Saint Francis calmly prepares to undergo the test by fire. He knows, and we know, he will emerge unharmed. Notice the Mohammedan leaders already look uncomfortable and can be seen creeping away on the left. Their defeat is indicated by their facial expressions and by the disarray of their drapery. This is what I mean when I state that with Giotto, for the first time, figures begin to look and act more like real flesh and blood, more human in their bodies and in the arrangement of their clothing.

"The two African slaves standing beside the Muslims are the earliest representations of people of color in Western Art and are sensitively understood by Giotto not only in the color of their rich skin tones, but in the careful analysis of facial structure." Emma paused, waiting for reactions.

"Giotto reminds me of Piero," Elizabeth spoke up. "We have seen much and traveled far, but those two artists stand out in my mind," she finished shyly, lowering her eyes.

"Good point, Elizabeth," Emma praised her. "You have hit on the theme of our entire tour, that is, to discover the tremendous, albeit naive power of Early Renaissance art."

Marigold, usually quick to blurt out pronouncements, surprisingly raised her hand. "I like the final scene of Saint Francis's funeral. The faces of the mourning monks show such grief and affection for Saint Francis."

Marigold's voice was unnaturally subdued. The group, including Emma, looked her way in amazement. Marigold appeared to have been genuinely moved. She, at least for the moment, had undergone a miraculous rebirth from the critical, fault-finding bully who carped at everyone, to a sensitive and caring human being. *Tutto e possible!*, Emma thought.

"Look," Marigold continued. "Above the scene there are angels bearing the soul of Saint Francis up to heaven. I don't think I have ever seen anything so beautiful."

The students were silent, wondering if they could be witnessing a minor miracle in the transformation of Marigold before their eyes. Lettice spoke.

"Marigold, you have made us all appreciate this fresco more. You have helped us see the true meaning of the Renaissance, a movement whose purpose was to bring more humanity into art. We thank you for your insight."

Emma felt a lump in her throat. Not only was she proud of Marigold, but of Lettice and all the others. In spite of the hardships of the tour, Emma knew she herself had gained rewards beyond her wildest hopes. She had earned and kept the respect of her students, and they in return had gained rich experience of the profound nature of great art.

The girls were free to lunch on their own as Emma and Barbara returned to the hotel to place overseas calls, Emma to Director William Clark at the Celia Drummond school, then to Sam in Aberdeen, and Barbara to her mother. Emma snatched a private moment to tell Barbara that Luigi sent best wishes to

"*Signorina* Barbara" when he telephoned earlier. She did not fail to note the radiance engulfing Barbara's face.

On a poor and crackling telephone connection to London, Emma related a complete account to Dr. Clark of the Celia Drummond School on progress of the tour. He asked many questions, and she conveyed to him the enthusiasm the girls had experienced, at the same time she kept details of the stolen painting to tell him when she was back in London and presenting her full report.

Emma and Barbara had reserved places on a local coach to Pisa airport for the group on the morning of departure for London. Emma told Dr. Clark about the fate of their coach driver, Mario. The story was complicated, but she gave the facts briefly and succinctly, saving the lengthy account for later, when she arrived back in London. She assured him they were completing a successful and memorable visit to *Toscana*.

When she asked permission to stay on in Florence as the girls would be accompanied by Barbara on the flight to Heathrow she explained she had been invited to stay at a villa near Castellina-in-Chianti with the aunt of her friend Charles St. Cyr of Scotland Yard and his wife Jane. He readily gave his assent.

Her next call to Sam in Aberdeen brought whoops of joy, even though she knew Sam must be speaking from the crowded lounge the young doctors shared. She could sense the longing in his voice, a longing she also shared. *How could I ever have* doubted that Sam was the right person for me, Emma wondered as they finalized plans to meet in Florence.

She rang off, knowing they would see each other soon and have time to talk to their hearts' content. Sam planed to arrive the day after the girls departed for London.

Barbara joined Emma in her room, and the two leisurely made their way to a late lunch.

"I've been thinking, Emma," Barbara said when they were seated in a little *espresso* bar enjoying *caffelatte* and *panini*. "Remember the first stop we made after we left Pisa, at the little chapel of the Pregnant Madonna? I'm not sure of the town—Monteverde, Montclair, something like that."

"Yes, Monterchi, the *Madonna del Parto*, the Pregnant Madonna. Certainly I remember."

"Do you recall how agitated Anna became when she saw us? I've thought about this a lot, how she hurried to speak to her brother, then the two left in a rush."

"Yes, apparently they didn't want us to see them," Emma said. "We never did find out why, did we?"

"Well," Barbara went on, "I don't think she was trying to keep us from seeing *her*. I think it was *Mario* she wanted to avoid, and she recognized his coach when he drove us up to the parking area."

Emma looked fixedly at Barbara as her brain raced forward. *Barbara is right!* Perhaps it was seeing Mario, not me and the students, which upset Anna so much. And what could the brother and sister have been doing that they did not want Mario to see? Searching for a safe place to hide something? A painting perhaps? The bizarre, almost *louche* suggestion was too outrageous to mention so she did not express it to Barbara or to anyone else. But Barbara's idea took hold in her brain and she resolved to tell Luigi.

"Barbara, you are brilliant, of course that must be it! We have been looking at the incident the wrong way 'round. What business do you suppose the pair could have had at that little chapel?"

"Well, the Pregnant Madonna fresco is too huge to think about nicking," Barbara laughed nervously at Emma's reaction. "So that isn't it. But maybe there was something else they were planning to hide in the little chapel. You recall Mary and Caroline thought earlier there was something in the chapel Anna wanted to conceal."

Emma's fingers began beating a tattoo on the table. "If only we had looked about more. Or maybe just our being there was reason enough to cause alarm. Anna did not want anybody to suspect, so when the coach turned up, she left."

Returning to the hotel, Emma and Barbara heard the short rings of the telephone as they approached Emma's room. It proved to be Luigi, ringing from San Sepolcro.

"I rang up to tell you that you were right again, Emma; the Cortinas are in deep water now. When we arrived at the house, they were just getting into their car with small traveling cases. Sure enough, they had tickets for a flight to Rome then another flight on to Brazil. They were not happy to see us, I can tell you."

"Brazil!" Emma let out an undignified screech. "Why Brazil, for goodness sake?"

"To get as far away as possible, I imagine," Luigi replied in a dry voice. "We found something amazing in Anna's studio, Emma."

"What?" Emma could hardly contain her excitement. Was it the stolen Piero? She felt she was choking, the suspense was so great. "Don't procrastinate, Luigi. Tell me."

"Remember the Madonna by Ghirlandaio stolen from the cathedral in San Gimignano a few weeks ago? Well, we found it in the studio, hidden as nice as you please behind one of her awful copies." At this revelation by Luigi Emma's heart fell off a precipice. "It is not the Piero painting, but one by Ghirlandaio, another Renaissance artist."

"Yes, I remember reading about the theft in the London papers," she answered dully. "Well, anyway, one missing masterpiece by a Renaissance artist is safe. That is cause for rejoicing. Good work, Luigi! What about our Madonna?"

"No such luck there I'm afraid. But we have Anna and Pietro in custody, they won't get out of the country. Finding the Ghirlandaio in their possession erases any doubt they were the ringleaders. We'll find the Piero sooner or later. And by the way, the lab in San Sepolcro is finally taking a look at those earlier pictures of Anna's. They'll go over them slowly and carefully."

"You are right, Luigi. The recovery of the Ghirlandaio is encouraging. Surely the Piero will turn up soon." She looked over at Barbara, patiently hanging on her every word.

"Luigi, Barbara is here with me and she has a brilliant idea about the missing Piero I want you to hear. It's something we've overlooked."

Emma passed the phone to Barbara who tentatively, in her softest voice, offered her thoughts to Luigi, telling him about the incident at Monterchi. By the sounds of his reply and Barbara's happy face, Emma could tell Luigi was listening with interest.

When the discussion ended, a flushed and sparkling-eyed Barbara put down the phone and said in a voice that resembled pealing bells, "He's coming up to see us tomorrow, after dinner."

13

Charades and a Surprise at the Farewell Dinner

Emma had planned a special farewell dinner and her students were practicing their surprise entertainment for the last evening. The hotel generously had offered their private dining room. Animated discussions about what to wear were taking place among the students.

Nonetheless, Emma felt somewhat discouraged. Luigi's latest telephone call brought bitter news: he told her all of Anna's pictures had been tested and examined in the police lab, and there were no more paintings secreted behind the slap-dash copies. After the Ghirlandaio Madonna from San Gimignano was found, Emma had allowed her hopes to soar; the Piero Madonna might be discovered underneath one of Anna's careless copies. But that hope was dashed now.

Missing in Toscana

Emma flipped through her closet for a suitable dress. She knew that in Anna the police faced a formidable opponent. Anna gave new meaning to the word duplicitous; she was both cunning and tricky. Where could the picture be hidden? In the end, Emma chose an older frock, a blue linen she had worn often the previous summer when she and Sam were in London.

She had been wearing that dress with the wide collar and flaring skirt the night she and Sam discovered the missing Apollo Amulet, hidden in the corner of her scarf earlier by someone at their little hotel in Greece, *Pensione Anastasia*, where the University of London group was stopping. Sam called it his favorite dress from that night on, she recalled with a smile. Maybe it would guide them toward the missing Madonna if I wore it tonight for good luck, Emma thought.

Luigi told her the police ransacked *Il Giardino*, the house of Anna and Pietro Cortina in San Sepolcro, searching painstakingly through its contents. He was certain the picture was not there. Then police drove to Fiesole to question the senior Cortina at his villa high in the hills.

Luigi told her Paolo Cortina, father of Anna and Pietro, lived like a king on inherited wealth. He doled out to his children sparingly, very sparingly. He managed his vast estates, rich with grapes and olives, and enjoyed the best life had to offer. The villa, crammed with paintings, sculptures of the finest travertine, was oppressively dark and over-decorated Luigi thought. Rooms were cushioned, draped and upholstered in the finest silks and brocades, but the atmosphere felt stifling and lifeless. There was a garden worthy of the dei Medici within the ochre colored walls of the estate, a garden filled with rare flowers, sculptures, shrubs and trees. Luigi told her the entire pile, in his opinion, seemed stuffy in its pretentiousness.

Luigi added that when Paolo Cortina heard the unwelcome news that both daughter and son were in police custody, charged with the theft of a priceless painting by Piero della Francesca from the Ducal Palace at Urbino, he lifted world-weary brows and coughed delicately behind a silk handkerchief before speaking.

"They know I will not spend one lira, not one, to extricate them from their folly," he repeated several times, muttering something that sounded like "*stupido, stupido,*" into his handkerchief. How very cruel, Emma thought, feeling sympathy for Anna and her brother in spite of their crimes. Surely if one did not receive love and support from one's parents, why that was true hopelessness. She was grateful for a loving, supportive mother and father, even though they were half a world away in Virginia.

She slipped the blue linen dress over her head, again recalling the evening with Sam when she wore it last summer. That night they had walked to Beauchamp Place in Knightsbridge for dinner, to the restaurant San Lorenzo, and it had been filled with young people.

Emma remembered how she and Sam, oblivious to any distractions, reveled in each other's company, talked about his dream to help two younger brothers study medicine; she told him of her wish to take a job as an art historian with a famous gallery.

As they left the restaurant that night, a London mist was falling, and Emma reached in her purse for a scarf to throw over her head. There, secreted in the folds of the scarf, the lost Amulet of Apollo shimmered up at her! By summer's end, the entire mystery had been unraveled, the perpetrators caught and imprisoned, and she and Sam became engaged. Emma stood before the mirror, recalling that happy time. She glanced at her watch and hurried to the party.

Her students had put forth great effort Emma saw, entering a room bright with all the colors of a butterfly reflected in dresses the girls wore. Even the most studious, who paid scant attention to appearances, sparkled. Each one looked smashing Emma thought, whether the dress came from Marks and Spencers or from Liberty's, representing London's lower and upper ends of the fashion spectrum.

Barbara, wearing Italian silk in pale green, a discovery on her shopping trip along Via Tournabuoni, seemed transformed and startlingly beautiful. Was it the color which flattered her complexion or the tell-tale light in her eyes? Emma knew Barbara was longing to see Luigi Rovere again, and she was thankful she had invited him to the farewell banquet for Barbara's sake. Somehow it put a touch of finality on the tour, having the dashing inspector from Urbino as a special guest. However, she admitted it would have been much more festive if Sam could have been there, *and* if the genuine Piero had been found.

Anxiously Emma looked for Lettice in the group. Was she still suffering from a broken heart? But Lettice, dressed in pale rose, looked radiant, unburdened by any thoughts of her attachment to Mario. If she was still crying inside she excelled in hiding it from her friends. Probably the attraction flared up so suddenly it hadn't time to develop much depth, Emma decided.

Luigi entered the banquet room bearing two enormous bouquets of roses ensconced in florists paper, one for her, the other for Barbara. Such Mediterranean gallantry, Emma thought, hiding a smile as she buried her face in the blossoms, thinking how unlike Sam this extravagant gesture. She accepted her tribute graciously, admitting Luigi indeed possessed considerable charm.

She noticed Barbara gazing at him, trying but failing to hide her admiration. Dinner that evening took a very long time, and after the final course of fresh fruit, preceded by toasts to the Queen, to Italy, to the memory of Piero, the meal ended and it was time for the long-awaited entertainment.

"What could they possibly have pulled together in such a short time?" Barbara whispered across Luigi to Emma.

"I've no idea," Emma whispered back. "One of them asked me if I had brought a bathing suit, but I had to tell her I had not. I do know they are very clever, resourceful girls."

Emma noticed a large screen had been placed at one end of the room and various boxes of props were stowed behind it. One by one the girls disappeared behind the screen, from which came muffled noises, as though costumes were being put on and adjusted.

The door to the dining room suddenly opened to reveal Sam, standing uncertainly on the threshold, blinking in the dim light as he searched for the only face for him in the entire room. Their eyes met, and Emma rose from her chair with a cry.

"You're early, how wonderful," Emma said in his ear, ignoring everyone in the room as she flew into his arms.

"I wanted to surprise you," he said, holding her close, whispering 'darling Emma' over and over.

She took his hand and led him back to her table, introducing him first to Barbara who greeted him with a warm handshake and a beaming smile. Next she introduced him to a solemn looking Luigi who bowed low and welcomed him to Italy with a show of formality.

Emma noticed that the two men stood apart, as though taking each other's measure. But it only lasted a few seconds as the lights blinked, signaling the beginning of the program. A quick-thinking waiter hurried in with a chair for Sam and inserted it next to Emma.

Sam whispered to her that he was unexpectedly given an extra day's holiday and decided at the last minute to fly out early. She pressed his hand, leaving him in no doubt as to how delighted she was, wondering if he had a place to stay.

Sam replied that one of the Aberdeen surgeons had recommended a *pensione* across the River Arno, and he had dropped off his bags before making for Emma's hotel. Emma, searching the handsome face, blond hair falling so engagingly over his forehead, marveled at how grand he looked, after being so far away from her for so many months.

Lights in the room dimmed and stage spotlights brightened. Mary stepped tentatively from behind the folding screen into the strong light, announcing that the entertainment for the evening would be charades.

"Probably she was too shy to take a part," Emma whispered to Sam, "so they made her the narrator."

Intense activity ensued behind the screen. Patricia, Lavendar and Fiona presently emerged carrying folding chairs and a small table. The two girls took seats as Fiona, dressed as a waiter with a huge white towel wrapped around her waist and a charcoal mustache drawn on her face, spread a white cloth over the table and carefully set two places. Then she disappeared.

She returned bearing two dinner plates with miniscule servings of green peas. Nothing else. With great ceremony she shook napkins into their laps and bowed. The diners carried on a spirited conversation in pantomime as they picked up forks and ate the peas one by one. After this went on for several minutes the props were removed, the girls disappeared behind the screen.

"That was the first syllable," Mary announced. "Does anyone know?" Several at the table ventured a guess.

"What could it be? Dinner? Banquet? What?" Barbara's face was a puzzle.

Luigi seemed completely at sea. Charades had not been a part of his American childhood all those years ago in California. Emma realized it was more of an English parlor game and recalled all those charades organized by her father on Christmas visits to her grandmother's home in Surrey. Sam looked thoughtful. Emma, her heart joyful at the surprise appearance of Sam, watched the performance wrapped in a a rosy glow.

Preparations for the second act began. An open air scene emerged as two girls stepped from behind the screen carrying cardboard replicas of small trees. They shook the trees gently, simulating breezes. The audience applauded their efforts.

Couples dressed in drapery inspired by the myths wandered into view. Dressed as boys, some girls wore sandals and tight fitting hose topped by long smocks cinched in at the waist with wide belts. The remaining girls wore flowing draperies in a variety of colors. The couples posed affectionately, arms draped over each other's shoulders, talked quietly, strolled about the wooded area. With a little imagination, it was easy to guess this was a view of some Arcadia, a scaled down *fete champetre*.

Dashing from behind the screen, Caroline entered, a willowy shape encased in a flesh tinted bathing costume and tights, looking very boyish. A quiver of arrows hung from her shoulder, she held a bow in her hand. She playfully aimed her arrows at the couples while dancing around them.

"Well, she's obviously a cupid," Barbara whispered, brows knitted in thought.

"Or an Eros," Emma said, but only Sam heard her.

Props were removed, The actors disappeared behind the screen and once again the stage was bare. Mary's cheeks were flushed, she hid a smile on her face. She was beginning to enjoy her part in the evening. Members of the hotel staff who had gathered behind the small audience, appeared captivated by the spectacle. As couples and cupid left the stage they applauded with great enthusiasm and cries of *Brava! Bravissima!, Signorine!*

"Now we come to the second word. There are two syllables. Here is the first. Good luck," Mary said, disappearing behind the screen.

Apparently no props were needed for this scene. Marigold and Vanessa walked out and began fiercely exchanging insults. As seconds went by, their anger escalated. They began shoving and boxing ears.

"Does anybody guess yet?" Marigold called gaily to the audience.

"We know you are unhappy with each other," Barbara answered. Nobody else spoke and presently they left the stage.

For the final scene there were minimal props. Two figures in elaborate period costume appeared. Winkie Taylor-Davies wore the costume of a Spanish bull fighter complete with cape and her tightly braided blonde pigtail pinned to a short length. Her upper lip sported a charcoal mustache. She looked so solemn, so serious, the audience immediately burst into laughter when she stepped out in front of the screen. Winkie frowned in mock disapproval.

"Where on earth do you suppose they found those costumes?" Barbara whispered.

Emma shook her head as she looked at Lettice, flamboyantly gowned in a brilliant red satin flamenco dress with tight-fitting bodice and flaring skirt. She had piled her blond hair on top of her head, held in place with magnificent jeweled combs. A rich shawl of yellow silk embroidered with flowers draped over her shoulders.

"You look ravishing tonight my sweet," Winkie cooed in a falsetto voice with a gallant sweep of her hand. "Yes, Donna Teresa, you look ravishing." Again, titters and applause for Winkie.

"A thousand thanks, Don Riccardo," Lettice replied modestly, fluttering enormous false eyelashes which made the cornflower blue eyes seem even larger. She opened and shut an enormous fan provocatively as she bowed.

The couple paused, allowing Winkie a moment to offer an arm, then they nodded sedately toward the audience and promenaded around the stage. At this point unrestrained giggling erupted behind the screen and the cast tumbled out for final bows to enthusiastic applause.

"So what is the final clue, do you think?" Mary asked.

"A Spanish Don, probably Don Juan, and a Spanish lady, a 'Donna'?" Emma's smile gave her away.

"You *know*, Miss Darling, you *know*, only two words!" Marigold shrilled, hardly able to contain her excitement. "Name the two words of the puzzle!"

Barbara looked at Emma and scratched her cheek absently. "I thought the first syllable was about a banquet or a meal," she said. "But the second one is a complete mystery to me. What is that gathering in the woods all about? A band of gypsies?"

"You are ice cold," Marigold answered her gleefully.

"At least Marigold is happy," Sam murmured in an aside to Emma.

"That's just Marigold, you have to take her with a grain of salt," Emma whispered back.

Luigi sat straight in his chair at attention. Suddenly he spoke up.

"I did think *Signorina* Caroline in her beguiling bathing costume with her quiver and arrows, made an enchanting Eros figure."

Wild clapping broke out among the cast. "You've guessed the second syllable of the first word, Inspector Rovere," cried Winkie. "Now, what about the first syllable of the second word? What do you think?"

"Whew," Luigi let out a long breath and tapped his forehead anxiously with long, tapering fingers. "A fight? A quarrel?" He let out another sigh. "Who knows?" He threw up both of his hands.

The hotel workers, challenged by the language although greatly interested, were without a clue.

Emma looked quickly toward Sam. He gave her a look full of meaning and nodded. The message was, "Go ahead. Speak up. I'm keeping well out of this. It's for you and your girls!" She pronounced the words softly. "Piero's Madonna."

"Oh, Miss Darling," Caroline clapped her hands. "I knew you'd come through!"

"Tell us, Emma, how do you figure it?" Barbara demanded as the applause died down, "I'm as much at a loss as our waiters."

She smiled helplessly at Luigi. Emma cheered her silently. That's the way, Barbara, play to *him!*

"Remember?," Emma said, "The first scene is of people eating peas. PEA, pronounced the same way as the 'Pi' in Piero. Then the scene of the romantic couples with a cupid, or Eros, as Luigi said. Put them together and they make PI-EROS."

"The first syllable of the second word is 'Mad', and Marigold and Vanessa certainly looked angry. didn't they? Finally, Lettice of course is the beautiful Spanish 'Donna', or lady, to Winkie's 'Don.' There you have it, MAD-DONNA. PIERO'S MADONNA. Very neatly done, girls, I must say. Congratulations." The actors bowed to the applause.

Barbara and Luigi slipped away for a quick stroll in the moonlight. Emma caught a glimpse of them as they turned the corner of the hotel. She wondered if the beautiful Italian night would work its spell on Luigi and Barbara. The street was still humming with activity, people walking, talking, pairs of lovers, arms entwined, looking into each other's eyes as they moved along the street.

Emma and Sam strolled arm in arm to the hotel's garden where they sipped *espresso* and tried to reclaim the weeks and months they had been apart. Such a lot of missed conversation, long walks together, and most of all, the wedding of Jane and Charlie.

"Your arrival tonight was a great surprise. I was already counting the minutes, and to see you a day early is truly wonderful, Sam,"

Emma smiled as they sat, contented, holding hands at a secluded table surrounded by flowers in pots.

"It was a last-minute thing, to have the extra day given to me. But there was also this powerful feeling that I needed to be here. I felt I should come ahead, even if unannounced. Is everything all right?"

"Perfectly fine, now that you are here." Emma gave his hand a reassuring squeeze. "But let's never be apart for such a long time again."

Emma looked into his eyes. There was a plaintive longing in her voice she could not disguise, and she hoped she would not have to explain to Sam how she very nearly fell in love with a charming Italian police inspector some years older than she.

Sam said nothing more. He simply put an arm around Emma's shoulder and pressed her hand. He said nothing about the brevity of her recent letters, their lack of affection. He was content to enjoy the present moment, taking in the perfume of some unknown vine flowering in the pergola over their heads as he held Emma's hand, sipped the fragrant coffee, and wondered why he had made the mistake of staying apart from her for so long.

Now things would return to normal, Emma hoped, just as though nothing had happened. She thanked the fates for pushing Sam in her direction the past summer, realizing he deserved to be cherished. Long after Sam had left to go to his *pensione* across the River Arno, long after the sounds of talk and music faded along with dimming streetlamps, Emma lay in bed looking out her window into the soft night's ceiling of blue black enlivened by twinkling stars.

Her thoughts turned toward Sam and his dream of setting up a surgical practice someday, of her dreams to carve out a career in art history. I love teaching, love passing on what I can to others eager to learn. She thought of her students, Marigold, surprisingly moved by the Giotto frescoes of Saint Francis in the Bardi Chapel of Santa Croce. Emma knew the power of art could change people. It had certainly changed her, she mused, remembering the moment in San Marco looking at the Madonna which reminded her of her friend Jane, painted by Fra Angelico in one of the monks' cells. Maybe the experience at Santa Croce, standing in front of the Giotto frescoes, changed Marigold as well.

Tomorrow morning would be hectic, getting the girls off on the hired coach in time to catch the London plane in Pisa. Someone was sure to have forgotten something, to need her help. She was calm in the knowledge that she possessed the inner resources to rise to the demands of the occasion, whatever happened. Emma knew having people depend on one made one grow.

14

A Difference of Opinion in the Room with the Iris Draperies

Once the students departed, Emma and Sam planned to take lunch in a pretty, vine-covered restaurant near the *Galleria dell'Accademia* on *Via Ricasoli*. Sam had expressed a wish to see the sculptures of Michelangelo on his one day in *Firenze*.

Earlier on this departure morning, Emma helped the girls prepare for the long trip home. All the extra souvenirs presented problems. With her help they secured the suitcases. Emma and Barbara stood aside when all cases were ready as they waited in the hotel lobby for the coach. Snatching a few private minutes, Barbara told Emma that Luigi had accepted an invitation to come to London in August during his holiday.

"Why that's wonderful, Barbara," Emma quickly gave Barbara a hug.

"You don't mind do you? I, I thought you found him appealing."

A denial sprang readily to her lips, but Emma reconsidered and said quietly, "No, I do not mind. But, Barbara, you are right. I did find him appealing. How did you know?"

"It was the way you looked at him, and what you didn't say, more than anything you did say." Barbara's answer surprised Emma; she turned a becoming pink in the face.

"I guess I was not so clever at disguising my feelings, after all," she smiled ruefully. "But you must know, it was a fleeting thing. I was so grateful to him for finding me, saving me from Mario's clutches not once but twice! But, Barbara, be assured, Sam was always first in my heart. We're going to be planning our wedding in earnest now."

What was it Luigi said to me not long ago, Emma mused. Something about being loved by an Italian in his own country of Italy? Well, love certainly had transformed Barbara. And apparently Luigi was becoming serious right away. How could I ever have thought Barbara was plain? Emma wondered as she recalled Luigi's words about love.

She and Barbara discussed plans to meet when Emma returned to London. Emma knew that in Barbara, she had found a true friend. As the students boarded the coach which would take them to Pisa, Emma reflected that her first experience leading an art tour had been a rewarding one. She felt a real affection for each girl. She realized what they had seen and experienced would remain with them all their lives. She had embraced each girl, asked her to remember their trip together as she wished her a safe journey.

The coach pulled away from Hotel Il Giardino leaving her standing alone at the entrance. Emma experienced sadness, at the same time she felt glad to have time alone with Sam. And of course, she looked forward to the reunion with Jane and Charlie.

The missing Piero Madonna had been her only disappointment, Emma realized, as she watched the coach disappear into the morass of Florence's morning traffic. Hopefully Piero's Madonna would be found and returned soon to its rightful place in the Ducal Palace at Urbino.

When she and Sam sat down at the little *ristorante* shaded by luxuriant vines on *Via Ricasoli*, they began to make plans, his move from Aberdeen, where they should live in London after they were married. Could they afford Kentish town? Hampstead? Fulham, off the King's Road? Or perhaps a flat in Dulwich? They devoured a big platter of *antipasti:* salami, roasted peppers, eggplant, olives and cheeses, then ordered coffee.

Sam leaned back, replete, then asked Emma to tell him about the tour and the stolen painting.

Alice Heard Williams

Emma related everything, including her stint as a prisoner in the Ducal Palace, later being taken captive by Mario at his house off the Via Santo Spirito in Florence. She watched as Sam began to frown and a white line formed in a tiny furrow on the bridge of his nose. He was obviously displeased at this bit of news, especially after Emma revealed how surprised she was to see Mario, thinking he had already been taken into custody earlier that morning after he dropped them off at the Uffizi Gallery.

"It really wasn't anybody's fault, Sam," she added, sensing his anger. "I assumed something had occurred. It hadn't. If I had known for sure Mario was still on the loose, it probably wouldn't have made any difference. I had no idea he lived on that street."

"Well, that bit isn't exactly true," she reflected. "If I'd known Mario was *not* in custody and that he *did* live near the Church of the Carmine and the Masaccio frescoes, I wouldn't have gone off alone to that backwater section of Florence. I'd probably have joined Barbara on Via Tournabuoni for shopping and persuaded her to go with me later to the Carmine church." But Emma hated going over what was past, assessing blame. Best move forward, even if Sam's thoughts were obviously headed in the other direction.

"As for where the painting is now," she said lightly, spooning a froth of whipped milk from her cup, "it's anybody's guess." She glanced at her watch. Almost three. But she reminded herself, this was Italy and nothing interfered with leisurely mealtimes.

"One thing does trouble me," she continued. "We saw the Cortina brother and sister in Monterchi on the first day we arrived in Italy. We saw them leave the little chapel suddenly, as though they wanted to get away from us. Much later Barbara thought it might have been Mario they didn't want to see, not our group. The coach pulled up and parked right beside their sports car, you see. But the big question is, why were they there in the first place? What were they looking for? What business did they have? I have a peculiar feeling that when we get those answers, a few remaining bits of the jigsaw puzzle will fall into place."

"Were there other works of art on display there? Works more, ah, portable, than a huge fresco?"

"Not that any of us remembers," Emma admitted. "But I'd like to go back and give the place a thorough going over."

"It's not that far, Monterchi, from Castellina-in-Chianti. I saw it on the map earlier today. Maybe we could check it out. I'd like to see the Madonna del Parto." Sam's voice was thoughtful.

"That would be topping," Emma answered quickly. "That is, of course, if Jane and Charlie haven't planned our schedule."

"To that pair the possibility of solving a crime is like throwing red meat to starving dogs," Sam grinned. "Believe me, Emma, they'll fight to go with us!"

"Remember the energy Charlie displayed in pursuit of the Apollo amulet last summer? Besides, you don't think I'm taking you to romantic *ristoranti* covered in vines *every* day of the week, do you? A picnic combined with a visit to the Madonna del Parto sounds great to me! Come on." He smiled and took her hand as they left the restaurant.

Arm in arm, they strolled toward the *Accademia*. The street seemed marginally quieter now as Florentine citizens observed the daily *riposo*. They came to the *questura*. As they reached the entrance, they heard a voice call, "*Signorina* Darling!" at their backs.

Emma whirled around to find herself facing a young policeman, one whose face seemed vaguely familiar.

"I am Orazio Bruno, Signorina. I was working with Inspector Rovere from Urbino when we freed you and picked up Mario at his house a day or two ago." Bruno had a stout figure, a short haircut to match his height and beautiful, earnest brown eyes, reminding Emma of a friendly Labrador puppy.

"Of course. Now I remember, Orazio. You came crashing into Mario's house where I was imprisoned and I thought a miracle had occurred. This is my friend, Doctor McGregor from Aberdeen." Introductions over, the men shook hands.

Missing in Toscana

"What is the latest news of the stolen Piero Madonna?"

"I know only that almost everybody has headed over to Monterchi today to look at that chapel one more time, the one with the Pregnant Madonna fresco by the same fellow. Hardly anybody is left at the station. Bad luck I drew patrol duty myself." He looked around mournfully as a couple of *vespas* carrying young men and shrieking girls whizzed by.

"Officer Bruno, it would have been wise to send you along, but I am sure they felt you were most needed here. By the way, any news of Anna and her brother?" Emma asked.

"We heard from the station in San Sepolcro the pair of them are still fuming in jail because their Papa hasn't shown up with a lawyer. As for Mario, he went crazy when he found out the picture he had been hiding was a fake, swore to tear the Cortinas apart limb from limb when he can get his hands on them, which is unlikely, as you know. A nasty business, when thieves turn on each other, but *Dio Mio*, we learn a lot!" He tapped the side of his nose lightly and grinned.

He tipped his cap respectfully and walked on down the street. "So they are searching at Monterchi today. This might be the break we are hoping for. The inability of the police to come up with the real Madonna is making everyone anxious," Emma said.

It was late afternoon when they left the *Accademia*, almost closing time, and they strolled toward the *Piazza della Signoria* to see the copy of Michelangelo's David in the place where the original first stood. Emma wanted to photograph it, so they made a detour by the hotel to pick up her camera.

She left Sam in the small reception room with the iris upholstery and draperies and hurried upstairs. She found the camera, checked her makeup in the bureau mirror and returned downstairs. Before entering the little reception room, she heard angry voices spilling out into the corridor. Sam and Luigi! She stopped, listened.

"Your failure to tell Emma of the change in plans put her in grave danger, you do realize that, don't you Inspector?" Sam's words reminded Emma of crashing waves beating against cliffs.

"What are you talking about, Dr. McGregor? Surely you know I would not harm a hair of Emma's head. That she ran into Mario was a complete coincidence. I had no idea where he lived when I spoke to her the night before; later, when I learned where his house was located, I did not dream Emma would be strolling alone nearby on the Via Santo Spirito. She had mentioned only the Uffizi and the Pitti Palace to me." Luigi's voice had turned icy cold.

"Inspector, she could have been bodily hurt or worse. One of the Florence policemen, one Orazio Bruno, told Emma and me just a couple of hours ago that the man Mario was completely out of control, a maniac. It seems to me you should have checked out his address for starters, but you chose to go blindly ahead.

At any rate, I find your failure to tell Emma of your change of plans irresponsible, bordering on negligence."

Sam, arguing so heatedly in her defense! Emma could not believe this was the mild, even-tempered Sam she knew so well. Quickly she stepped into view before the argument resumed. Both men looked embarrassed, at a loss for words.

"Luigi," what a surprise! You must have just arrived from Monterchi. We ran into Orazio Bruno this afternoon and he said you were over there."

"Yes, well, that is true. I thought you might be interested to hear what we accomplished," Luigi answered primly in an injured tone. Sam turned away to inspect the majolica plates on the fireplace mantel. Bright red flushes darkened his cheeks.

"How nice that you thought of us. Shall we go into the garden for an *espresso*? The hotel is named for the garden, you know. It is quite pretty." She beamed a smile toward them.

Luigi and Sam trailed meekly behind Emma in silence down the corridor and out into the garden where a large umbrella tree's spreading limbs cast welcome shade over the patio. Giant tubs of red geraniums filled niches in the walls. Emma noticed Sam's blue eyes were flashing fire, and Luigi was desperately struggling to regain composure. Emma hoped for a return to civility which would soothe everyone's nerves.

"I have been assigned to Florence for another week," Luigi said stiffly. "We are looking at new leads."

"And today? What did you find at Monterchi?"

"Precious little, and that with the combined might of police from Urbino, San Sepolcro and Florence," he admitted as he sipped the little cup of black coffee. "The chapel at Monterchi was thoroughly searched. As you know there are no other works of art there. Only the gigantic Piero fresco which has been reattached to canvas, covered with glass and hangs on the wall. Oh, there are a few framed diagrams explaining Piero's fresco technique in the entry hall, nothing else."

"There is a tiny crypt below. We looked it over thoroughly. Nothing there but a few very old tombstones and some broken down chairs and rubbish. It's a shame, really. The place could be cleared out and the old tomb slabs would be quite attractive. As it is, the whole area is nothing more than a repository for junk. Sometimes." he sighed, "I despair of this country."

"So the Madonna del Parto fresco is no longer painted on the wall?" Sam spoke up in an interested voice and Emma slowly relaxed. Peace seemed to be forthcoming.

"That is correct," Luigi answered politely. "It's condition is very fragile. How they transferred it and got it into a frame is a miracle the art historians and techno types can take credit for. Sometime when we have a couple of free hours, Emma, you might explain it to us. But nobody in his right mind would ever think about trying to steal it because of its size and condition."

Emma nodded and turned to Sam. "Sad, isn't it? It's condition I mean. However they have done the right thing by detaching it from the wall. This will be a much better way to preserve what is left." It was looking to Emma as if they might possibly enjoy a civilized conversation.

"And there is nothing else to attract a thief in the chapel?" Sam asked Luigi.

"Nothing whatsoever we could see. We spoke at length to the attendant of course. He does not seem that well informed, frankly, and has been on the job only a short time, about a month, he said. He promised to notify us of any strange visitors or unusual goings-on."

"Is he a young man?" Emma asked.

"Young, about twenty or so. Thin and wiry. Dark hair and eyes. Brows firmly knitted together over the nose. Right eye has a slight cast to it."

Whew, Emma thought, Luigi's photographic memory was bound to help him in his work; she too remembered the attendant, the same one on duty when she went there with the students. But weren't there two people? Surely she recalled another figure in the chapel, taking tickets. A female, old, somebody's aunt or mother.

But Luigi was certain. No such person was on the premises, at least not during the police visit.

"So we still haven't a clue why Anna and her brother were there on the day we arrived?" Emma reflected thoughtfully.

"No idea at all," Luigi admitted, "unless of course they wanted to look at the Pregnant Madonna like everyone else. She is quite famous in these parts, you know." Luigi looked over at Sam.

But Emma, though she said nothing, did not think that was the reason. Anna seemed the type of person who never performed an act without a purpose. To go on a pleasure jaunt to see a painting? Surely that was not her style. But she applauded silently the discernable lessening of hostility at the table; the tension between Sam and Luigi was disappearing.

Luigi coughed slightly and prepared to leave. "One last thing I almost forgot to mention. There's been a letter from Paolo Cortina's lawyer up in Fiesole."

"The father!" Emma exclaimed "Is he going to try to bail them out?"

Castellina-in-Chianti: Market day

"There's no way he can do that, Emma. Italians take their art seriously. The theft of a painting is a major crime."

"I see, of course. Then why?"

"He wishes to speak to them. Possibly to arrange for legal help, I don't know, but the police have agreed to a visit. There will be an officer present of course."

"Surely he wishes to talk to them about suitable counsel to defend them?" Sam said.

"Probably you are right, Dr. McGregor," Luigi looked at Sam thoughtfully. "I hope his heart is softening a little toward his children. So far he hasn't been able to get beyond the *disgrazia* brought down on his head by Anna and Pietro."

"Not likely," scoffed Sam. "His type thinks only of himself."

Emma sighed. Sam and Luigi, like the North Pole and South Pole, would take opposite sides of any question. Emma felt it would always be that way.

Could Sam's intuition have revealed to him the possibility of something between her and Luigi? Tact and restraint had kept Sam from inquiring, but Emma knew the moment would arrive when she would be forced by her conscience to discuss Luigi with Sam. She knew her future with Sam trumped everything in importance.

15

A Return to the House with the Walled Garden

Emma's bags were packed, her bill with the hotel for one additional night settled, and she waited in her room for Sam. He planned to collect her and they would enjoy a leisurely drive to Castellina-in-Chianti to meet Jane and Charlie at midday.

Early that morning Emma went out with her camera, photographed the David sculpture by Michelangelo in the morning sunlight, then took photos of several historic churches: Santa Maria Novella, San' Lorenzo, the Duomo, Santa Croce and its Pazzi Chapel, the Church of Santo Spirito and the nearby Ospedale degli Innocenti, the foundling hospital designed by Brunelleschi. She planned to add them to her growing collection of lecture slides. Who knew how useful they might be in future.

As she waited for Sam she wondered idly if Paolo Cortina had appeared yet at the police station in San Sepolcro to see his children. Had he undergone a change of heart? At least, he was well able to pay for competent representation in the courts. And Luigi? The chance she would see him again was unlikely. Not after last night. An ugly scene had been avoided, but Emma knew Sam's accusations had wounded Luigi's pride.

Emma had discussed the facts of the case with Sam at dinner the past evening, carefully skirting around mention of Luigi. But Emma knew it would be only a matter of time until the subject came up. She dreaded the look in Sam's eyes if he asked her what Luigi had meant to her. Hopeless at concealment, Emma knew the truth would tumble out, impelled by an energy of its own.

Luigi was aware they were leaving for Castellina-in-Chianti and then on to the Villa Signorelli nearby. That was all. She did not plan to propose an invitation to visit. She would be forced to learn about the case from Italian newspapers now. She took one last look around the room, recalling the final few days of the tour. Roused from her reverie by the ringing of the telephone, she stood up to answer, sure it must be Sam. He must be leaving his hotel. But it was Luigi.

"Just a final briefing, Emma, before you leave for Castellina. I am in San Sepolcro. I thought you would be interested to know that Signor Cortina has just left here. He's been talking with his children."

"And was he overcome with fatherly feeling when he saw his children incarcerated?" Emma spoke lightly, Luigi chuckled.

"It was not quite like that. He met them in one of the interrogation rooms. There was an officer there of course, but he kept his distance while they talked. I was there too, but in the background. The father really is an unforgettable figure. Roared up in a red sports car with the top down, wearing a cravat and an English tweed jacket, grey flannel trousers. He looked more like the Duke of Devonshire than an Italian vineyard owner to my mind. Had a perpetual smirk or scowl spread across his face."

"What are his features like?"

"Very long nose, a slightly receding hairline, very thin lips. I'm not sure how women feel about these things, but I would call him handsome and attractive for a man of sixty or so. The amazing thing about him is his presence. He exudes confidence."

"Intimidating as a father?"

"Whew! I should say so. To incur his displeasure would be bad, very bad."

"And the officer in the room overheard nothing?"

"It was Alvise, and he's smart. He picked up a little. I was there too, but in the background as I explained. He said the pair appeared to be trying to persuade the father to do something, pleading with the older man. But he could not make out what exactly. Alvise and I will talk again when he comes on today. I have some ideas of my own about Paolo Cortina, head of the Cortina clan. I will have to file a report on my findings and I'll send you a copy if you want. I just think he may be in this up to those arrogant eyebrows of his! Would you like me to send it?"

"That would be fine, Luigi," Emma answered, but she did not offer her address. "By the way, Barbara told me you are coming to London to visit in August."

"Yes, well, I am finally realizing that I should think about settling down. My parents have been nagging at me for years, my mother especially. So when Barbara invited me, I accepted."

"You could not find a more loyal, supportive woman than Barbara. She accepts responsibility, she is sincere too," Emma spoke softly. "I wish the best for you, Luigi."

"Admirable qualities, Barbara has," Luigi agreed, not commenting on her final words. "And we are close in age. A mere ten years difference. In Italy, that is standard."

"I had not realized," Emma murmured. "At any rate, Luigi, I applaud your choice."

"*Ciao*, Emma," he said suddenly. "Until we meet again sometime." She stood there holding the telephone, realizing that Luigi had not wanted her approval. He was still stung by her refusal of his attentions. He'll get over it, she thought, replacing the phone in its cradle.

~~~~

When Sam arrived at the hotel half of the morning remained to explore the Tuscan countryside, once they negotiated the clogged traffic of Florence and environs in the little Fiat. Emma, in a flash of inspiration: suggested they drive by way of San Sepolcro to their one o'clock destination, the square at Castellina-in-Chianti.

"Sam, San Sepolcro is only a few kilometers away, and I'll show you *Il Giardino*, the house where Anna Cortina and her brother live. We can only see it from the gate of course, but it is such an interesting old place, the garden is lovely. And you would get a look at the town where Piero della Francesca lived most of his life, the Piero park, the cathedral, the museum, just in case Jane and Charlie have already been and we don't make another trip. Looking at the house where the Cortina brother and sister live, mulling over what we know about the missing Piero, we just might uncover a fresh lead. The house might suggest something about where the painting is hidden. We have loads of time before lunch."

"Jolly good, Emma. I've been thinking about what Luigi said yesterday, and there are quite a few pieces of the puzzle to slot in, before the missing picture is found. Let's have a look at the map."

Heads together, they poured over the *Toscana* map. They saw that the journey would take them only a few kilometers out of the way. They both were eager to leave Florence behind and explore the beautiful *chianti* country.

Sam stowed the bags in the snug boot of the black Fiat and they moved off. They spoke little as Sam maneuvered through heavy traffic of Florence toward the south. Castellina—in—Chianti, where Charlie had suggested they meet for a bite of lunch, was in the heart of the wine country.

"Did you know the British have jokingly named this part of Tuscany 'Chiantishire' because so many Ex-Pats make their home there?" Sam's voice was thoughtful.

"Well, Charlie's Aunt Olive is one of them, much to our good fortune," Emma replied, grinning.

The drive through rounded Tuscan hills was so predictably lovely it put a lump in Emma's throat. In places the road was hemmed in on either side by inclines covered in neat rows of sprouting vines. Later, when the grapes were ready for harvest, the road would be filled with tourists visiting the vineyards. Today, however, they had it to themselves, occasionally passing a tractor, a farm truck, the lone *vespa* buzzing along. The few open fields as often as not were planted in rigid rows of giant sunflowers, turning faces toward the morning sun.

San Sepolcro was only a short drive and Emma guided Sam smoothly into the old part of the town within the walls. Leaving the center, with the cathedral dominating the square, they parked the Fiat and walked along side streets, past the small church of Saint Agostino, and soon arrived at the locked gates of *Il Giardino*. Anna and Pietro Cortina, now in police custody, were no longer in residence.

The place looked deserted as they peered through the gates. As before, the scent of lilies from the garden swam around them through the air. Emma looked right and left, trying to see if the menacing gardener was about, but all was quiet. *Il Giardino* slumbered, cocooned in memories of a happier, more lively past, when young children ran shouting and laughing through its rooms, Emma imagined.

In a few minutes they turned away and began retracing their steps toward the Fiat. Emma's hopes for gleaning information had withered. Suddenly they heard running footsteps behind them.

"*Signorina!*" Emma whirled around to face Maddalena, the cook.

"I saw you at the gate," the plump cook gasped. "I wanted to speak to you. Oh, *Signorina*, the sadness of this house! My mistress and young master have been taken away by the police. *Signor* Paolo has come from Fiesole and taken away the gardener. I am the only one left here. I am afraid I will lose my job!"

Emma quickly took her hand. "Now Maddalena, don't be sad. Surely that isn't going to happen."

Emma introduced Sam, telling Maddalena they had stopped briefly on the way to Castellina where they would be staying with friends.

"Castellina is near to Monterchi?" Maddalena asked. Emma nodded. Why should Maddalena ask about Monterchi?

"That is where Bepe, the young gardener at Il Giardino has gone, sent there with his old grandmother by *Signor* Paolo. She was nursemaid for the Cortinas when they were *ragazzi*, I mean children," she smiled broadly, proud she knew the right word in English. "*Signorina*, remember the old dragon who was so cross when you were here before? Domenico has been sent to Fiesole to *Il Signor's* villa. Oh you don't know how nice it was, working here when the children were small and the house was full. And now, I am here all alone!"

"But Maddalena, I don't understand. Why would *Signor* Paolo send everyone away?" Emma was puzzled, her thoughts flying back to Luigi and his findings about the elder Cortina. Could it be possible, that the man was secretly in league with Anna and Pietro? The mastermind of the theft? What if he too was planning to leave Italy and go somewhere far away? Brazil perhaps? Emma's mind traveled at breakneck speed. Sam looked askance at her. He knew she was concentrating hard.

"Anger and frustration, I believe, *Signorina*," Maddalena replied. "He was furious when his children got in trouble with the police. Truly, they have caused him much heartache, you see. When it came out that they were mixed up with stealing paintings he threw up his hands in disgust. I saw him myself, the day the police came and searched the house from top to bottom. *Che disgrazia*! I think he decided he won't let anyone stay in the house since the children have shamed him so much. That's what I think!"

"And did he have a good place to send Bepe and his grandmother in Monterchi?" Sam's voice was thoughtful as he struggled to keep up with the musical Italian streaming from Maddalena's mouth as he observed Emma's strange behavior.

"He owns some farms in the area of Monterchi, *Signor*. The family has had land there for centuries. He would be able to get a job for Bepe if he wished," Maddalena answered as certain as the chance of tomorrow's sunrise.

"And is he kind, Maddalena? I mean *Signor Cortina*." Emma asked, wondering just where Bepe and his grandmother might have found employment in Monterchi, perhaps at the little museum? And to what end? Something devious, she thought.

"Yes, even though he frowns and looks gruff, and has had much sadness in his life, yes, he is kind."

"Then surely he will take care of you," Emma said softly. "He wouldn't just turn you out." Her words were meant to reassure, but privately, Emma was beginning to fear the motives of the elder Cortina's actions. Did he protest too much about the disgrace his children had brought on him? Or was it a smokescreen to disguise his position of mastermind of the theft of the Piero? She wanted very much to read the report Luigi was preparing now.

"That is what I keep hoping, *Signorina*. Even if it means I must move to Fiesole, or even to Monterchi, I will have work, and I will try to do my best. But this house, this garden, the lilies, I, I love. To me, they are home."

Emma took the woman's hand and pressed it. The parting was a sorrowful one. What would happen to Maddalena? Paolo Cortina might possibly sell the house. But Emma, thinking furiously, recalled the Italian love of land, and doubted things would come to that. But if he were involved in the stealing of the Piero, a clean break to freedom might be uppermost in his mind, whether abandoning loyal retainers and his children or not. She must talk this over with Sam and get his opinion.

~~~~

"So what do you make of everything?" Emma asked Sam as they left San Sepolcro and Sam expertly found the outskirts in record time, setting the little Fiat on the road to Castellina with a minimum of fuss.

"I think Bepe and his grandmother may have been sent to Monterchi for a specific reason. Maybe to get them out of the way of the police or for some other unknown purpose."

"To work there on his farm?" Emma's tone was despairing. That didn't seem to fit into the puzzle at all. Except for a bit of detail about the family she already knew, they hadn't learned a great deal in San Sepolcro. But Sam was patiently reflective.

"Not necessarily. In that little hamlet suppose Pietro, the Cortina son, had control over some matters he managed for his father. What if the Cortinas secured a post for Bepe at the little museum? Taking tickets or something similar. What then? He would have a loyal family retainer in a spot if he ever needed him, wouldn't he? And there was already one gardener at San Sepolcro."

"Then surely the next question is, WHY would he need them there? What special purpose?" Emma felt dejected. "Was the father involved in the children's clandestine plans? I know Luigi thought so but he had no proof. He promised to send me his findings on the elder Cortina. However you must be right: Pietro and Anna planned the theft, before the police became interested in their activities. Their father may have joined in later, or perhaps he didn't."

"We'll have to find that out, won't we? Don't be discouraged, Emma. With Jane and Charlie on board too, we'll surely do some unraveling. But now, we better push on so we won't be late to meet those newlyweds, right?"

They followed signs leading them to the center of Castellina. The meeting place was a *trattoria* on the square with bright umbrellas shading the tables. It was market day in Castellina and the square was buzzing with noise, laughter and music. They found the *Trattoria Tonio*, but Jane and Charlie had not arrived so they decided to have a quick look around. Their eyes feasted on glistening piles of fruit and vegetables, plump chickens, stalls selling terra cotta pots from Impruneta, the legendary pottery village nearby, even a stall selling a dozen varieties of specialty pastas made by hand. They found *orzo*, the tiny rice-like grains and other shapes and colors unfamiliar to them. They bought a tempting assortment of pasta and a basket of fresh green and purple plums to take to Villa Signorelli and Charlie's Aunt Olive. They were accepting their purchases when Jane and Charlie found them.

Emma and Jane embraced while Sam and Charlie shook hands and indulged in a bit of manly back slapping, a tribute to Charlie's elevated status as a new husband. In a few minutes they had settled at a table under the yellow market umbrellas and were ordering plates of antipasti and huge salads from chef Tonio, who had become a friend of Jane and Charlie.

Sam was brought up to date on every detail of the wedding he was unable to attend. Charlie and Jane wanted to hear about Sam's move from Aberdeen to London. The news that he would join them in London soon provided another reason for celebration.

Jane described the high gothic arches, the beautiful stained glass windows of St. Margaret's, the church next door to Parliament where their wedding vows were exchanged. Jane and Emma told Sam about the students from their summer trip to

Greece who showed up, along with Professor Maria Crawford. Charlie described the butterfingers of the last minute best man he asked to take Sam's place—he almost dropped the ring at the most solemn moment of the ceremony. But there was no doubt in the minds of Sam and Emma that Jane and Charlie were perfectly suited as husband and wife, and that they were clearly relishing the married state.

Jane described the reception at Browns Hotel in Picadilly to Sam, reminding him it had been their favorite gathering place the summer before, for Charlie's tea party announcing the solving of the case of the missing Apollo Amulet. Charlie's role was much more difficult this time Jane suggested slyly: he had to eat a slice of their wedding cake decorated with icing like concrete in front of the whole assembly of guests looking on. She agreed completely with Emma that English pastry cooks desperately needed help in the frosting department. Charlie was afraid he'd cracked a tooth on that icing!

Following lunch, the three quizzed Emma about leading her first student group on tour and the stolen painting. As Emma recounted being twice captured by one of the thieves, Jane's eyes widened. They had not realized she was taken prisoner.

"We must get ourselves over to Monterchi and Arezzo to see these wonders of the Piero Trail before thieves cart them all off," Charlie said. "We could make a run over to Monterchi tomorrow if you like, that is, if you girls don't mind dragging along the uneducated members of the party who remain ignorant about Piero's work." He raised an eyebrow at Sam.

"Yes, let's do it," Jane agreed, "if Emma isn't sick to death of herding students around. Emma, I promise you, I'll not let Charlie and Sam ask stupid questions."

Emma reassured them her students were positively brilliant, and as for Charlie and Sam, "Why they know almost as much as we do, Jane!"

"Seriously, Emma, it's not like you to harbor an unsolved mystery. What's the problem? Wherever is the missing Piero masterpiece?" Charlie asked.

"The problem, Charlie, is that every lead has fizzled. The police found the ring leaders, a conniving brother and sister. We found their helper Matteo, or Mario, his alias, who turned out to be our coach driver. All three of them are now in police custody. We even located the painting, but later found it was only a copy, a very good copy, I might add. Everyone seems now to have run out of options as to where the genuine Piero is hiding!" Emma shrugged.

"Where do you look for a stolen masterpiece? Monterchi, the place where the Pregnant Madonna hangs, figures in it somehow, I know it does, but the police can't discover why, as yet." A frown creased Emma's smooth forehead.

"Nor can we," Sam added. "Emma and I took a run through San Sepolcro on the way down. Emma wanted me to see the house where the brother and sister lived. But all we gained was a conversation with the cook and some information about the

Cortina connection to Monterchi we can't seem to process into solving the puzzle of the missing painting."

"Never mind, Uncle Charlie and Aunt Jane are on the case now! We can help." Charlie leaned back, draped his arm protectively over Jane's chair and smiled benignly. Scotland Yard's youngest inspector was enjoying his honeymoon, being married to the lovely Jane, Emma could tell. But marriage had not distracted him from the thrill of pursuit of a missing masterpiece.

Emma glanced around the table. Charlie, assured, elegant of figure, with eyes that could turn to steel when tracking down a criminal, dedicated to his job at Scotland Yard; Jane, tall, lovely, grey eyes following Charlie adoringly, a gifted student of art history; Sam, unassuming, relaxed in dark blue button down shirt and chinos, a brilliant surgeon, thoughtful, patient, her compass.

It *was* good to be with friends after the roller coaster ride of the past fortnight. And devoted as she was to her students, it was heavenly to shuck the responsibility. No worries about who turned up late, or who became involved in unsuitable romances. Emma, visibly relaxing, began to enjoy her final week in Italy.

16

The Magic of Villa Signorelli and Chianti Country

It was no wild speculation that British tourists had jokingly renamed the region Chiantishire. British motors with UK tags transporting fair-skinned tourists with bad cases of sunburn seemed to be everywhere. Sam was right, Englishmen were positively swarming in this part of *Toscana,* Emma observed.

The remote Villa Signorelli's faded coral walls with shutters of a watery viridian gave it the appearance from a distance of a blurred mass of antique roses, Emma thought wistfully as they approached. She knew it was built in the early 1900s, replacing a much older, smaller house. And she had researched this area thoroughly enough to expect the vineyards to go right up to the lawns surrounding the house, customary in many of the old vine-growing estates in *Toscana* where the landowner's house began as merely a farmhouse, the title of villa tacked on by subsequent descendants.

When Charlie's aunt Olive came to Florence to study art after World War I, she met and married Umberto Signorelli. Olive was forty when she and Umberto made their vows. Twenty years later he was dead, but Olive chose to stay on at the villa rather than return to the cold damp of England. She had transformed into an Italian now, living the life of a gentle recluse, far from family and friends in England.

She spent her days painting large, splashy landscapes in striking colors which when dry were stacked against the walls of her studio, an airy, light-filled former ballroom occupying the entire third floor of the villa.

When she was not painting, Olive roamed the half-wild remnants of her garden where ivy and thyme ran untamed and old roses clambered over everything. A nymph's arm protruded from the lacy covering of a clematis vine, a tipsy Bacchus stood uncertainly in a sea of purple iris, the fragrance of lavender and rosemary perfumed the air, assaulting senses already on overload from the rioting pinks, purples, blues and lilacs the eye registered.

Charlie scoffed at the disorder, for his aunt was well able to employ gardeners to impose discipline. In fact, there was a gardener on the property, but Olive loved the garden in its semi-wild state, and insisted it be kept as it was when her beloved Umberto was alive. Only Olive and the old gardener knew how many hours of labor were required, patiently pruning and trimming, to maintain it barely within its untamed exuberance. Emma and Jane thought it surely was the most beautiful, romantic arcadia they had ever seen.

Inside the villa Emma felt she was in a time warp. The furniture, dark and ponderous, handed down through Umberto's family, consisted of knobby-legged chairs of a reinvented baroque design; gigantic, camel back sofas piled with flotillas of pillows; mushroom-shaded lamps winking with strands of sparkling beads; needlepoint fire screens and heavy porcelain potpourri jars with pierced lids from which delicious scents of rose petals wafted through the air. Shepherds and shepherdesses gamboled around the surfaces of these jars in a delightful way.

The heavy ponderous furniture was offset by the room's light, whimsical feeling, helped along by filmy, sheer curtains hanging from ceiling height on wrought iron rods and pushed open on either side to reveal the room's generous casements.

Upholstery of a faded blue brocade embroidered with a fleur-de-lys pattern lightened the heavy woods, reminding Emma a little of motifs in the little parlor of the Hotel *Il Giardino* in *Firenze*. The walls were another of Olive's concessions to modernity: the original patterned wallpaper had vanished and walls were painted a mottled cream. Sunlight now flooded in from the large windows. Emma felt the presence of an artist in the villa, a very good artist who had created a canvas of the senses within the four walls. The result was magical, surprisingly airy and comfortable.

Missing in Toscana

Emma's room, upstairs on the *piano nobile*, was reached by a sumptuous marble staircase, clearly intended by ancestral Signorelli who commissioned it to be the showcase of the villa. Impossible to ascend or descend without feeling like a queen Emma thought, making a stately climb to her assigned room to unpack.

It adjoined Olive's suite and had its small, private entrance and bath at the end of the corridor. Probably designed for a maid's room but perfect for one guest, Emma decided, admiring the dainty, white-covered single bed, airy lace at the windows, spectacular views of vineyards on the hillsides beyond. The walls were the same mottled ivory of the reception rooms downstairs. Sam occupied a room a the end of the opposite wing, but dressed in a more tailored décor, next to the suite occupied by Jane and Charlie.

Life at the villa revolved around the kitchen, an enormous room managing to look cozy and comfortable in spite of functional necessities. Bare terra cotta tiles waxed and polished to a startling brilliance covered the floor. A fireplace surrounded by majolica tiles, a fireplace big enough in which to roast a steer, had the look of being used daily in times long gone; today however the kitchen gleamed, equipped with every modern convenience. Here Olive had allowed time to fast forward to the present.

The kitchen was presided over by plump, bustling, red-cheeked Maria, whose smile and laugh were as jolly as her robust complexion, ruddy from long hours bending over the range.

Maria was Olive's link with the real world, her confidante and friend. Square like a slab of *polenta*, hair peppered with grey and scraped into a bun on top of her head, gold loops dancing in her ears were her only concession to adornment; Maria possessed arms and legs with the sturdiness of rolling pins.

She arrived every morning on her *vespa*, first bringing Olive up to date over cups of *caffelatte* on the happenings in the village and news of her husband who worked at a nearby vineyard. Then she sprang into action, cooking, cleaning and polishing every visible surface in the villa until late afternoon, when she hopped on her machine and sped over the undulating road toward Castellina, the overnight ironing tucked neatly in a basket strapped to the side of the *vespa*, dinner for Olive left waiting in the warming oven of Villa Signorelli's kitchen.

Olive, on the other hand, reminded Emma of a water sprite, delicately splashing about here and there, her fluid movements full of grace. As Olive flitted restlessly around the house and garden, she seemed like some mythical creature, untouched by time. The wonder of nature and delight in the everyday world had never deserted her, even after the crushing blow of her husband's early death. She was tiny, hardly five feet tall, thick grey hair springing luxuriantly from a well-shaped head. Emma could not imagine her hair another color. Somehow the pewter color suited her. Hair touched by winter frost Emma described it.

"I do so hope she likes me," Emma mused, listening to the muted movements of Olive in the next room preparing for bed. "It is so wonderful she invited Sam and me to visit."

Earlier they all had sat around the big pine table in the kitchen and enjoyed a delicious meal, dining by candlelight. Maria had prepared *frito misto*, a mixed grill of meat and fish dipped in the lightest, most delicate batter Emma had ever tasted. Replete, they remained at the table, talking and enjoying the last sips of *chianti*, the robust wine of *Toscana*, long after Maria had finished tidying up and had zoomed off toward home on the *vespa*.

"You must come with us to Monterchi tomorrow, Auntie," Charlie said. "We're off to see the famous Pregnant Madonna by Piero della Francesca Emma and Jane have been raving on about."

"Oh yes, Olive, do come, we would so love to have you with us." Jane added quickly.

"Dr. McGregor is a very careful driver," Charlie said. "You can motor over with him and Emma." Sam and Emma exchanged glances. Charlie's reputation as a speedy driver on the open road seemingly had preceded him to Italy.

"You must," Emma said, "The *Madonna del Parto* is so beautiful."

Olive's eyes took on a faraway look. "Ah yes, the *Madonna del Parto*. I wanted so much to paint religious art. Women and their babies, you see. But I could never get the figures quite right, so I painted landscapes instead. Yes, that painting. I remember it." Her voice trailed off in a wistful whisper, like the falling of a veil over an object once loved.

"The landscapes you paint are inspired, drenched in the most marvelous colors." Emma's voice held admiration.

Olive seemed not to be listening, lost in her own thoughts.

"There were four of us that day, looking at the *Madonna del Parto*. I shall never forget. It was a day to remember. Sometime I must tell you about it." She addressed the group, but she looked at Emma. She took a sip of wine and rose from the table. "Excuse me, please. I must check on the moon outside." And her sweet, vague smile bestowed a blessing on them all as she left the room, lost in some rediscovered paradise in the sepia world she inhabited with memories of Umberto and their life together. Jane and Emma gazed at each other, caught up in the romance of the person, the place.

Although nothing was said, Emma wondered if Olive would rouse herself to accompany them on the following morning, or would she prefer to spend the day painting in her sunlit studio and dreaming in the tangled garden, her thoughts far away?

"I wonder, how changed would she be today if there had been children before Umberto died so suddenly?" Jane's remark triggered Emma's thoughts as she climbed the great staircase.

17

A Surprise on the Pillow

Entering her room, Emma realized she was certainly ready for bed after a day filled with the excitement of a reunion with Jane, Charlie and Sam as well as her introduction to Olive and Villa Signorelli. On the fresh white pillow of her bed, however, she discovered one more object demanding her attention. She lifted the large white envelope addressed to her with no postage, only the words "Delivered by Courier" mysteriously written above the address. What on earth, she wondered, opening the flap?

It was Luigi's report. How had he found out where she was staying, and so speedily? Then she realized, she had probably mentioned where she was going earlier, and, in any case, he had ways, the police could find out anything. The Signorelli name would certainly be known about these parts, located in the heart of the wine country of *Toscana,* so very near San Sepolcro. She began to read.

"Emma, you probably did not wish to hear from me again, I sensed this when I saw you last, but this is a professional matter and as a servant of the people of my city, I ask for your help, plain and simple. I want you, and Dr. Sam too, if he will, to read this and tell me if you think I'm right—or have I let my feelings for the man drive me way out onto an unsupportable limb? You can let me know by a note to the *questura* in Urbino—we do not have to meet again. I'm not suggesting a meeting, but I do need your hunches and instincts about what I've found before I file this report with the *commisario.* You know as I've said many times, you've been right in your thoughts at almost every turn in this wacky investigation. I mean that. You've made spectacular discoveries and led us along on the case. Now I'm asking for your reaction, nothing more. No hidden agenda here. Read on:

CONFIDENTIAL REPORT

Subject Paolo Cortina, Villa Esperanza, Fiesole, Toscana
San Sepolcro Questura, 15 June, 1975
By Luigi Rovere, Inspector, Urbino Questura, and Alvise Damiano, Inspector, San Sepolcro Questura

Subject arrived at the San Sepolcro Questura for a scheduled visit of fifteen minutes with his children Anna and Pietro Cortina who are being held there.

Missing in Toscana

Inspector Damiano in charge. Inspector Rovere observing in the room.

(1) A close rapport was quickly established between subject and his children even though he tried earlier to give the impression to police he had washed his hands of them. We observed the three in deep conversation which they attempted to keep private. It was definitely a conversation of importance, not just the niceties, such as "How are you? Etc . . .

(2) In answer to some request which we could not overhear, subject promised his children to undertake some kind of action. But the words we were able to make out were not "suitable counsel to represent you". Rather we heard words like "the Doctor is a good dealer" and "Get help safely" and "London or Paris." We think it may refer to the stolen painting and efforts to either get it out of Italy or turn it over to an underground art dealer in Paris or London—or both.

(3) Subject was extremely agitated and uncomfortable during the visit. He constantly wiped his forehead of perspiration. We heard him say he had received communication from "that friend of yours" then something about "doing us all in." We took this to possibly mean Matteo—Mario—Caponi, behind bars in *Firenze* charged with theft of the Piero painting along with the two Cortinas. Rovere

had read an earlier report from the Florence questura that Caponi went wild when he found out the painting in his possession when the police arrested him was a copy. He swore revenge on all the Cortinas during that outburst.

(4) Subject was heard to say he was "going tomorrow to check things out with Bepe" and there would be news soon about "further developments." We thought it might mean getting the painting safely hidden or perhaps making arrangements for its departure from the country. We do not know who Bepe is or where he lives, but we will check that out immediately.

(5) We heard subject say to his daughter, "your mother is disappointed in you" and as he told us earlier when we visited the villa in Fiesole that his wife had been dead for years, this must be investigated. This was another example of subject's duplicitous behavior. We will pay another visit to him and ask for straight answers, hoping he will lead us to the painting and to "Bepe."

"We believe these observations are substantial enough to warrant close watching of the subject."

Beneath his signature, Luigi had penciled in his thanks to Emma in advance for giving her reaction to the report.

Emma thought about what she had read. So, another suspect to add to the mix. Nothing seemed simple anymore, but she recalled she also had thought the elder Cortina might possibly be involved in the theft. She could at least tell Luigi who Bepe was, probably a childhood name given the young gardener who had been sent to Monterchi to work in the little chapel. If Luigi filed this report, the investigation would broaden. Who knew when they would find the Piero and return it to its home in Urbino? Emma was not sure how she felt. She resolved to sleep on it and confide in Sam in the morning.

~~~~

Surprisingly Olive was downstairs, dressed and settled in the kitchen as they gathered for *caffelatte* and *pane Toscana* the following morning. The front hall was cluttered with small rugs and a ridiculously large hamper already prepared by Maria for their picnic. Olive was dressed for the outing in a filmy, loose-fitting white linen dress lined in silk, setting off a finely woven straw hat with a large floppy brim. She had pinned a fresh rose to the hat and wore sunglasses, making her look even more vulnerable and wraithlike.

When they opened the massive doors of the villa after breakfast, their eyes were drawn to an ancient, beautifully polished grey Bentley idling in the drive, brought around by the old gardener on instructions from Olive who handed the keys to Sam with a smile. Olive took a seat beside him while Emma scrambled into the back, relishing the voluptuous cushions and well-preserved luxury of a bygone age. Emma realized with Olive in the car she was not going to have a chance to confide in Sam about Luigi's mysterious report on Paolo Cortina until later

Jane and Charlie led off in their small sports model. It was a late spring morning filled with promise, acres of blue, unblemished sky presiding over undulating hills covered in vines. The air felt pure and cool as crystal, slow to absorb the warmth of the sun.

Emma noticed that Charlie was on his best driving behavior as leader of the convoy, curbing any impulse to let his open car test the road. Several motors shot past, including a sleek, red sports model which, according to Sam, must have been doing one hundred kilometers. Poor Charlie, Emma thought. Moving restlessly but sedately ahead of the Bentley in his car with Jane, he would *certamente* be a blob of frustration.

"Italian drivers are a menace," Olive spoke up suddenly through tightly drawn lips. "They are demons; Umberto agreed with me on that." Her eyes followed the speeding red car disapprovingly until it vanished over a hill.

Their plan was to drive straight to the chapel at Monterchi, have a good look at the Madonna del Parto while at the same time carry out their own investigation, checking every inch of the chapel. Afterward, they would search out a perfect spot for the picnic.

A chattering coach load of American tourists and a trio of nuns preparing to enter the chapel crowded the tiny parking area. The group from the villa quickly hurried inside to purchase tickets. For Sam and Charlie seeing the fresco for the first time, a careful noting of the technical details as well as studying the artist's painting style would add to their enjoyment.

Olive, perhaps lost in secret memories of earlier visits, stood to one side, her eyes widening as she absorbed the beauty of Piero della Francesca's composition. She said nothing to anyone and her obvious desire to enjoy the work alone kept her guests at a distance. A solitary creature most of the time, she obviously preferred to let her thoughts flow uninterrupted as she gazed at the familiar painting again.

Had she perhaps wanted children herself but for some reason been unable to have them? Or was it Umberto who was unwilling? Emma pondered the question Jane had raised the night before as she made the rounds of the two rooms searching for something, anything suspicious, perhaps a small painting earlier overlooked.

Why would the thieves choose an obscure chapel to hide another famous work by the same artist anyway? It didn't make sense, unless it was so outrageous it might work and, throw the police off track. Emma frowned The idea seemed so louche the thieves might possibly get away with it. Why did Anna go to England to copy Piero della Francesca in the National Gallery? Why did she wear the blonde wig? She just might have the type of personality which compelled her to behave in a perverse way, nothing more than that. But Emma knew there was great complexity to the persona of Anna Cortina. What secrets did she hide? Was there a connection between the attendant and the younger Cortinas? Did Anna and Pietro confide in Bepe, the man mentioned by Maddalena the cook and also mentioned in Luigi's report? Of course they knew him. He had been the junior gardener at *Il Giardino*.

"If they did not know him, then how," she said aloud, "could the Cortinas possibly be able to hide anything for safekeeping in this place?"

"And if they did, the attendant must have been privy to the plan." Jane, at her elbow, whispered softly. "If he were acquainted with Anna and Pietro, he might have been persuaded to let them hide something, even if he didn't know what it was, in this remote place."

Emma turned and looked at Jane. "You may well be right Jane. The old woman selling tickets, has been around a long time, she looks almost eighty. She probably spent most of her working life in service to Anna's family. But Luigi was adamant that only the young man was here the day the police came."

"And did you notice the young man who sold the tickets?" she added as though thinking aloud, "He has the same nose as the old woman and the same hooded eyes. He must be a grandson, don't you think? It would fit what the cook Maddalena told us about the pair being relocated in Monterchi. And Paolo Cortina spoke of "Bepe" to his children when he visited and Luigi overheard him. The father, Paolo Cortina, may be in on the plan too."

"Remember, Emma, I wasn't with you earlier. What could be the link of these people to Anna and Pietro Cortina? They couldn't be relatives, could they?"

"Not relatives, simply loyal retainers, which I'm told, often amounts to the same thing in these hills. Certainly the history books are filled with examples of loyal servants dying for their masters and other examples of loyalty in the extreme. Yesterday, when Sam and I stopped at the house in San Sepolcro on our way down, the cook Maddalena told me the young gardener, Bepe, and his grandmother had been sent to a farm Signor Cortina owned near Monterchi. But what are they doing at this little museum? She mentioned nothing about them working here. Jane, we'll never find it out if we don't ask. I think I'll see what I can learn from the old woman."

Emma thought over what Maddalena the cook told her and Sam, that the young gardener and his grandmother had been relocated to Monterchi, as she strolled toward the old lady taking tickets. But that was on a farm Paolo Cortina owned. As she began to speak to the woman, Emma saw Jane covertly watching from her post in front of the fresco.

Once Emma smiled and offered a few friendly words to her in rudimentary Italian, the old woman seemed only too happy to talk. Poor thing, Emma thought, noting the worn but respectable black dress, the spotless white collar. This new life had turned into a lonely business, away from the charming house in San Sepolcro. The old woman replied to Emma's questions, taking over the conversation, embellishing her rapid flow of words with extravagant gestures and nodding her head, touching the ornate combs holding her white hair in place as Emma struggled to keep abreast of the magical fountain of words falling so rhythmically from the old woman's smiling lips. She was obviously enjoying the attentions of the young *Signorina*. After a few minutes Emma gave her a fulsome smile and moved back toward Jane.

"She has only come here to live in the past three months," Emma whispered. "Before that she lived in San Sepolcro, where she and her husband worked for many years for a family with two small children. She was nurse for the children, her husband worked as gardener until he died. Now that the children are grown, she has retired." Here Emma paused for breath.

"Her husband died many years ago. Her 'family', the people she worked for, were able to get this job for her grandson Giuseppe, and he invited her to come and keep house for him. She misses San Sepolcro, a lovely house near the old city walls with its pretty garden. Sound familiar? She surely must have been nursemaid for the Cortinas. The house sounds awfully like *Il Giardino*. I couldn't pry out the name of the family, however. They must have warned her not to mention it to anybody."

"Let's go down to the crypt and tell Sam and Charlie."

Olive was still studying the fresco while nearby the American coach party continued to chatter. The three nuns were gazing attentively at the Blessed Virgin. Jane and Emma slipped down the stairs. In the crypt, Sam and Charlie appeared engrossed in examining the floor which at some stage had been roughly paved with huge slabs of flagstones between the tombstones.

"Probably nobody has been buried here for many, many years," Emma said. "According to legend, Piero's mother was supposed to have a grave somewhere in the cemetery near the chapel. She came from Monterchi. That would explain why Piero accepted a commission in such a tiny hamlet." Emma looked around. "It seems unlikely her tomb would be here, surrounded by stacks of old newspapers and discarded chairs with three legs."

"You're right." Jane peered doubtfully at a stone on which a skeleton's head grinned wickedly at her.

"I don't believe anyone would leave a picture here. It's so damp, any picture would deteriorate very quickly," Emma spoke firmly.

"Right, again, Emma, and I would be very surprised if anything had been buried under these stones, certainly not recently. They haven't been disturbed." Sam looked downcast. Emma relayed to Charlie and Sam her conversation with the old woman.

Sam whistled. "The Cortinas! So there is a connection?"

"Yes, possibly, Sam, but we mustn't jump to conclusions," Emma warned. "We can only guess she worked for the Cortinas. San Sepolcro is a very small town. On the other hand, she was careful not to reveal the name of her employer."

"Sounds like you've arrived at the truth, Emma," said Charlie.

"Then there must be a hiding place somewhere in this chapel, but where?" Emma's frustration was unbearable. Where could the painting be? She was beginning to believe the Piero Madonna had perhaps already left Italy.

They tapped lightly on the walls but could locate nothing sounding hollow. No new plaster seemed to have been put up. If there were secrets in the crypt, they remained hidden, Emma decided, despondent that once more the *Madonna del Parto* had revealed nothing. The stolen Piero Madonna had eluded them. Would she ever be found?

"Should we try to question the nephew, Charlie?" Jane asked as they went up the narrow stairs.

"Wouldn't hurt," Charlie drawled, "but don't expect overly much. He may not prove as eager to talk as the old lady."

They returned to the main exhibition room, finding Olive deep in conversation with a man of her own age, a man impeccably dressed in silk trousers, jacket and fulsome cravat. His supple leather shoes, Emma noted, were cousins of Mario's black shoes with gold tassels. Expensive. Fussy. But this man was of a type completely different from Mario, Emma realized, studying him covertly. His profile was aristocratic, brows permanently set in a disdainful frown, making him seem critical of everyone his glance rested upon. The man's facial expression reminded her of someone, lodged firmly in the far reaches of memory. But who? She knew her subconscious was dancing all around it, but she could not unlock what was hidden in her brain, at least for the moment.

When Olive saw them, she quickly put her arm on the man's sleeve, whispered, then walked over to her nephew and his companions.

"I have run into an old and dear friend," she said. "Give me ten or fifteen minutes and I will join you at the parking area."

She quickly returned to the man who had been looking in their direction with displeasure written all over his face. What can be his problem? Emma studied the face. Where, oh where have I seen that same pouting look before? Emma racked her brain, but the answer eluded her.

"Auntie seems to have found an admirer," Charlie murmured.

"A very well-to-do admirer, by the looks of him," Sam added.

"Who do you suppose he can be?" Jane whispered.

"Oh, just some long ago friend of Umberto's, I imagine," Charlie said as he strolled toward the young man selling tickets at the entrance. "Italians are the most gregarious people in the world."

18

Aunt Olive Undertakes a Mission

The grandson of the old woman had revealed little to Charlie in spite of his pleasant inquiry and innocent questions. In fact he seemed nervous, constantly swiveling his eyes toward the room where the fresco hung, where Olive and her mysterious friend were still deep in conversation. Charlie was able to confirm the grandson's name as Giuseppe, but nothing was said about a "Bepe", although Emma suggested it was probably a nickname.

The American coach party filed by, the three nuns following some distance behind them.

As for Emma, the need to speak to Sam about the courier-delivered letter from Luigi was pressing on her like a weighty stone; there had nor been a moment when she could have a word with him in confidence. Could Paolo Cortina be an accomplice, not the grieving father so repulsed by the crime of his children, as he pretended to be?

"He certainly seemed very nervous," Charlie was saying of the young man he questioned as they all waited for Olive outside, standing between the Bentley and Charlie's open car. "I'd guess he had been warned very recently to keep quiet."

The coach carrying the Americans pulled away and the nuns climbed into an ancient Rover and glided off, waving gaily.

"Where do you suppose they got the Rover?" Sam wondered. "English cars aren't that common in Italy."

"Some British expatriate died and left it to their convent, I'll bet," Charlie answered. "Doesn't it sound reasonable?" Seeing the nuns sitting sedately in the British car brought a smile to Emma's lips. A little bit of England in faraway Italy. Only one other car beside their two cars remained in the parking area, a red sports model, obviously owned by Olive's unknown friend.

"Isn't that the motor that shot past us when we were on the road earlier?" Jane asked.

"Careful, Jane, you know how sensitive Charlie is about being overtaken." Sam's eyes sparkled with mischief.

"You are right about that, Sam." Jane agreed, patting Charlie's arm. Emma noticed that Jane had begun to acquire certain wifely gestures. Will I be that way with Sam, she wondered, envisioning a quick vignette of middle age, both she and Sam wearing bifocals and wrinkles.

"This surely isn't the same one," Charlie remarked. "That chap we saw earlier is probably in Rome by now." He failed to keep a certain amount of envy out of his voice.

"I believe it *is* the same car," Emma said quietly. "I remember the registration number."

It took only a few seconds for the others to digest this bit of information. "So he is the chap talking to Olive," Charlie stroked his chin thoughtfully.

"Perhaps Olive will bring him out soon for an introduction," Jane offered.

Emma was thinking hard, remembering Luigi's description of just such a man. She had a prickly feeling at the back of her neck, but no facts to go on. Just an idea. And she knew better than to raise everyone's hopes. Besides, they had searched the crypt and the two rooms upstairs with no success. She sighed. Maybe they were on the wrong track, again. But in a flash of perception, she remembered who the man's disdainful looks recalled: *Anna Cortina*! The puzzle piece fit!

"What is the matter, Emma? You look like a cat whose been at the cream!" Jane looked suspiciously at her friend.

Emma smiled and shook her head. This was not the time for speculation. She would have to be certain before saying anything. "Sorry, just my mind meandering, nothing else." But thoughts were tumbling out rapidly, teasing her.

Olive appeared at the door of the little museum and began walking briskly toward the group. Alone, hat in hand, her large purse tucked under her arm, she appeared nervous.

"Charles, you must drive us to San Sepolcro at once." Olive's voice sounded tense and her face projected a roadmap of worry lines.

"But Auntie, it is almost lunchtime. What about our picnic?" Charlie's voice registered dismay. "Must we do it first?"

"I am sorry that our luncheon plans must be delayed, but I cannot postpone this errand. We must go to San Sepolcro quickly, before we can have our luncheon." She took a deep breath.

"Sam, you and Emma and I will lead off and Charles and Jane can follow. This is an emergency. I will explain everything to you all later, *after* we reach San Sepolcro.

Time is of the essence. We must fly!"

Solemnity in the tone of her voice alerted them to her purpose and they quickly scrambled into the two cars. Whatever the reason, Emma reflected, this was extremely important to Olive and they all must rally around.

Charlie capitulated with good humor to her wishes. "Of course, Auntie. We're with you wherever you lead us. Let's get started. San Sepolcro isn't far."

Charlie and Jane followed Sam's lead behind the Bentley. Charlie, hunger pains gnawing at his stomach, recalled that he had warned Jane earlier, and Sam and Emma too. His Aunt Olive was an eccentric! He could not imagine what the two occupants of the Bentley with Olive were thinking at this moment.

Olive sat ramrod stiff beside Sam in the passenger seat looking straight ahead, not speaking, clinging to a parcel wrapped in heavy paper which Emma had overlooked as Olive's hat and handbag had earlier shielded it. Emma tensed, hardly daring to breathe as she perched on the edge of her seat. Her heart was pounding. They were silent as Sam guided the purring car through the little hamlet of Monterchi on to the open road. Charlie and Jane were following close behind.

"Just what street are we looking for, Signora Signorelli?" Sam asked breaking the silence as the industrial area surrounding San Sepolcro at last loomed into view. They were passing the gates of the huge Buitoni factory where pastas of all kinds were made.

"The *questura*, the police station is in the town center. There will be directions signposted presently," Olive answered softly, still looking straight ahead. Except for twitching fingers which gripped the package, she was motionless. Two red spots burned in her cheeks.

The *questura*! Emma was shocked. Olive Signorelli, the semi recluse, making for the police station! How traumatic. Sympathetic as she was to the turmoil Olive must be feeling on this bizarre mission, a little burst of hope began flickering. But she dared not fan it into a bonfire. Not yet.

"The road signs will clearly indicate the direction," Olive added in a faint voice, noticeably trying to calm herself by keeping her voice soft, her face smooth.

Following signs leading toward the city center, they soon saw the *questura*. Olive turned to look back at Emma.

"Will you go inside with me please, Emma?" she asked, a look of pleading covering her face, a slight tremor in her voice. Again Emma was reminded of a reluctant child.

"Of course, Olive. I'll be glad to go with you. And I know Charlie . . ." Olive interrupted quickly. The look of the child disappeared.

"No! Not Charles, just you for now, please. He and the others should wait outside." The voice of an older aunt speaking firmly to a child, Emma's sentence was left dangling.

The car glided to a stop at the entrance. "Tell the others we won't be long," Olive called over her shoulder to Sam, as she opened her door and sprang out so quickly Emma could barely keep up. Olive tucked a stray wisp of hair under her hat with her free hand as Emma hurried beside her. Olive was tightly clutching the package beneath her large handbag.

She is dreading this more than anyone can imagine, Emma thought, sensing the pain a shy person endured when forced to act. And Charlie, a Scotland Yard Inspector, must be in a right old state, seeing his aunt marching into a police station in a foreign country without him! She wondered if Sam thought Olive had taken leave of her senses. But I know she hasn't, Emma reasoned. She's promised something to this man she met in front of the fresco and she's carrying out her promise. I know that's it. She's going to do it even if she finds it the most frightening thing she's ever had to do in her entire life. This much Emma felt she had guessed.

As for what Olive was carrying, Emma refused to dream. If only! But so many earlier hopes had been dashed. She couldn't let imagination run wild over this amazing turn of events.

They approached the desk and Olive asked to speak with the police inspector in charge. Something in her manner, her presence, her wistful air, perhaps the sight of an older woman, obviously a lady of a gentler age, wearing so simple yet distinguished a dress, propelled the officer into action. He left his desk abruptly and returned in seconds to usher them to a small office at the end of the corridor.

An enormous desk covered with layers of papers in obvious disarray almost obscured the man sitting behind it. Emma could see he was tall, slender of figure, with abundant red hair framing a noble head, a rounded bald spot at the crown, horn rim glasses resting on a well-shaped nose and the most penetrating hazel eyes Emma had ever seen.

So this was San Sepolcro's chief inspector, the man the Urbino police and Luigi Rovere had been working with! To her, he looked more like a university professor than a policeman. Try as she might, she could not imagine the glamorous Luigi Rovere in such a room, behind such a desk, cluttered with mountains of papers. The chief inspector rose and looked them over, hazel eyes beaming like lasers.

"I am chief inspector Francesco Barzoni. May I help you?" He motioned them into two chairs in front of his desk. Emma, studying his head, noting the fringe of fine red hair, was reminded of a monk's tonsure.

"I am Olive Signorelli," Olive began nervously, "Widow of Umberto Signorelli, living in Villa Signorelli outside Castellina-in-Chianti."

Olive's voice was steady, but faint. Barzoni nodded, pressing the fingers of his hands together as he sat down again, leaned back slightly in his chair and looked intently at Olive through heavy-lidded eyes which seemed to dip sleepily, but eyes which Emma sensed were completely alert and awake, taking in every detail of the two women seated before him.

"This young lady is my houseguest, Emma Darling, an American art historian, working at present in England. She has been leading British students around Toscana and Umbria the past fortnight." Olive continued in her soft voice. Did Emma imagine it, or did his eyebrows lift slightly when her name was mentioned? He surely had heard of her, the woman abducted first in Urbino, then in Florence, by one of the criminals who stole the Piero Madonna. His nod was noncommital however.

Olive struggled a few seconds arranging her thoughts, then resumed. "I have come directly from the small chapel at Monterchi where I, my nephew from England and his wife Jane, Miss Darling and Dr. McGregor from Aberdeen were visiting the Piero della Francesca fresco of the *Madonna del Parto* this morning."

Barzoni nodded. "Continue." His hands formed a pyramid over his chest as he leaned back in his chair. The hazel eyes never left Olive's face.

"We looked at it together about fifteen minutes, perhaps twenty, then the young people left to go downstairs. They wanted to see the crypt. I stayed because as a painter, I wanted to study the figures in greater depth, you see."

Olive paused as though gathering strength. But Emma noticed with alarm that her face was as white as the rose she had pinned to her hat when they left Villa Signorelli earlier. She knew poor Olive's heart beneath the linen of her dress must be beating like the wings of an imprisoned bird. Since her husband's death all those years ago, she had inhabited a gentle, remote world of her own creating. Now, to find herself in a *questura*, facing a stern faced *commissario*. Poor Olive, you can bet I'd be having palpitations too, Emma thought.

"There was a small coach party of Americans," Olive continued. "They left and it became quieter and I was able to concentrate, really concentrate on the frescoes. Three nuns who had also been in the museum left and at last I was alone." Olive paused for breath and Emma quickly looked at her. Was she not going to say anything about the man driving the red sports car?

"I wanted to examine the angel on the left side more closely," Olive continued. "I moved to the extreme left of the fresco. The fresco has been detached from the wall you know, in order to better preserve it. It is in a thick frame, behind glass, and now stands away a slight distance from the wall. I had a silly notion that somehow the perspective was off. So to test it I stepped to the side, closed my left eye and sighted along the figures. I could see what I wanted to observe more clearly then. The perspective was flawless, it just *appeared* to be off. In fact, Piero had not erred in the slightest. I stood there admiring it, admiring the genius of an artist long gone, then it happened." She paused, Barzoni gave the slightest nod of encouragement.

"I had seen something else from that exaggerated angle. Something flat, about the size of a twelve by fourteen canvas, similar to many in my studio. It was brown. It had been tucked in just behind the fresco frame in the space between the frame and the wall." Quickly she looked at Barzoni. "As I just said, the fresco has been removed from the wall and is framed now, for preservation." He nodded. "The gesso of the frame was ornate, and had almost hidden the package, so close to the wall was the fresco frame mounted. I touched it with my finger. It was paper, stiff brown paper, but I knew that was only the covering. Below it felt hard, like wood. I lifted it out. Here is what I found." Solemnly she handed over the parcel with both hands. Barzoni had not yet said a word.

He accepted the parcel from her outstretched hands, his long, tapering fingers lifting the paper covering as carefully as a monk handling precious vellum containing the calligraphy and jewel-like paintings from a medieval *Book of Hours*.

Again Emma was reminded of scholars she had known. The red fringe of hair, the kindly face, the thoughtful, probing gaze from those hazel eyes. A quick vignette of a monk of the Middle Ages, body swathed in enveloping robes, bent over a desk, copying texts by candlelight in some dim monastery library, sprang to Emma's mind. Yes, scholarly, monk-like. Only the penetrating eyes betrayed his calling. As he slowly removed the stiff, heavy paper something more solid loomed into view. In all her glory the *Urbino Madonna*, the missing portrait by Piero, looked solemnly back at the occupants of the room.

Emma's parted lips attempted an involuntary cry, but only a croak of surprise emerged. Tension had rendered her vocal chords almost silent. Joy momentarily overshadowed everything she felt, that the painting was found, including the fabrication

Olive had presented as fact to the Chief Inspector. *Not one word has she uttered about the strange man she spoke with so earnestly in front of the fresco,* Emma realized, and her heartbeat quickened, fear took over. She felt the dampness of perspiration on her face and palms. What was Olive playing at?

Olive sat motionless, like a condemned prisoner awaiting sentence. She looked frightened, unconvinced that her story would be believed. Inspector Barzoni transferred his gaze to Emma. Emma felt heat on her face, she knew she was turning beet red. Would he realize Olive had invented this, this fantasy? The searchlight gaze of the Inspector settled on her face.

"And when did your hostess make this, ah, discovery, *Signorina?*" His clipped tones bored into Emma's consciousness.

Her voice wavered as she replied. "Only about an hour ago. We all hurried here immediately." She lowered her eyes and waited, her heartbeat sounding like thunder in her chest.

"And you were present when *Signora* Signorelli ah, extracted the picture?" His eyes locked on Emma's with all the intensity of a floodlit stage setting.

"No sir." Emma lapsed into the response of a Virginia-raised child, remembering the mandatory 'Sir' and 'Ma'am.' "I was outside in the parking lot by that time. The four of us finished looking around in the crypt and as we came up we could see Olive was not quite ready to leave, so we decided to go outside and wait for her in the parking area." Emma was feeling like a frightened rabbit in a cage, as the menacing hand moved ever closer.

"And were there any other automobiles in the parking area by this time?" His question shot out so quickly, Emma was thrown off guard.

Confused, she blurted out, "There was one, a sports model, beside our two cars, Chief Inspector."

"And whose car was it, do you know?" He asked in a soft voice almost a whisper.

Again the hazel eyes locked on her. For a moment their eyes met. Emma felt her mouth go dry, the thundering in the region of her heart deafening her.

"I, I thought I might know, Sir."

"Whose motor, Miss Darling?"

"Wait! Stop! Don't torment her! She is blameless!" Olive's voice rang out, her eyes bright with tears. "I have the answer to that question! I have deliberately tried to mislead you, Chief Inspector. I, I was not alone in that room. What I have said is false about finding the painting! I invented that, to shield him! There was someone with me. *He* removed the panel of the Madonna from behind the fresco. *He* knew where it was hidden because his children told him it was there and begged him to retrieve it and hide it for them. The man I met was *Signor* Paolo Cortina." Olive's voice lowered several decibels and grew cold as the Russian steppes. Her voice was barely audible, so despairing it sounded.

"I, I couldn't turn my back on him, don't you see? We had been friends long ago, oh so long ago. Then his wife died. My Umberto died. There was so little left. I couldn't turn my back on an old friend." The pain on Olive's honest face brought tears to Emma's eyes.

"Just what exactly did he ask you to do, Signora?" Barzoni's voice was as soft as a kitten's purr.

"Why, to turn the picture over to the *questura. Certamente*! Do you think he would have wanted anything else? But of course not! He felt so ashamed of his children he asked me, on an impulse, if I would do it for him. We only met by accident, you see. He didn't have any idea I would be at the museum. Nor did I have any inkling he would be there. He told me the whole story, how his children begged him to go to Monterchi and pick up the painting, to hide it in a new place, to keep it for them until they were set free. To keep it! Can you imagine?" Her voice was incredulous. "He was undone by their greed, their insensitivity, their hardness. His children! It was the ultimate despair for Paolo."

"It was to save him the humiliation and pain of being the instrument to further incriminate his children that made me want to help him. Why he had been driving around the countryside all the morning, trying to get up enough courage to remove the painting and turn it in to the police himself. He was outraged by their request, his own children, already guilty of such a despicable crime and then asking their father to assist them in committing another! Wanting to hide it to feed their greed! Paolo was horrified. He wanted to turn it in to the police. Surely you can see . . ." Her voice trailed off and she buried her face in her hands and sobbed.

"There, there," Chief Inspector Barzoni reached across his desk with a large, immaculate handkerchief. As Olive accepted it, her face took on the misery of a naughty child. His face held the look of a patient parent.

"You did what you thought was right. And we've finally got the Madonna safe and sound, if indeed it is the right one." Emma noted the irony which had crept into his voice and the slight shake of his head. So many times the wrong one had turned up, he must have been thinking.

"Oh, I believe this is the genuine Piero, Chief Inspector," Emma said softly, finding her voice. Her eyes had hardly strayed from the painting on the desk in front of her. "There is no doubt in my mind this time. I've certainly seen enough copies! This is the missing Madonna I believe, minus its frame, of course. The Cortinas may have burnt the frame or disposed of it in some other way."

"They may well have done," Barzoni replied with bitterness. "That brother and sister have behaved wantonly all along. Now we'll see what happens."

Emma looked over at him quickly in surprise, such a mild looking man. His voice deepened with emotion.

"Oh yes, Miss Darling, I know we police are supposed to act as robots without displaying our feelings. I can tell you, I have been outraged by this theft. When such works of art are stolen, the unborn generations are deprived of a part of their heritage. It is a travesty. Doubly so because the perpetuators were citizens of San Sepolcro, the artist's birthplace!"

"Of course you are right, Chief Inspector," Olive spoke up in impassioned agreement. She had regained her composure. "Paolo felt that way too. He told me so. It made things so very difficult for him, you see, because the guilty ones were his own children."

"Yes *Signora* Signorelli. Life gives us much to deal with, is it not true?" His voice was gentle, *simpatico.* He turned to Emma, who was beginning to believe the unfortunate father of the Cortinas might indeed be blameless, and might truly be sickened by the actions of Pietro and Anna. And that would render Luigi's suspicions mistaken. She would need to get word to him soon with these new developments, before he filed the report. She returned her thoughts to the present as Barzoni asked her to bring in her friends waiting outside.

When Emma reappeared with the others, Charlie hurried directly to his aunt. "Are you all right, Auntie?"

"She is perfectly fine, Signor. And who might you be?" Francesco Barzoni quickly took charge.

Castellina-in-Chianti: Shopping Street

"Pardon, Chief Inspector. I am Olive Signorelli's nephew from London, Charles St. Cyr, and this is my wife, Jane." He took Jane's arm and gestured toward Sam. "My friend, Dr. Samuel McGregor of Aberdeen."

Barzoni gave the briefest of nods and, as there were no vacant chairs, sent the desk sergeant to fetch some. At last they were all seated, with barely enough room left to close the door. Emma wondered afresh about such cramped quarters, and for a Chief Inspector! She decided funds must be very scarce in San Sepolcro.

Barzoni quickly confirmed the sequence of events at the chapel in Monterchi. He extracted an amazing amount of information in a very short time, Emma thought admiringly. When Charlie told him he was an Inspector with Scotland Yard in London, Barzoni's eyes bored into him.

"Ah, now I see why *Signora* Signorelli preferred Miss Darling, not you, to accompany her. She knew you would, ah, persuade her to reveal the *entire* truth at once, no?" He permitted himself the smallest of smiles as he looked at Charlie, then at Olive, whose cheeks immediately flushed bright pink, confirming his suspicions.

"Yes, well, Auntie is the only one of us who actually knew Paolo Cortina," Charlie offered. "I think Emma, Miss Darling, had strong suspicions from bits and pieces she had collected. But the rest of us were in the dark. I was worried about Auntie, who is frail as you can see, and she came out of the chapel carrying a heavy parcel concealed under her purse. I had no idea, however, she was carrying the wooden panel of the Piero Madonna, never having actually seen it, wrapped or unwrapped. Emma, Miss Darling, must have guessed the truth."

Charlie's look of admiration toward his aunt showed he had misjudged the small, grey-haired figure in a crumpled linen dress sitting quietly. He underestimated his aunt's grit and determination, and needless to say, her wiry strength to see that the painting was turned in to the authorities.

Barzoni turned to Emma. "Were you aware, Miss Darling, that police from here and from Florence spent a whole day recently in Monterchi searching for the missing painting, the needle in a haystack, and found nothing?"

Emma coughed delicately to hide a smile. Barzoni seemed as proud of his American colloquialisms as Luigi. She wondered if he had been reading American thrillers, watching the telly, or perhaps he picked up phrases during an extended stay in America; of course, she was too polite to ask.

"Yes, I did know that. Inspector Luigi Rovere of Urbino told me."

"And yet you decided to return again to search?" Barzoni's brows lifted slightly.

"Yes, Sir. The first day I arrived in Italy, at the Monterchi chapel with my students, I saw Anna Cortina, the copyist we'd encountered earlier in London at the National Gallery. I wondered why she was there. And why she seemed so nervous when she saw our group. I always believed the chapel somehow was linked to the missing painting, absolutely nothing based on fact, only a feeling. Now I think I know why: on that first day when I saw Anna and the young man who turned out to be her brother, they must have been making arrangements in advance to hide the painting as soon as they could steal it."

"What makes you think so?" Barzoni's voice was almost a whisper; he was obviously wondering what an amateur could possibly have gleaned when an entire day's search by the police netted nothing.

"Today I spoke to the old woman who takes the tickets. She is a former childhood nurse of Anna and Pietro Cortina. Her nephew is in charge of the chapel, a job which pays little, but it certainly made it convenient, to say the least, for the Cortina brother and sister. An obscure, out of the way place. Who would think of looking there for another Piero painting? Of course I was disappointed when I learned the police turned up nothing." She paused.

"But I also learned the old lady was nowhere to be seen on the day the police arrived. Today I gleaned information from her that she had been sick a few days. I observed that she does love to talk. So it is possible she wasn't really sick, just given a few days' rest by her nephew, knowing if the police spoke with her, they would get every scrap of information out of her easily enough, if she were anywhere about the chapel. And he'd probably been warned to keep silent by Anna and her brother."

"I had better luck today. She talked freely to me. Except for one thing: I could not persuade her to reveal the family's name. Now, after Olive's information, I'm certain it was the Cortina family she worked for all those years. Also, another reason I wanted to return to Monterchi was because Inspector St. Cyr and Dr. McGregor had never seen the *Madonna del Parto*. That was another purpose of our visit."

"I see, very logical." Barzoni's answer was matter of fact. Clearly his mind was racing ahead.

"I must notify Rovere in Urbino that we believe we have found the painting at last. No doubt the curator will come flying over the mountains as he did before, swoop down and bear it away to subject it to more tests before declaring the victory. That will be easy." He is thinking out loud, Emma realized. Resignation in his voice told her the police will once more be forgotten when bouquets were handed out.

"I will go and confront the Cortina brother and sister again. Finding the missing painting makes the case against them virtually water-tight. But that Cortina woman has the tongue of a *vipera*," he muttered under his breath. *Snake,* he meant, Emma realized.

"*Signorina* Emma, the evidence you have given me about the Cortina's connection with the chapel attendants will be a great help in tying up loose ends, plus the fact that the father, unwilling to join in their scheme, made arrangements to have the painting safely brought to the *questura*, thanks to help from this brave lady." The hazel eyes bestowed a gentle gaze on Olive.

"You have been most helpful, *Signora Signorelli*". Barzoni smiled at Olive. "Please leave me your address and telephone should I need to speak with you. I see no reason to detain you and your guests any longer." He stood up. They were dismissed.

"At last," Charlie sighed when they were outside. "We can have our picnic. I'm famished."

19

A Picnic under the Piero Statue Serves Up Some Insights

Emma suggested, as they were already in San Sepolcro, they should enjoy a picnic at the little park dedicated to Piero della Francesca, opposite the house where he once lived. Sam found a space for the two cars just outside the old city walls, a short distance from their destination. The five made their way carrying provisions, spreading the rugs and a cloth on the grass in a secluded spot, but with a good view of the sculpture of Piero. It was time for the *riposo*, the afternoon rest; the park was deserted.

Soon they were devouring sandwiches of ham, tomato and cheese, too hungry to say much at first. There was salad dressed with Maria's special olive oil and herbs. Only Olive seemed indifferent to the food, breaking off tiny bites of her sandwich. After assuaging hunger pangs they began conversing, reluctant to leave, lingering over lemonade and cookies Maria made for dessert.

The mood was one of elation among the four young people; Emma felt jubilant that at long last the Madonna by Piero had been found. Soon it would be back where it belonged, in the Ducal Palace in Urbino. This time she felt no doubt about its authenticity.

Charlie, lounging on the grass with a rolled up rug for a pillow, stretched his long legs and gave every indication of dozing off. Emma and Jane quietly gathered up the remains of the lunch and repacked the hamper, but nobody suggested leaving. It was too peaceful to be in the Piero della Francesca park, celebrating in their quiet way the painting's recovery. Olive sat silently, lost in her own thoughts, eyes fixed on the Piero statue presiding over the little group. There was a look of melancholy in her eyes, she resembled someone in a trance. Presently she began to speak and Charlie, suddenly roused to attention, sat up.

"It was long ago, the first time I went to Monterchi to look at the fresco, but I can remember the day as though it were yesterday. There were four of us, Umberto and myself, Paolo and Giulietta his wife. They had not been married as long as Umberto and I, and it was the first outing we had taken together since our marriages."

"You see, I met Paolo Cortina soon after I arrived in Florence, even before I met Umberto, and Paolo quickly imagined he was in love with me. I can't think why." A puzzled look came over her face. "I never gave him any encouragement along that line, none at all."

"We met at a famous villa in Fiesole adjoining the Villa Esperanza which belonged to Paolo's family. He grew up there as a boy and lives there now, but when he and Giulietta were married, they went to live in San Sepolcro, in a charming old house with a big garden which had been in Giulietta's family for generations." She means *Il Giardino*, Emma realized as she listened, captured by Olive's dream-like voice.

"I had recently come over from England when I met Paolo," Olive continued. "I'd only arrived a few weeks earlier to study art, and did not know many people. A girl in my life drawing class, an American, had a friend who worked as a secretary at a lovely villa owned by an American university. *I Tatti*. the villa, had belonged to a world famous art historian. When he died, he left it to the university. That is where the party took place."

"So there I was, just over from England, already madly in love with Italy, gawking at original works of art on the villa's walls, paintings I'd seen pictured in art history books for years. I was content to look and admire. I was never what they called "a mixer" at parties, absolutely hopeless at small talk. I was never popular. Oddly enough, I've never minded that. So the party ebbed and surged around me while I paid scant attention, lost in the beauty of all those paintings."

"Then along came this tall, handsome man about my age, who happened to live in the adjoining villa. Heaven knows what he saw in me, but he took charge at once, bringing plates of sandwiches and small flutes of sherry out onto a lovely terrace off the main reception room. The terrace overlooked the cedar-dotted hillsides of Fiesole, punctuated by the occasional red tiled roof of a villa peeking through. It looked like paradise. It *was* paradise. And far in the distance we could see Florence, laid out like a king's ransom in jewels on velvet. We could make out the dome of the *Cattedrale,* Santa Maria dei Fiori, the twisting River Arno bisecting the city. It was magical."

"Paolo was very good looking in those days. His face was smooth, not marred by a perpetual frown or smirk. Life has not been kind to Paolo. In spite of great wealth, he has suffered much." Here Olive stopped and looked at each of them, to be sure they understood.

"So before I knew it, Paolo was occupying a lot of my time. He would be at the *Accademia* to meet me when my classes finished. I should have realized what was happening. I viewed Paolo as a friend, but he was much more serious. He made sure I saw all the treasures of Florence. It was on one of these excursions, to the church of Santa Maria del Carmine, that I met Umberto." Emma looked quickly over at her, remembering how she herself had been on her way to see the same frescoes by Masaccio when she encountered Mario. She shivered in spite of herself.

"In those days there was no special entrance to view the frescoes. You just walked into the nave of the church and there they were, in the Brancacci chapel. Only one other person was there, not the constant stream of visitors you have today, and he was a lanky, thin man who looked as though a capricious wind might blow him away. He held a hat in his hands. I remember looking at his hands with long, tapering fingers before I looked at his face. An artist's hands, I thought."

"But he wasn't an artist, much as he loved art. He was a farmer because he had to take over the family estate, deep in *chianti* country, where he grew grapes on the land as countless ancestors had done before him. A shock of straight brown hair fell over his forehead and he was always impatiently pushing it away. Clear brown eyes of indescribable beauty, a skin tanned by the winds to a warm honey color, a prominent hooked nose carried, as I later learned, by generations of Signorelli men." Olive paused, close to tears, coughed, then resumed.

"Paolo had met him before, at some wine growers' meeting. They were acquaintances rather than close friends. At that time, *Toscana* had scores of small vineyards. Most of them are gone now, sold out to the big *cooperativos*." Olive returned to her narrative after a moment of reflection.

"Paolo introduced us. I still recall Umberto fidgeting with his hat as we stood in front of the fresco of the *Tribute Money* by Masaccio, with Jesus speaking to his disciples and to the Roman soldiers, saying the familiar words, 'Render unto Caesar the things which are Caesar's and unto God the things which are God's' as Peter took the coin from the fish's mouth at the side of the main group of figures. The work was so powerful, believable!"

"This is when I remember thinking, 'Someday I will marry this man.' It was very silly of me of course, I had no inkling of how he felt about me, but women are often silly, don't you think?" She smiled at Emma and Jane, listening enthralled to Olive's account of meeting her future husband.

"So there we stood, talking about Masaccio and the frescoes. I could tell he was a man who really loved paintings. He looked at the frescoes so hungrily, a yearning look. Then Umberto suggested we find a small place near the church and have an *espresso*. Sure enough there was a little bar near the church entrance. The church is in a working class neighborhood, you know. The bar was a plain little bar but I didn't mind, I didn't even notice." Emma nodded, recalling her recent venture into that neighborhood, near Mario's house.

"I remember how Paolo rather fussily insisted on putting down his handkerchief over the seat of my chair, which was none too clean, how Umberto kept quizzing me about England and the farms there, how we all speculated about Masaccio and why he painted in such a monumental new style."

"Umberto told us that in 1771 a disastrous fire destroyed much of Santa Maria del Carmine's interior, damaging some of the frescoes. When the remodeling began, it was decided to tear down the frescoes. Then the artists of Florence rose up, demanded that the Masaccio frescoes be salvaged and restored, and they prevailed. They understood his genius and would not allow the destruction."

"By this time the sun began to go down, and I think Paolo was beginning to realize how I felt about Umberto. He was the sweetest, most guileless person I ever knew." Olive paused, almost overcome by emotion. "Am I becoming tedious?" she asked, looking at each of them in turn.

"No, Auntie, carry on." Charlie, like the others, was hanging on every word.

"Yes, Paolo understood how I felt immediately, and to his credit, he accepted it. He began inviting Umberto up to Florence and Fiesole for gallery openings, exhibitions and parties, giving us a chance to know each other better."

"There were so many parties then. Florence is still a very social place, like any small town where everyone knows everyone else. When Umberto asked me to marry him, Paolo was the first person he told, and Paolo gave us his blessing. There was never a moment's hesitation on my part. I loved Italy and as my parents were both dead by then, I had no responsibilities nor immediate family back in England. There was no reason I couldn't live wherever I wished. And of course, I was deeply in love."

"Shortly after this time Paolo began seeing Giulietta. He knew it was time to marry and settle down. He had the responsibility of a large estate to look after. Giulietta was beautiful, blond and blue eyed, not dark like many Italians. They made a handsome couple."

Toscana: Looking out toward the
Mountains of the Moon

"After they married she insisted they live in San Sepolcro, her town, in the lovely old house with the garden which belonged to her family, and good sport that he was, Paolo consented, although it meant many trips for him back and forth to Fiesole. Uncomplaining, he would drive up during the week to manage the Fiesole properties and return to San Sepolcro on the weekends."

"After the four of us were married, we made plans for an outing together, a visit to Monterchi to see the *Madonna del Parto*. It was more famous then as a holy icon rather than a painting by Piero della Francesca as it is today. There was nothing like the legendary Piero Trail. That would spring up later, brought into existence by Piero's growing reputation. Brides in the Monterchi area prayed to the Madonna there so that their babies might be safely brought into the world. I imagine they do still."

"As we looked at it, Giulietta whispered to me that she and Paolo were expecting a child. This was a bittersweet revelation for me, because I had not yet been able to conceive. The doctor had told us there was a possibility we might never have children, because of my age. I was already forty, you see. More than anything, Umberto and I longed for a child. Giulietta knew that. She could have postponed her announcement until a later time, but she was perverse in that way. I think she knew Paolo had cared for me earlier." Olive shrugged.

"It proved to be our last outing together. Later in the pregnancy she almost miscarried, and her doctor confined her to the couch after that. She was delivered of a fine, healthy boy, Pietro, and of course Paolo was over the moon when he wrote us the news. Two weeks later she was dead."

At her words Emma jerked to attention. But Anna, she thought. What about Anna?

Before she could question Olive, however, Sam asked, "What did she die of?"

"The reasons Paolo gave were vague. He was undone by grief, of course. Umberto thought it must have been an infection. Everyone had their babies at home back then. A careless nurse, a slovenly maid, it is not hard to imagine what could happen. Paolo was inconsolable. Under that sophisticated exterior beat a sincere heart. He was a man who felt—and still feels—deeply. After her death, he was like a motor car with failed brakes careening down a slippery hillside; by that I mean he seemed to have, or want, little control over his life."

"But Olive, what about Anna, Pietro's sister?" Emma asked.

"Oh, didn't I mention? Anna is adopted. Paolo did not want to raise Pietro without a sibling, so he adopted a child from his family. We heard about it later, after Anna had already arrived. There was a disgraced cousin of Paolo's who abandoned a wife and young daughter. This cousin was into all sorts of trouble with the authorities we heard, and for whatever reason, the wife did not want to raise the child. Paolo agreed to adopt the daughter."

Anna adopted! And from a disgraced father! She might not have fit into the family! Emma felt a rush of sympathy for Paolo Cortina.

"And there was never any indication from Paolo about how the adoption worked out?" she asked.

"Not a peep," Olive answered. "In *Toscana,* we rarely discuss family troubles, not even today. We did not see much of Paolo after that happened. He seemed to be occupied trying to cope with two lively children. But it is true, he became very reclusive. We heard rumors as the children grew older that they were unruly. But never a word from Paolo about them."

"As the years passed, he saw people less and less. He withdrew to the villa in Fiesole and the children were left at the house in San Sepolcro with a housekeeper."

"So if Anna is an *adopted* child, then why would she have the same disdainful expression?" Emma wondered aloud, suddenly remembering the haughty expression of Paolo Cortina as he looked at her in the Monterchi chapel earlier that day. At last she remembered! It was the same look she noticed on Anna Cortina's face at the National Gallery in London, the first time she ever saw her!

"What do you mean Emma?" Sam looked puzzled.

"Oh, sorry! I was thinking out loud. I forgot I'd not mentioned this: You see, every time we ran into Anna, my students and I, she always had the same proud, unfriendly scowl on her face, exactly the same facial expression as Paolo Cortina wore this morning. And, if she were an adopted child, would she be likely to have the same mannerisms as her foster father? I don't think so."

"I see," Sam looked thoughtful. "Not likely that she would."

"Yes, Emma, I see what you mean." Charlie spoke up. "Unless, of course, she was Paolo's *natural* daughter, by some woman unknown, a carefully guarded secret."

"What an amazing thing to say, Charlie," Jane spoke up in her soft voice.

"That sort of thing does happen in Italy," Olive mused, "more often than you might suppose. The history books are full of examples. Usually the child is loved and taken into the father's household. Leonardo da Vinci comes to mind as a famous example."

Everyone was quiet for a few minutes mulling over this possibility.

"That certainly would explain why Paolo took her in, and he had the best of reasons: to have a companion for his motherless child, Pietro." Sam said. "And Giulietta was in her grave at this point. She certainly would not object."

"I never knew or heard a whiff of any scandal like that," Olive mused. "But I'm not denying it is possible. Umberto and I simply accepted the disgraced cousin story. Castellina-in-Chianti is a bit removed from Florence, and Fiesole too, come to that. And you all know, most of my time is spent at Villa Signorelli. The similarity of facial expressions Emma noticed is powerful evidence, it seems to me." The others were silent, thinking of the ramifications.

"How even more heartbreaking this must be for Paolo, if Anna is his own flesh and blood." Jane's tender nature was revealed as her eyes filled with tears. But as Charlie reminded her, this was only speculation.

Emma had been busily thinking of some of the accusations Luigi set down about Paolo Cortina in his written report, notably the fact that he told Anna her mother was disappointed in her. Of course he meant her real mother, who apparently was very much alive!

"Did Paolo mention either Paris or London to you in your talk this morning Olive?" Emma asked suddenly, thinking the mother might live in another country.

"Why yes, he did," she replied. "How odd that you should ask. He told me his doctor was concerned about his health and strongly suggested he visit clinics in both London and Paris where some gifted doctors had offices. He planned to go soon to get help." So it was medical doctors he had referred to with is children, not an underhand art dealer!

And as they begin trooping back to the two cars, Emma's silent speculations told her Luigi could indeed have mistaken the reference to a "Doctor, a dealer in art" to a "Doctor, a healer" at clinics in Paris and London who might cure him. Emma knew she needed time alone to sift through the points, one by one.

~~~~

When they returned to Villa Signorelli, Emma slipped quietly into the small, book-filled library smelling faintly of old leather and lavender polish, asking Sam to join her. When he arrived, she showed him the report delivered by courier from Luigi and asked for his thoughts.

While the others were lounging in the kitchen, enjoying cups of Maria's famous *caffelatte*, Sam read the report and then insisted she ring Luigi in Urbino at once, telling him of today's events before he filed his report.

"He should forget that report now, Emma. Knowing what Olive told us, it is highly unlikely Cortina is mixed up in anything underhanded. Better warn Luigi *rapido*."

Emma did not wish to speak to Luigi again, but Sam thought a letter would not be quick enough. She should act now. She made the call, and in short order gave pertinent facts to Luigi which quickly convinced him he had overreached in his report. She told him apparently "Bepe" and Giuseppe, the young attendant at Monterchi were one and the same, and that the possibility had arisen that Anna Cortina was either the natural daughter, or adopted, with a live mother somewhere. Luigi agreed the elder Cortina's only crime appeared to be failing to turn the picture in himself, and he knew how hard that would be for any man. But after ringing off, Emma still had some nagging questions that needed answers. Taking fresh paper from the drawer of the desk and unscrewing her fountain pen, she began to write.

Unanswered Questions

Why did Anna Cortina go to England to copy masterpieces in the National Gallery in the first place?

Why did she disguise her ability to paint by producing slipshod copies? The copy of the Piero Madonna she and Pietro passed off to Mario was extremely well done.

Were the Cortinas responsible for other art thefts, in addition to the Ghirlandaio Madonna taken from San Gimignano? If so, where are they hiding them?

Is Anna Cortina the natural daughter of Paolo Cortina? If so, where is Anna's real mother?

~~~

But when Emma showed the list to Sam, he urged her to let it rest. "Things don't always get completely solved, you know that, Emma. I'm beginning to wonder if we might have a quiet, stress free honeymoon when we finally tie the knot, or will you be galloping off to solve some mysterious disappearance, or theft, or a forgery in the art world! You've got to admit, mystery seems to follow you like a magnet!"

Emma put down the pen, closed her eyes and leaned back in the old leather chair. Her brain was too tired to think any more. All right, why not drop it, now that the stolen Piero was safely returned to Urbino? Let Chief Inspector Barzoni find the answers she thought drowsily as she allowed herself to drift into sleep in the quiet of the library, her head resting on the desk while Sam, not wanting to disturb her, quietly tiptoed out.

20

An Unexpected Visitor; Some Questions Resolved

A few days later the two couples motored into Castellina-in-Chianti for a light supper under the market umbrellas, tightly furled now to reveal the panoply of stars blinking in blue-black heavens. Every night in Italy seemed destined to produce perfect skies worthy of a stage set, Emma mused, remembering the often opaque, rainy skies of London evenings.

Olive had not accompanied them. There was a recording of *Turandot* on the wireless she wished to hear. The events of the past days had taken their toll she admitted. When they returned after a leisurely drive after dinner, they discovered she had retired to her room. Jane and Charlie opted for an early bedtime, pleading exhaustion. Emma and Sam decided to wander about the wild, overgrown garden.

"Let's hope we aren't assaulted by bats," Emma joked as they made their way around the paths overgrown with wild thyme which sent up a pungent fragrance as their shoes crushed the tiny leaves pushing up between the flagstones.

"Scant worry that," Sam said reassuringly, placing an arm around her shoulders. "About the only danger I can think of in this spot is being wounded by one of Cupid's darts. The wee man belongs in a place like this."

"It is terribly romantic, isn't it, Sam?" Emma agreed "If only we could stay in Italy forever."

"You really have fallen head over heels for Italy, haven't you?" He tightened his arm around her shoulders.

Emma took a minute to reply. "I admit I find Italy terribly compelling, *simpatico*."

"Including certain handsome Italian police inspectors?" Sam's voice sounded playful. So he *had* guessed, Emma thought.

"All right. I admit it. I did find Inspector Rovere attractive, Sam. I am only human, you know. And he rescued me from my abductor, not once, but twice. And you and I had been apart for so long; you yourself said you hardly remembered what my face looked like. But it was all innocent. We never so much as went out on a date. I suppose, Sam, that owing one's freedom, and possibly one's life, to someone can be a powerful attraction."

"I should never have left you and gone off to take the job in Aberdeen. It was a big mistake, especially since it turned out that I could never get away." They stood embracing in the garden, surrounded by silvery shapes of foliage-draped statues, gleaming in the pale light of a half moon.

"I don't want to lose you Emma. I really envy Jane and Charlie, seeing them say their goodnights, go up that grand staircase together and head for their own room. I want that privilege too, with you. I mean to lead you to the altar as soon as I can, so we can begin living the real life."

Emma reached up, gently pulling his head toward her and kissed him on the lips, leaving no doubt as to her own feelings. She was very much aware they had waited almost a year since Sam slipped the garnet and rose diamond ring on her finger.

"I agree, Sam. Let's decide soon when and where our wedding will be."

~~~

Several days after newspapers had proclaimed the safe return of the Piero Madonna to Urbino, Emma realized that her Italian idyll would soon be only a fond memory. But she knew when she and Sam boarded the plane at Pisa for Heathrow, she would be taking with her a part of Italy in her mind and in her heart.

They had begun to make plans for an autumn wedding. When they returned to London they would reserve the church, order invitations and announcements. She would select her dress. They both wanted a small wedding, small compared to the wedding of Jane and Charlie. What Emma and Sam preferred was a ceremony in the company of their families and only a few close friends.

They were sitting together, ensconced in the library of the villa. Jane and Charlie had driven up to Florence for the day to see an exhibition of watercolors painted by an old school chum of Charlie's. Olive was painting in her studio. Maria had departed on her *vespa* after lunch to visit her brother and his wife in their flat over the *gelateria* on the piazza in Castellina.

Sam was busily jotting down the list of distant relatives in Scotland who should receive announcements and Emma had finished a similar list of her American and English relatives when the drowsy silence of the afternoon was shattered by the clap of the huge wrought iron door knocker.

"Who on earth?" Emma hurried to the door hoping to deal with the intrusion before Olive's painting was interrupted.

She opened the big door to Chief Inspector Barzoni, peering down at her behind owl-like spectacles, a mild expression on his face. He was neatly dressed in the standard dark suit coupled with a subdued red necktie, patterned in small flowers. I do believe it's a Liberty's tie, Emma noted fleetingly as she welcomed him, inviting him in. The Inspector remained something of an enigma to her.

"Good afternoon, *Signorina* Darling. I wonder if I might have a few words with *Signora* Signorelli? You may tell her I have come to reclaim my handkerchief, if you wish," he smiled, eyes twinkling.

"Of course, Chief Inspector, she is painting in her studio. I know she will wish to see you. I'll take you up to her." Emma answered, aware that Sam had joined them. Greetings were exchanged by the two men.

"The St. Cyrs have motored up to Florence for the day. Dr. McGregor and I are the only ones downstairs," Emma explained.

"Then I am very lucky," he smiled, "Because *Signorina*, I would like to ask you a few questions first, *permesso?* Perhaps I can do that before I go up."

Francesco Barzoni settled comfortably into an ancient, tapestry-covered wing chair in the reception room, crossed his legs and began.

"We have learned about an international ring of art thieves working in Europe, stealing art works, then finding buyers for them in America and Canada. It seems they have headquarters in London. The chap in charge is an antique dealer. I wondered with your knowledge of the London art world, if you had ever heard of a man named Martin Kline?"

Emma thought for a moment. "No, Chief Inspector, I haven't heard of Martin Kline or of such an organization, but

I must say, it does not surprise me. The offhand way some museums and galleries protect their art is bound to tempt the unscrupulous."

Barzoni shrugged and gave a wry smile. "Of course, my country is one of the worst offenders. But you are quite right, *Signorina* Darling."

"Oh I was not being critical of Italy," Emma answered hastily. "England is hardly exemplary, especially in some of the provincial museums. London security is somewhat better."

"Is there some reason to think the Cortinas are linked with this man or his group?" Sam asked.

"Yes there is, Dr. McGregor. We know the Cortina brother and sister went to London shortly before they stole the two paintings." Here he nodded toward Emma. "They were given instructions there, we think, on how to execute the theft. Anna Cortina was sent to the National Gallery to study the work of Piero della Francesca in order to be able to make the colors of her work identical to those of the master. The plan was to make a copy to trick Mario, their co-conspirator."

"Then she wasn't thinking of *form* so much as she copied," Emma's voice held amazement. "It was *color* she was focusing on."

"*Scusi?*" "Excuse me?" Barzoni's searchlight eyes swiveled toward Emma.

"Chief Inspector, my students and I first saw Anna Cortina in London, copying at the National Gallery. Subsequently we saw her in Italy. But we could never understand why her work was so amateurish, and what on earth she was doing in London copying Piero masterpieces in such a slipshod fashion. Now you tell me she was working on color values, not composition and design. It explains somewhat the carelessness: she was in a hurry and expertise did not matter. She certainly did not want to be remembered by anyone as a copyist reproducing Pieros; the more rapidly she worked, the fewer who would see and observe her."

"It concealed her real ability also," Sam added thoughtfully.

Barzoni broke in. "You are right. This whole business is riddled with deceit, concealment and double dealing. It's anyone's guess what they are capable of. By the way, Miss Darling, the possibility she may be linked to the London based art ring is intriguing, don't you agree? Did you ever see Anna Cortina wearing a wig?"

"I didn't see her myself, but two of my students did, on two separate occasions," Emma replied. She frowned. "But I am positive I told that to Inspector Rovere in Urbino shortly after the theft."

"Ah yes," Barzoni said softly. "When so many different police are at work on a case, the information sometimes is overlooked, misplaced, or even forgotten. We all are human, you know." His smile was melancholy Emma thought.

"Do you think it might be important?" she asked.

"It could be," he admitted cautiously. "It could provide a solid link to the London operation. I'm not at liberty to discuss it more at this point." He stood up. "And now, I will see *La Signora*. Did you say her studio is at the top of the house?"

His gaze toward the staircase seemed wistful to Emma as she hurried to guide him. Perhaps he and Olive might become friends. Olive needed to be in the world more. She noticed the light which brightened Olive's face as she greeted the Inspector. Emma quickly closed the door and hurried down to tell Sam. An hour later when the Inspector reappeared, Emma rose to see him out.

"Please, do call again, Inspector," Emma said. "I am afraid Olive will be lonely when we all leave."

"Yes, I will, *certamente!*" The Inspector gave them one of his rare smiles, and hope leaped in Emma's heart.

"I will need to keep her informed of progress in the Piero Madonna case, so she can relay it to all of you back in England." He waved goodbye, climbed into his modest black motor bearing the seal of the San Sepolcro police on the driver's door.

"Emma, do all women have that matchmaker gene in their makeup?" Sam's question was delivered in all innocence, but Emma, undeceived, lobbed a pillow at him.

The visit of Chief Inspector Barzoni cleared up several of the questions about Anna Cortina Emma had set down on her list. But would she ever learn for certain if indeed Anna was the natural daughter of Paolo? More delving was needed there, she realized.

Jane and Charlie returned later in the afternoon from *Firenze* with a farewell present for Sam and Emma. As Emma opened the flat package she gave a cry of delight. It was a small watercolor sketch of the Ducal Palace in Urbino.

"What a beautiful reminder of my, er, visit there!" Emma, her eyes mischievous, smothered Jane in a big hug.

"I was afraid it might cause you to focus on the 'Unpleasantness,'" Charlie said, a smile escaping the corners of his mouth. Emma looked up from the painting in surprise.

"Why Charlie, of course not! When I look at it, I'll be thinking of the Piero Madonna, returned at last to where she belongs! At this particular moment I am thinking of where to hang this lovely present in our flat, when we find one, that is!" She looked at the small watercolour fondly.

"Do you suppose we'll be able to find a wee place?" Sam added, but no one seemed to harbor any doubts.

"So a wee wedding is in the cards," Charlie drawled, waiting for a reaction. But neither Sam nor Emma seemed to have any doubts whatsover as they moved closer together for a kiss of confirmation.